FIRST TASTE OF TEMPTATION

He cupped her face in his two hands and, for a brief moment, studied her upturned face with his remarkable eyes. As if in a dream, she felt his lips brush the shadowed hollows beneath her eyes, her fevered cheeks, the tip of her nose. Finally, when she thought her pounding heart would surely burst from her breast, his lips covered hers—firm, as she'd known they would be, yet softer than she had ever imagined, and so incredibly warm she felt their heat penetrate to the very core of her being.

When his arms tightened inexorably around her, she wound her own about his neck and gave herself wholly to the strange and wonderful magic of his lips, his very breath intermingling with hers.

Dazed and trembling, she opened her eyes to meet his intense silver gaze. "So that is what it is like to be kissed," she murmured, at once wondering what was to come now—and hungering for it. . . .

The
Duke's Dilemma

~

Nadine Miller

Ø
A SIGNET BOOK

SIGNET
Published by the Penguin Group
Penguin Books USA Inc., 375 Hudson Street,
New York, New York 10014, U.S.A.
Penguin Books Ltd, 27 Wrights Lane,
London W8 5TZ, England
Penguin Books Australia Ltd, Ringwood,
Victoria, Australia
Penguin Books Canada Ltd, 10 Alcorn Avenue,
Toronto, Ontario, Canada M4V 3B2
Penguin Books (N.Z.) Ltd, 182-190 Wairau Road,
Auckland 10, New Zealand

Penguin Books Ltd, Registered Offices:
Harmondsworth, Middlesex, England

First published by Signet, an imprint of Dutton Signet,
a division of Penguin Books USA Inc.

First Printing, February, 1996
10 9 8 7 6 5 4 3 2 1

 REGISTERED TRADEMARK—MARCA REGISTRADA

Printed in the United States of America

Chapter One

~

London, 1812

"So, the day of reckoning has finally arrived." A wicked glint brightened Lady Sophia Tremayne's sharp old eyes. "You have danced to your own tune for thirty years, my lad, but the time has come to pay the piper."

Jared Neville Tremayne, Eighth Duke of Montford, Marquess of Brynhaven, and various other titles too numerous to mention, raised his quizzing glass and stared down his elegant nose at the crusty old woman. Lady Sophia was both his aunt and his godmother, and one of the few people in all of England rash enough to address him with such a lack of deference.

"If there is a point to that obscure statement, Lady Sophia, please make it and be done with it," he said stiffly. In truth, he knew all too well what her point was; it was the very reason he had given up his morning to this duty call on the two old tabbies who inhabited this stuffy, overfurnished town house in Grosvenor Square. More to the point, it was what had afforded him countless sleepless nights during the past month and had soured his outlook on every aspect of his formerly pleasant existence.

Lady Sophia matched her godson's haughty stare with

one of her own, and the temperature in the small salon chilled at least ten degrees. "My point is, your grace, I remember a promise you made your dying grandfather some ten years ago and I feel it my duty to inquire how and when you intend to honor it." She raised a questioning eyebrow. "You do remember the promise of which I speak?"

"Of course he does, Sophie. The dear boy has a memory every bit as retentive as your own. I'm the only one in the family so dreadfully forgetful." Lady Cloris Tremayne, lace cap askew and ribbons flying, fluttered through the open doorway like a small brightly colored moth to perch on the rose velvet settee next to her austerely gowned sister. "What is it he is supposed to remember?"

"That today is his thirtieth birthday, of course, and—"

"Thirty years! I simply cannot credit it. Why, it seems only yesterday I was listening to him recite his sums." She fixed her nephew with her usual vague, sweet smile. "I suppose, my dear, I must try to remember to address you as 'your grace' from now on."

"And," Lady Sophia continued, scowling at her chatty sister, "he promised the old duke he would make a suitable marriage in his thirtieth year, if he had not already done so, and produce an heir."

"A family wedding! How delightful!" Lady Cloris's faded blue eyes took on a new sparkle. "And what a stroke of fortune that my friend Lady Hargrave taught me to knit last spring while we were chaperoning dear little Lady Lucinda's dance classes. I shall have no trouble at all keeping Jared's children in caps and mittens." She smiled shyly at her nephew. "Is she exceedingly lovely and good-natured?"

The duke frowned. "Who, my lady aunt?"

"Why, the girl you have in mind to marry."

"I have no one in mind," he said tersely. "No one at all. In fact, considering the disastrous marital history of the previous dukes of Montford, I am more inclined to remain a bachelor forever." He raised his hand to forestall the objection he could see forming on Lady Sophia's tightly pursed lips. "Be assured you need not remind me of my obligation to secure the title, my lady. I am fully aware of my responsibilities and if nothing else, the thought that that blithering fool Cousin Percival is next in line to inherit would compel me to set up my nursery."

Crossing one impeccable buckskin-clad leg over the other, the duke surveyed his two elderly relatives through narrowed eyes. He had learned one sad fact during the soul-searching month he had just endured—an awareness of his obligations to the title did not make the idea of taking on a set of leg shackles one whit easier.

He was an intensely private man; the last thing he needed was some silly female cluttering up his life. Not that he lacked appreciation for the gentler sex; he'd had a series of very engaging mistresses in the ten years since he had reached his majority and had thoroughly enjoyed every one of them. But a mistress didn't live in a man's house and share his table, nor did she have the right to expect him to spend the season in London when he would much rather be at one of his country estates—and when a man's passion for a mistress abated, he had only to present her with a suitably expensive bauble and send her on her way. It was not so easy to dispose of a wife!

He sighed deeply. But as the Duke of Montford he was obliged to produce a legitimate heir, and to accomplish that he must take a wife. At times like this, he found himself wondering if the obligations of nobility didn't sometimes outweigh the privileges.

But, to the business at hand. His two aunts were already eyeing him speculatively, and he schooled himself to hide his seething frustration behind the mask of aristocratic indifference he had inherited along with the ancient title.

"I am aware the time has come when I must marry," he

said as dispassionately as if he were discussing changing the method of tying his cravat. "But since I have no inclination to expend a great deal of effort on the tedious business, I was hoping I could count on the two of you to take care of the preliminaries for me. It is the sort of thing I feel would best be handled by a woman, but somehow I cannot picture any of my birdwitted female cousins rising to the task."

"What preliminaries?" both ladies asked simultaneously.

"A list, if you will, of whom you consider the five most eligible young women to come out this season. Nothing less than an earl's daughter, of course, but spare me those two horse-faced creatures spawned by the Duke of Ashford. The ladies' bloodlines may be unexceptionable but I should not care to risk producing progeny with features so closely resembling one of my prize stallions."

The duke momentarily toyed with his quizzing glass; then thrust it impatiently into the pocket of his fawn-colored vest. "I am leaving this afternoon for the races at Newmarket," he said, brushing an offending speck of lint from the sleeve of his beautifully tailored coat of forest green superfine, "but I shall plan to inspect the candidates when I return and consequently make my choice."

"And just where do you propose to 'inspect' these candidates, your grace?" Lady Sophia asked acidly. "At Almack's? You have not entered the halls of that hallowed establishment in years. If you should do so now unannounced, the hostesses would undoubtedly all be taken with apoplexy."

Montford's stern mouth curved in what, in a less imposing man, might have been thought humor. "Never fear, my lady. I am not *that* anxious to conclude the business at hand."

He crossed to the window and stood for a moment looking at the small formal garden at the rear of the town house. "Arrange a house party, in my name, at Brynhaven and invite all five of them, with their parents, for a fortnight's stay beginning Friday next. That is where I shall expect my"—he nearly strangled on the word—"wife to live until she produces the necessary heir, so it will be well to observe them in that venue."

"Let me see if I have the straight of this," Lady Sophia said. "You refuse to shop for your bride at the season's social functions like the rest of the eligible bachelors of the *ton* but propose to hold a private marriage mart of your own at Brynhaven starting Friday next."

"Precisely," the duke declared with an impatient scowl.

"Surely you jest. Not even *you* could be that autocratic, your grace. You cannot expect people of consequence to leave London at the height of the season with less than ten days' notice. They will already have accepted other social obligations for that weekend."

"Which they will cancel, I am sure, once they sniff out the reason for the invitation. From what I have seen of the rapacious matrons of the *ton*, they will harness themselves to the family carriages and trot to Brynhaven before they'll miss the chance of obtaining the title of Duchess of Montford for their vacuous little daughters."

Lady Sophia's smile was a bit thin around the edges. "You may be right at that. Ah well, if nothing else, such a blatant disregard for convention will certainly enhance your already legendary reputation."

"As well as accomplish my aim with the least possible inconvenience to myself," the duke said dryly. With that, he strode across the room, yanked the gold tasseled pull cord, and retrieved his stylish brushed beaver-and-gray kid gloves from his aunts' ancient butler. "I leave you to your list making, dear ladies, certain that the commission will be well and truly accomplished."

Lady Sophia raised a deterring hand to halt his exit. "I cannot say I entirely approve of your unconventional behavior, your grace, but I commend your good sense in allowing responsible female relatives to separate the wheat from the chaff in the matrimonial mill. Men are notoriously bad judges of women; witness the deplorable mistakes your predecessors have made by relying on their own judgments."

The duke nodded. "My thoughts exactly, my lady."

"But," Lady Sophia continued, "for the sake of propriety, I feel we must also invite a suitable number of young gentlemen as well. There will, after all, be four very disappointed young ladies who will not come out the winner in this high-handed lottery of yours. We should consider their tender feelings."

"You are right of course, as usual, Godmother." Montford sighed deeply. "Very well. Invite whomever you wish. I, for one, intend to mention it to Brummell when I see him at Newmarket. The Beau is always amusing and I suspect I shall have sore need of a diversion before the infernal fortnight is over."

With a last perfunctory bow, the Duke of Montford took his leave of the two ladies, secure in the knowledge that with two such *arbiters elegantiae* in charge, this blasted business of arranging a socially correct marriage would soon be a fait accompli.

For the first time in all her twenty-four years of hand-to-mouth, catch-as-catch-can existence, Miss Emily Louise Haliburton found herself deeply grateful she was the plain-faced daughter of a penniless third son.

Listening in horror as her aunt, the Countess of Hargrave, read aloud her note from Lady Cloris Tremayne, Emily even counted herself fortunate that she had inherited her mama's mousy brown hair and pudding bag figure. At least *she* would never have to worry about being caught in the kind of insidious trap she could see closing around her beautiful young cousin Lucinda.

The note had arrived at an unseemly hour, as if of too much import to wait until fashionable London was officially astir. Lady Cloris's elegantly liveried footman had hand-carried it to the Earl of Hargrave's equally elegant footman, who in turn had handed it to the earl's austere butler, who had delivered it on a small silver tray to the countess while the ladies of the house were still at breakfast.

"My stars and garters, I cannot take this in with just one reading. I must read it again," the countess said, and promptly proceeded to do so.

Dearest Hortense:

Enclosed you will find an invitation addressed to the earl, yourself, and Lady Lucinda to spend a fortnight at Brynhaven, one of the country homes of my nephew Jared Tremayne, Duke of Montford. The duke has decided the time has come when he must consider taking a wife and setting up his nursery, and has requested my sister and me to recommend five eligible young ladies from whom he might choose his duchess. Naturally, because of the warm friendship we share, I insisted Lady Lucinda's name head the list. I do not know the names of the other four who, with their parents, will join you at Brynhaven, as they will be my sister's recommendations, but I am certain your dear little daughter will outshine them all.

With most heartfelt regards,
Cloris Tremayne

Emily could scarcely believe her ears. What kind of cold fish was this Duke of Montford to blithely relegate the choosing of his wife to two elderly spinsters? Lady Hargrave's cook gave more personal attention to choosing the mutton for Sunday dinner than this peer of the realm did to choosing the future mother of his children.

In the two months since she had joined the earl's household as her cousin Lucinda's companion, Emily had observed that most of the high sticklers of London society were a shallow, jaded lot. But this toplofty duke must surely be the most outrageous of them all.

She shuddered. A cruel twist of fate had landed her amongst these Philistines and here she must stay for the next four months until she could receive the modest portion her grandmother had willed her. But then, God willing, she would leave the dirt and decadence of London behind forever and return to her beloved Cotswolds.

Warily, she looked to her aunt to gauge her reaction to this amazing missive just received. As she might have expected, a smile as bright as the sun flooding the window of the cheerful morning room lighted Lady Hargrave's plump face. Laying the note aside, she reached across the table to clasp her daughter's hands. "Never say your mama has not looked out for your welfare, my darling. Now do you wonder why I spent all those tedious hours teaching Lady Cloris to knit? Just think of it. My little girl a duchess!"

Lady Lucinda's already pale skin blanched a shade whiter. She was a timid little thing who at the slightest provocation swooned gracefully away. Emily normally found such missish behavior very off-putting, but in this case she could scarcely blame her cousin for feeling faint.

"But, Mama," Lucinda gasped, clutching the edge of the table as if it were a lifeline. "I do not think I would like to be married to the Duke of Montford. He is so . . . so stiff and so grand."

"Of course he is, you silly goose. He's Montford. The

first Tremayne crossed the Channel during the reign of Charlemagne and they have been rich as Croesus ever since. Why, even the Regent and the Royals compete for the honor of entertaining the Duke of Montford." Lady Hargrave breathed an ecstatic sigh. "Just imagine, you may soon be visiting Carlton House on the arm of your husband, the duke!"

Tears welled in Lucinda's china blue eyes. "I should be absolutely terrified," she declared, "but at least the Regent is rather fat and jolly-looking and when I was presented to him at Lady Halpern's musicale last Tuesday, he tweaked my chin and said I was 'a rare little beauty.' The duke just walked right past me without a single look."

"Well, he won't ignore you at Brynhaven, my pet."

Lucinda gulped back a sob. "But what shall I do if he expects me to talk to him? I am not at all clever like cousin Emily."

"He won't," Lady Hargrave said with absolute certainty. "The last thing a man like the duke is looking for in a wife is clever conversation. Just curtsy and smile prettily and make certain you never step on his toes when he dances with you."

"I shall be required to dance with him?" Lucinda shrieked. "Oh, Mama, never say you expect me to do such a thing. I would simply die if he touched me. He does not look at all kind."

Lady Hargrave shrugged. "Dukes rarely do. I am sure it has something to do with being catered to from the moment one is born. But"—the corners of her mouth lifted in a sly smile—"I know this is not a topic for innocent young ears and I only mention it so you will understand what is at stake here."

Her voice lowered to a discreet whisper and, fascinated, Emily leaned across the table to hear her aunt's latest *on-dit*. "Montford is rumored to be excessively generous to his paramours. That emerald necklace of Lady Crawley's which you admired at the opera Sunday last was a gift from the duke—and she is merely his mistress and unattractively plump at that. Think, my precious darling, how generous such a man would be to a beautiful young wife who presented him with his heir!"

Lucinda's finely arched brows drew together in a puzzled frown and she looked to Emily as if for guidance. "I would very much like an emerald necklace like Lady Crawley's," she admitted.

"And furs and jewels and elegant dresses and a carriage of your own with the duke's lozenge on the door," Lady Hargrave prompted.

"Of course, Mama. Who would not? But I still would not like to marry the Duke of Montford. My abigail said that any man who marries me will expect to share my bed. I most certainly would not want to share my bed with *him*! I am quite certain I should die of mortification if he ever saw me in my night rail."

Two angry red blotches stained Lady Hargrave's cheeks. "That insufferable chatterbox will be given her walking papers today and without one word of reference," she declared vehemently.

Emily turned away, afraid the disgust she felt for her aunt must surely be stamped on her face. It was difficult to believe this crass schemer could be dear Mama's only sister. Aunt Hortense had the sensitivity of a turnip; without the slightest compunction, she was tossing Lucinda to this wolf who was currently prowling London's fashionable marriage mart without explaining any of the more intimate aspects of marriage to the poor innocent.

While Emily had no actual experience in the ways of men and women, she had, like most country girls, a working knowledge of the breeding of sheep and horses and dogs. The correlation with human procreation seemed fairly obvious. She was very much afraid her pretty little cousin would find there was much more to the marriage bed than being viewed in one's night rail.

She saw the fear in Lucinda's eyes, and her heart ached for the girl. She found herself wondering just how sensitive to such fears a jaded aristocrat like the duke would be.

Lady Hargrave had maintained a long moment of ominous silence while she gathered her forces. Now she resumed her attack on Lucinda's objections to the duke's bizarre invitation with a vengeance. Emily listened as words poured off the countess's tongue like rain off a clogged gutter spout, one tripping over the other in their eagerness to be said. "I will hear no more of this foolishness," she screeched. "The die is cast. We have been invited to Brynhaven and to Brynhaven we will go. I cannot believe you are such a featherhead as to think we would dare refuse the hospitality of the Duke of Montford, even if we should want to. We would be social outcasts, my girl. Pariahs. Every door in London would be closed to us. Is that what you want?"

"No, Mama."

"I should think not! And if you care not a whit for me, at least give a thought to your poor father. With all the financial reverses the man has suffered this past year, he was forced to cash in his precious consols to give you your season. 'But never fear, my lord, your daughter will not fail you,' I assured him. 'With her pretty face and winning ways, she is bound to attract a rich *parti* who will keep you out of dun territory.' "

She pressed her hand to her ample bosom and sighed dramatically. "But Montford! Oh my stars and garters, never in my most blissful dreams did I hope to reach that high. Wait until I tell the earl.

"But first things first," she declared, ignoring the fact that her daughter was still sobbing quietly into her soggy handkerchief. "Emily, alert John Coachman that we shall need the carriage in half an hour. I want to be away from here before that insufferable gaggle of fribbles who moon over Lucinda descend upon us."

Emily smiled to herself. Just yesterday that "insufferable gaggle of fribbles" had been delightful young men who, as potential suitors for Lucinda's hand, were welcomed with open arms by the countess.

"We must hurry to Madame Fanchon's salon and engage her services before someone else thinks of it," Lady Hargrave explained. "As it is, she will have to put on extra seamstresses to finish everything we need in time."

"But, Mama, have you forgotten how unpleasant Madame Fanchon was the last time we visited her. I am certain she meant it when she said we could run up no more credit."

"Nonsense. Watch that French needle-pusher change her tune when she learns she is dressing the future Duchess of Montford—which reminds me, one thing you absolutely must have is a new riding habit. The duke is famous for his brilliant horsemanship. He will most certainly expect his duchess to ride to the hounds."

"But, Mama," Lucinda cried, reaching for Emily's hand beneath the table, "I am not at all good with horses. They frighten me to death."

"You will simply have to get over it. Mind over matter, my girl."

"But, Mama . . ."

"But me no more buts, young lady. You have been blessed with the opportunity to make the most brilliant marriage of this or any other season. I expect you to make the most of it."

Lady Hargrave turned to Emily. "And I expect you to talk some sense into this foolish child. You know all too well what it is to be poor and without prospects. Tell her how humiliating it is to have to wear your cousin's ill-fitting, cast-off dresses and hire out as a paid companion to keep body and soul together." She shuddered. "Ask her what she thinks her life—indeed all our lives—will be like if her father is sent to debtors' prison . . . and all because she failed to bring the duke up to scratch."

With a last admonishing glance at Emily, the countess swept from the room clutching Lady Cloris's precious missive to her breast and demanding, at the top of her voice, that someone find the earl.

She had scarcely closed the door behind her when Lucinda flung herself into Emily's arms. "I cannot bear it," she sobbed. "I'd rather die than marry the Duke of Montford. He is a horrible man . . . and he must be a thousand years old."

"You are exaggerating as usual," Emily said, giving her cousin's heaving shoulders a comforting pat. "I was at Lady Halpern's musicale, too, you know. I remember the duke well. He was neither old nor horrible. A bit stiff-necked and proud, I admit, but quite amazingly handsome . . . in a chilly sort of way."

In truth, she knew exactly why Lucinda found Montford forbidding; she'd developed a few shivers of her own in the brief instant she'd come under his frosty regard. She had even found herself thinking of him at odd moments ever since, and each time she thought of his dark, brooding countenance, those same shivers traveled her spine.

She racked her brain for something to say that would comfort the frightened girl. "Think of all the lovely new gowns you will have to wear."

"What good will they be if I die of fright?" Lucinda wailed, dropping in a crumpled heap onto a nearby chair.

"Isn't it early days to be turning this into a Cheltenham tragedy? After all, there is only a one in five chance the duke will choose you."

Lucinda's eyes widened in astonishment. "How could he

not choose me? I am this season's incomparable. Everyone who is anyone says I am the most beautiful girl to make her come-out in years." She sniffed. "I cannot even imagine who the other four might be."

Emily grudgingly acknowledged that while not exactly humble, her cousin's statement was probably true. Even now, when such a fit of weeping would have left any other woman with puffy eyes and a mottled complexion, Lucinda's perfect golden beauty remained undiminished.

"Brynhaven is known to be one of the grandest country homes in all of England," Emily said, deciding to try a practical approach to the problem. "I sincerely envy you the chance to see it. And since you really have no choice in the matter, why not make the best of it and enjoy your fortnight." She paused. "And pray for a miracle."

Lucinda raised her head—her lovely eyes wide and frightened. "What do you mean, you envy me the chance to see Brynhaven? Never tell me you mean to let me face this terrible ordeal alone!"

"The invitation was addressed to you and your parents," Emily reminded her gently. "I do not remember any mention of other relatives."

"But surely it includes maids and valets and footmen and such. Everyone takes one's own staff to such affairs."

Emily gritted her teeth. She had grown very fond of her pretty, flutterbrained cousin in the short time she had spent with her, but there were times when the girl's tongue ran ahead of her wits. "Much as it may sometimes seem so, Lucinda," she said crossly, "I am not a servant. Just a 'poor relation,' as my aunt so aptly put it. I am afraid you will have to do without my services in this instance."

"I shall do no such thing! If I *must* spend a fortnight at Brynhaven with the dreadful duke, I shall need you beside me every minute to tell me what to do. You know very well thinking gives me a headache."

Lucinda's perfect, heart-shaped face assumed a mulish mien Emily had never before seen. "I'll tell Mama and Papa I will not go to Brynhaven unless I can take you as my companion. Not even if they lock me in my bedchamber with nothing but bread and water for the rest of my life."

She tossed her silky, burnished curls defiantly. "So you might as well begin packing your portmanteau, dear Emily. Mama will simply have to make the proper arrangements when she pens her answer to Lady Cloris."

Chapter Two

Darkness had fallen by the time the Earl of Hargrave's party reached the entrance to Brynhaven, but they were obviously expected. Beyond the massive stone pillars and heavy iron gates, grooms bearing torches waited to escort them down the elm-lined driveway that stretched more than two miles to the main house of the estate.

"I am certain we must be the last guests to arrive," the countess complained petulantly. "I shall never forgive the earl for forcing us to travel in such a disreputable fashion. How embarrassing to have everyone clipping by us as if we were standing still. I can still see that snide smile on Lady Sudsley's face when she passed me in her new barouche."

Emily made no comment, although it was her personal opinion they should consider themselves fortunate to have arrived at all—never mind late. The earl's ancient landau appeared to be held together by nothing more substantial than sticking plaster and prayer, and it was a sheer miracle the two spavined chestnuts hadn't given up the ghost by the halfway point of the long, nightmarish journey.

Furthermore, the landau had not been their only problem. Having long ago sold off all the other family carriages, the earl was forced to hire a common vehicle-to-let to transport his valet, the prodigious collection of family luggage, and the redoubtable Maggie Hawkes, Lady Hargrave's maid, now serving both the Hargrave ladies since the untimely departure of Lady Lucinda's loose-tongued abigail. Like most such rigs, the chaise had seen better days, and twice the rackety little caravan had had to stop to repair a loose wheel.

The earl, who rode on horseback beside the carriage, was the only member of the party traveling in style. The day before they had set out from London, he had visited Tattersall's and, much to the countess's disgust, had traded the last of his consol earnings for a magnificent bay stallion. "A man is judged by the prime blood he sits astride," he'd declared. "And I'll not be found wanting by such as the Duke of Montford."

The landau rounded a bend in the long drive and Emily finally got her first glimpse of Brynhaven Manor. Every window of the magnificent four-story structure was ablaze with light, and as they drew closer she could see that flanking the shallow, torchlit stairs leading to the great carved doors stood two lines of footmen in the dark blue-and-gold livery of the duke's household.

A slender figure in somber black descended the stairs to welcome them and Lady Hargrave, first to leave the carriage and obviously blinded by the brilliant torchlight, dropped into a deep court curtsy.

"Good evening, Lady Hargrave. Welcome to Brynhaven." The voice was deep and mellifluous, but the dark, bespectacled eyes perusing the top of the countess's head were most definitely not those of the duke.

"I am Edgar Rankin, the Duke of Montford's man-of-affairs," the voice continued. "His grace has not yet arrived, but we are expecting him sometime later this evening."

He turned his smiling gaze to Emily and her cousin. "Welcome, Lady Lucinda and Miss Haliburton," he said. Then with a graceful, fluid movement which took Emily completely by surprise, he leapt forward to catch the countess, whose carriage-weary legs had failed her at the apex of her curtsy. Like a great, foundering whale, she toppled forward into Mr. Rankin's outstretched arms.

"What the devil!" Behind them the earl dismounted and handed his reins to a waiting groom. His heavily jowled face was mottled with rage and humiliation, and he grasped his wife's ample waist with both beefy hands to haul her to her feet. "Damn blast it, madam, you've made a fine cake of yourself this time," he declared. "You are far too fat to be trying to do the pretty."

"Welcome to Brynhaven, my lord," Mr. Rankin wheezed, his bulging eyes and high color the only visible indications he had just exerted the kind of effort not generally required of a gentleman in his position. "If you and your ladies will follow me, I shall direct the staff to make your accommodations available."

"Lead on then, sir, by all means," the earl blustered, with a quelling glance at his countess.

Emily could immediately see the duke's man of affairs was far kinder and more gentlemanly than his haughty employer. The smile he bestowed on the red-faced countess was benign in the extreme and the discreet hand he placed beneath her right elbow was just the thing to help the flustered woman regain her composure.

"May I suggest a hot tub, my lady," he said gently, "and a light repast in your chambers after your long, tiring journey. The duke's other guests have all opted for an early night to prepare for tomorrow's activities." So saying, he led the small bedraggled group up the stairs toward the massive, wide-flung doors of the manor house.

Emily caught a glimpse of Lucinda's distraught face and took a firm grip on the girl's arm. "Don't you dare faint," she warned when she felt her cousin stumble. "I cannot carry you up these stairs and poor Mr. Rankin has already had his arms full of one Hargrave this evening."

Fairly dragging the limp-limbed girl past the interminable lines of stoic footmen, Emily followed the earl and countess into the great entry hall where an equally stoic butler and another row of footmen waited to greet them.

With a feeling close to awe, Emily stared about her at the huge mullioned windows and the magnificent Gobelin tapestries displaying the duke's flamboyant coat of arms, at the graceful curving staircase, and the high, narrow balcony which ringed the cathedral-like room.

Beside her, Lucinda sobbed softly. "Oh, Emily," she whispered, "it is even grander and more foreboding than I had imagined. I want to go home."

For the first time in the two months she'd been Lucinda's 'companion,' Emily found herself in complete accord with her flighty young cousin.

After a restless night that seemed never to end, Emily rose from her bed at dawn on her first morning at Brynhaven. She had been assigned the guest bedchamber next to Lucinda's—a surprise, since she was not actually a guest but merely a paid employee, albeit one who had yet to receive her first shilling.

She had been too exhausted to give the room more than a cursory glance before she sank gratefully into the steaming hip bath provided for her the night before. Now she could see that unlike the great drafty hall below, this room was of comfortable proportions and had obviously been decorated to suit a lady's taste.

A daintily executed mural on one stretched-silk wall depicted a group of seventeenth-century ladies of the court surrounded by cherubic children and gamboling lambs, and everything from the delicate embroidered hanging over the bed to the exquisite Gillows rosewood writing table was much too fragile and feminine to appeal to anyone of the male gender. Emily's sad little hand-me-down gowns filled one small corner of the intricately carved armoire, looking very much out of place in their elegant surroundings.

Since the morning was chilly for May, she dressed in one of the plain kerseymere frocks Lucinda had discarded once she left the schoolroom. It was much too tight across Emily's bosom—as were all the dresses she had inherited from her slender cousin—and a faded line showed where the hem had been let down. But it was warm and no one would expect a mere companion to be dressed in the first stare of fashion.

A pair of sturdy half boots completed the outfit, and since Lucinda never required her services before eleven o'clock, Emily made a spur-of-the-moment decision to spend her free time walking in the fresh, clean country air—an activity she had sorely missed during her sojourn in London.

No sooner had she stepped into the corridor and closed her chamber door than she encountered Maggie Hawkes. "For Miss Lucinda," Hawkes said, indicating the cup of steaming chocolate she carried. "It's that worried I am about the poor little scrap. What with sobbing her heart out and all, I doubt she closed an eye all night."

"Oh dear, I should go to her," Emily said.

"Beggin' your pardon, ma'am, but it might be best if you didn't. She's all cried out now and I think she may drop off once she has a nip of chocolate and a bite or two of the biscuits I pried out of the duke's cook."

"Perhaps you are right," Emily agreed, feeling guilty at how relieved she was that Hawkes's suggestion freed her to pursue her own desires for a few hours. "I'll look in on her when I return from my walk."

"You do that, miss." A frown darkened Hawkes's age-weathered face. "I know it's not for me to question my betters, ma'am, but I can't help but wish her nibs wasn't so set on making a match of it with Miss Lucinda and this high-and-mighty duke. To my way of thinking, she's not right for him, nor him for her. The man is too particular by half, if Cook is to be believed, and not one to tolerate anyone who don't live up to his demands—which we both know Miss Lucinda couldn't do no matter how hard she tried."

"How do you mean . . . particular?"

"Cook says the duke expects his house to be run like clockwork and there's no excuses allowed. Whenever he's here at Brynhaven, everybody from that stiff-rumped butler down to the boy who scrubs the pots in the scullery has to be on their toes every single minute. His fish has got to be so fresh it's just quit swimmin' when he's served it and he won't touch an honest piece of mutton, but must have the youngest spring lamb—if you ever heard of such flummery—and it's a special sauce for this and a special sauce for that."

She shook her head. "Why he's even given orders that every morning Cook must have fresh lye and lamb suet and olive oil for his nose-in-the-air valet to mix up his shaving soap—like even his graceship's whiskers is better'n those of ordinary folk. A recipe from the Duke of Marlborough's valet, so Cook says."

Hawkes searched Emily's face with worried eyes. "Now tell me, miss, how long do you think a little flibbertigibbit like Miss Lucinda would last with such a particular one as that?"

Emily shuddered. "It would be a miracle if the duke didn't strangle her within a se'nnight of the wedding."

"My way of thinking exactly, and it just don't seem fair. It's the earl what's punting on the River Tick due to spending his nights in the gambling hells and who knows where else. But it's the little miss what has to pay for the old humgudgeon's sins."

"It isn't fair, Hawkes, but there's little in life that is,"

Emily deplored, thinking of how she was paying for the ex-
travagances of her own father—and Farley Haliburton's
only vice had been an obsession with research into ancient
myths and legends which had driven him to spend every
guinea he had on obscure tomes that no one but another
scholar of his peculiar ilk would find of any value.

Emily had loved her father dearly and took great pride
both in the modest fame his erudite publications had earned
in academic circles and in the research and editing she had
contributed to them. But she couldn't help but wish he had
invested some portion of the meager family funds in something more practical than a collection of dusty volumes.

She looked up to find two chambermaids approaching,
their arms full of linens, and she held her finger to her lips
to warn Hawkes to silence.

Hawkes nodded sagely. "I'll be taking this chocolate to
Miss Lucinda now," she declared in a voice loud enough to
apprise any but the hardest of hearing of her intentions.
Then, in a hoarse whisper she added, "There's more I could
tell you about this fine Duke of Montford, Miss Emily.
Much more. Tales I've heard in the servants' hall about
goings-on at Brynhaven as would fair curl your hair."

"And I shall want to hear them, Hawkes," Emily whispered back. Ordinarily she cared nothing for servants' gossip, but in this case it behooved her to learn all she could
about the supercilious duke. How else could she hope to
save her poor cousin from a fate she was now certain would
be worse than death for a sensitive little innocent like Lucinda?

Moments later, with the help of a sleepy young footman,
Emily located a set of French windows in a small salon at
the rear of the duke's mammoth country house and stepped
through them onto a wide stone terrace overlooking an ex-
tensive parterre garden. She stood for a moment, fascinated
by the stylized beauty of the colorful display, yet strangely

repelled by the way the landscape artist had constricted nature to fit his own narrow concepts. To her way of thinking, the formal pattern of walks and flower beds and neatly clipped hedges more closely resembled one of Aunt Hortense's Aubusson carpets than a garden.

For nearly an hour she wandered down one gravel path after another until she came to a collection of topiary shrubs groomed to resemble horses and dogs and sheep and something she suspected, from pictures she'd seen, was meant to be an Indian elephant. This final desecration of nature might suit the "particular" duke; Emily found it an insult to the Creator. She shuddered, feeling a frantic need to escape this artificial world the frivolous Duke of Montford had designed for himself.

Hurrying down a gravel path, she passed a collection of Greek statuary and circled a miniature replica of the Parthenon; then, to her surprise, she found herself staring across a shallow ha-ha at a grassy meadow which looked amazingly like the one adjoining the cottage in which she had spent the first twenty-four years of her life.

The fence at the bottom of the ditch was just high enough to keep the sheep pastured beyond from dining on the succulent contents of the formal gardens, yet low enough to be hidden from the view of the manor house windows. Without a moment's hesitation, she scrambled down the rock-strewn bank of the ha-ha, climbed over the fence and up the other side to where nature had been left to her own devices. She breathed a sigh of relief. This was more like it—there was no evidence of the duke's fine hand here.

She could see a stand of birch trees at the far end of the meadow, their leaves fluttering in the breeze like a great flock of silver butterflies, and beyond them the crystal waters of a small lake sparkled in the early morning sun. Like a child released from a tedious schoolroom, Emily gave a joyous cry, picked up her skirts, and ran pell mell across the open meadow toward the inviting scene.

Minutes later, warm-cheeked and breathless, she stood on the edge of the lake. For the first time since she'd boarded the London coach in her tiny village in the Cotswolds two months earlier, she felt at peace with the world.

With a deep breath of the cool morning air, she spread wide her arms and reveled in the blessed silence of this lovely spot. None of the rude noises of the city here. No carriages bumping over cobblestones, no vendors hawking their wares, no babble of voices nor clatter of horses' hooves along congested streets. Just the sighing of the breeze through the trees and now and then the mournful bleating of a lamb for its ewe mother.

The bleating grew more insistent, and Emily looked about her to discover the source. It was immediately evident. At a nearby spot where the bank stood level with the lakeshore, a lamb that looked to be but a few days old stood withers-deep in the water. From the skid marks at the lake's edge, it was obvious the tiny creature had lost its footing while trying to drink and slid into the lake and now was too frozen with fear to try for dry land on its own.

Emily worked her way to within a few feet of the mired lamb, but it was too far out in the water for her to reach it. She tried coaxing it to come to her, but with every word she uttered its eyes grew wilder, its bleating louder.

Finally, in desperation, she removed her boots and stockings, knotted her skirt between her legs above her knees and waded in after it. She had just managed to get her arms around the noisy, dripping creature when she heard the sound of hoofbeats and looking up, found she had an audience. One glimpse of the black-haired man astride the midnight black horse and her heart nearly stopped. "The duke," she gasped, clutching the noisy, wriggling lamb to her chest.

Then she looked again. This man might have shockingly

similar facial features and coloring, but he was a far cry from the fastidious Duke of Montford. With his blue-black hair wildly windblown and his rugged jawline darkly shadowed by a day's growth of beard, he looked more like a highwayman than a titled aristocrat. Tight-fitting black trousers, mud-covered boots, and a wide-sleeved homespun shirt open at the throat completed the thatchgallows look of the handsome stranger.

He leaned forward in the saddle until he was almost directly above her. "The sights one sees on an early-morning ride," he remarked with a chuckle—further proof he was anyone but the Duke of Montford. Emily was certain *that* stiff-necked peer of the realm would never be guilty of anything as undignified as chuckling.

She took a closer look and found another striking difference between the two men. Unlike the chilling disdain she'd seen in the duke's pale eyes, these eyes staring down at her fairly sparked with laughter.

"I suppose you must have a reason for bathing that lamb," he said, surveying her with obvious skepticism, "but I cannot, at the moment, think what it might be."

Emily was not in the mood for idle banter—especially from this scruffy example of local manhood. Her feet and legs were turning blue with the cold, her stomach rumbled with hunger, and the smell of wet wool was beginning to make her feel decidedly queasy. "I am not bathing him, you looby," she stated indignantly, "I am rescuing him. He fell in the water and could not get out by himself."

"Looby?" One black eyebrow shot upward. "You have an incautious tongue, miss. I cannot remember when anyone has dared address me so before."

Emily raised an eyebrow of her own. "Well, how do you expect me to address you, sir, when you sit warm and dry on your fine horse and leave a lady to stand in freezing water. Anyone *but* a looby would have offered me assistance the moment he rode up."

The stranger's hearty laugh shattered the stillness of the morning. "I beg your pardon, ma'am. My wits must have temporarily gone begging. I was not aware I was in the presence of a *lady*. But then one so seldom finds a *lady* unescorted and knee deep in a lake at this hour of the morning." So saying, he leaned even farther forward in the saddle, grasped Emily around the waist and hauled her, lamb and all, onto the bank with the same ease as another man might lift a feather.

Emily set the lamb on its feet, watched it scamper away, and hastily untied her skirts, aware a bold, silver gaze had fastened on her bare legs, then traveled upward to where the bodice of her hand-me-down dress strained across her bosom. A strange, shivery sensation slithered through her. No man had ever before looked at her in such an assessing fashion; whoever this rakish fellow might be, he was certainly no gentleman.

She picked up her boots and stockings and stared him defiantly in the face. "If you will be so good as to turn your head, sir, I shall finish dressing," she said peevishly.

"As you wish, ma'am." He shrugged his powerful shoulders negligently. "But I wonder to what avail. I have already seen what you have to offer."

Emily gasped, too shocked at this man's effrontery to think of a ready answer. She quickly pulled on her stockings and boots and stalked away without another look in his direction. Moments later, to her disgust, she heard him ride up behind her. "You are heading in the wrong direction unless you mean to go to the manor house," he said conversationally.

Emily plodded ahead. "Not that it is any of your concern, sir, but that is exactly where I mean to go."

"You are not from the village then? How odd! You certainly have the look of a country woman."

"And you, sir, look amazingly like the Duke of Montford, which only proves how deceiving appearances can be."

"You know the duke?" He cantered forward and turned his horse to block her path.

"I do not *know* him, but I have seen him."

"And you can easily tell us apart? Now that is truly remarkable. I have been told we look enough alike to be twins."

"Hardly!" Emily took in his disreputable appearance. "Although I suppose, by some accident of birth, you could be a shirttail relation of sorts."

He grinned. "As a matter of fact, the duke and I did have the same father."

Emily stared at him mouth agape. This rogue was one of the former duke's by-blows. No wonder he looked so much like the present duke. Her cheeks burned with embarrassment. "Forgive me," she said stiffly. "My remark was most unseemly. Whatever else your shortcomings might be, you cannot be held to blame for the manner of your birth."

His grin widened, displaying a multitude of strong, white teeth. "Truer words were never spoken, Miss . . ."

"Miss Emily Haliburton," she said automatically, still mortified at the thought of unwittingly casting aspersions on the unfortunate fellow's lineage. "And you were right in your supposition. I am a country woman. From the Cotswolds, to be precise. I am just at Brynhaven for a fortnight. The duke is hosting a house party."

"So I'd heard." He hesitated. "Of course, I only know the fellow by reputation, but rumor has it he is shopping for a wife." He stopped short. "Never say you are one of the five . . ."

Emily laughed. "A mud hen amongst the swans. Not likely, sir."

"More like a plump little country sparrow, I should say." His pale eyes raked her with a measuring gaze that noticeably quickened her already erratic heartbeat. "So then, Miss Emily Haliburton, late of the Cotswolds, how come you to be one of the duke's guests?"

"I am not a guest—merely a companion to my cousin, Lady Lucinda Hargrave, which explains why I am, as you pointed out, unescorted. A companion scarcely needs a companion, does she? Besides," she added lamely, "I am no green girl straight from the schoolroom."

"I can see that," he agreed so readily Emily felt certain she must have suddenly developed a full measure of crow's feet and wrinkles.

He cocked his head thoughtfully. "I take it Lady Lucinda is one of the five beauties vying for the duke's hand."

"That is correct," Emily said, cautiously circling the restless black stallion to make her way down the bank of the ha-ha. "I am here to offer the poor child what support I can."

"Poor child! One would think your cousin had been sentenced to Tyburn," he said, sounding a bit taken aback. "From what I've heard, Montford has the title and wealth to make him the catch of the season."

"If one is looking for a *parti* so high in the instep he comes close to tripping over his own nose each time he puts one foot in front of the other," Emily acceded sourly. "It was inevitable that Lucinda should come to the attention of the duke; she is the most beautiful girl to make her come-out this season, but she is entirely too gentle and sensitive to cope with such a man."

"Which translates into 'the chit is a bit of a slow top' unless I miss my guess." The stranger's lips curled in a nasty smile. "So naturally, as companion to Lady Lucinda, the sharp-tongued Miss Emily Haliburton is expected to supply the brains which the lovely dimwit needs to trap the hapless duke into marriage. How could such a combination fail? I've been told the high flyers of the *ton* are a perverted lot. A *ménage à trois* may be just the thing to whet the appetite of a roué like Montford."

"Why, you insufferable . . ." Emily sputtered, struggling to keep her temper under control and her skirts in place while she climbed over the low fence at the bottom of the ha-ha. She scrambled up the far bank, made a few quick repairs to her collapsing hairdo, and looked back to find her tormentor watching her every move.

"How dare you address me as if I were one of the tavern doxies with whom your kind associates," she panted.

"My kind!" The handsome devil let out a howl of laughter. "And what would a prim little country puss like you know about 'my kind'?"

For that insolent question, Emily could think of no ready answer.

Under the circumstances, the only prudent move appeared to be immediate retreat. She had already stalked past the grecian statuary and well into the parterre garden when it occurred to her that for a baseborn ruffian, this annoying fellow she had just traded wits with had had a rather amazing command of the King's English.

Chapter Three

The duke had still not made an appearance when Lady Hargrave, Lady Lucinda, and Emily joined the others for breakfast in the cheerful green-and-white morning room at five minutes before the hour of twelve noon. But Lady Sudsley made a point of informing them that their interim host, Mr. Rankin, had advised her personally that his grace had arrived at Brynhaven, but would not join his guests until dinner that evening.

Lucinda was pale as a ghost. She had complained of a headache and begged to be allowed to remain in bed, but Lady Hargrave would have none of that.

Emily sympathized with her cousin. She had a headache of her own—one that had started with the worrisome thought that very few tobymen had the vocabularies of Oxford professors and had accelerated with her discovery that the tapes securing the back of her kerseymere gown had split open during her climb over the fence. No wonder that leering oaf, whoever he might be, had had such a smug expression on his face when she'd reached the other side of the ditch. He must have gotten an eyeful of "what she had to offer" from his vantage point atop that devil horse of his.

Lady Hargrave seemed totally oblivious to the megrims suffered by the two young women accompanying her. She was much too eager to assess the "competition," already enjoying the lavish display of food laid out on the sideboard to consider anything else.

"Thank goodness I thought to have Madame Fanchon make up this French green morning dress for me," she whispered when the guests looked up from their plates to cast critical eyes on the newcomers. She fluffed the neck ruffle of the fashionable creation which hugged her portly figure like a celadon sausage casing. "First impressions are so important."

Emily assumed it must be the four other anxious mamas she was endeavoring to impress since the duke had chosen to forego the privilege of viewing the ladies and their daughters in all their morning finery.

Mr. Rankin, who had leapt to his feet the moment they entered the room, stepped forward to introduce them to the assembled guests, including three passably pretty young blond ladies and Lady Sudsley's daughter, who was a ravishing redhead, four of London's most dashing young Corinthians, who looked enough alike to be brothers, and Percival Seymour Tremayne, the Earl of Chillingham, whom Emily had heard was the heir presumptive to the Duke of Montford's title and estates until such time as the duke produced a son of his own.

The earl appeared to be no more than twenty, with a thin, anxious-looking face, ears that protruded from the sides of his head like doorknobs, and an oversized Adam's apple which seemed to have a life of its own. He was a true pink of the *ton*, with collar points that stabbed his cheekbones, gleaming tasseled Hessians, and a cutaway coat and breeches in a remarkably vivid shade of rose. With his thatch of unruly straw-colored hair and attenuated physique, the heir presumptive closely resembled an up-ended broom with a pink handle, and Emily was hard put to keep from laughing when she saw his goggle-eyed reaction to her lovely cousin—until she caught Lucinda's blushing response.

Emily took another look at the gawky earl. Could this unlikely Galahad be the knight who would rescue the fair Lucinda from the dragon duke? Miracles had come wrapped in stranger packages than this, she told herself, and filed her observations away for future reference.

Breakfast completed, Mr. Rankin announced that the duke had instructed him to conduct a tour of Brynhaven for any of his guests who were interested. Lady Hargrave declined as her knees were still tender from her abortive curtsy, but she immediately pushed Lucinda forward. "Good way to see what will be yours one day," she hissed, and since Lucinda had a death grip on Emily's hand the two found themselves part of the group of eager young ladies gathered around Mr. Rankin. Lady Sudsley and the other mothers followed close behind, with the male members of the party bringing up the rear.

All except the Earl of Chillingham, who declared his intention of taking the tour even though he "knew the manor house as well as the back of his hand" . . . and promptly attached himself to Lucinda's side with all the fervor of a honey bee hovering over the perfect flower. Lucinda, whose hitherto pale cheeks had miraculously regained their usual healthy glow, cast him a shy smile, and the earl's Adam's apple took such a leap Emily was not the least surprised his precisely tied cravat ended up slightly askew.

"We shall begin the tour in the domed entrance hall," Mr. Rankin said and proceeded to give a brief history of the house and the seven eccentric dukes of Montford who had preceded the present owner. Emily was intrigued by both the colorful stories and the wry humor with which Mr. Rankin related them, but she could see he was drawing nothing but yawns from the rest of the group.

From there, he led them through the vast ballroom with

its banks of crystal teardrop chandeliers and rows of cheval mirrors extending from dado to ceiling, then into the duchess's private salon, also known as the gold salon, since the walls were covered with pale green satin embossed with paper-thin gold leaf foil in a floral motif.

Lady Sudsley plopped her ample frame onto the nearest Hepplewhite chair and announced that she was perfectly content to forgo the balance of the tour and spend the next hour in this delightful room. The other women, along with their wide-eyed young daughters, immediately decided to join her, and from the avaricious looks cast on the delicate *objets d'art* with which the room abounded, it was obvious to Emily that each woman was laying plans for the day when her daughter would be the next duchess to claim ownership of the salon and its priceless contents. For the first time, she found herself feeling a little sorry for the high-and-mighty Duke of Montford. With all his wealth and power, he would never know the kind of unquestioning devotion her sweet-natured mother had lavished on her impractical father.

Their next stop was the duke's library—an impressive collection of first editions that made Emily's mouth water just thinking about them. From there, they moved on to the games room, where they lost the male members of the party to the billiard table—all except the besotted young earl, who remained glued to Lucinda's side while Mr. Rankin and the three remaining members of his tour examined the manor's many other salons, including the green salon, the blue salon, the Grecian salon, and the pretentious Chinese salon, which the last duchess had furnished with a plethora of authentic fourteenth-century red lacquer furniture and exquisite hand-painted screens depicting the development of the arts during the Ming Dynasty.

Lucinda pronounced this replica of the Emperor's throne room "very pretty and cozy," and the earl fervently agreed, declaring it his favorite room at Brynhaven. Then, since

Lucinda complained she was exhausted from the strenuous tour, he tucked her slender arm into his and led her through a convenient set of French windows to a bench in the duchess's rose garden.

Emily watched them go with her blessing. With twenty-four guests and two hundred servants roaming about the house and grounds, she could see no impropriety in two starry-eyed young people sitting together in the spring sunshine.

"You are obviously a patient woman, Miss Haliburton, as well as one with a forgiving disposition." Mr. Rankin's dark eyes twinkled behind the thick lenses of his spectacles. "It is all too apparent I have bored the rest of our little group to flinders."

"I cannot imagine why," Emily declared. "I found both your discourse and your delivery quite fascinating."

"Why thank you, Miss Haliburton." An appreciative smile brightened Mr. Rankin's thin face. "Would I be assuming too much then to hope you might wish to see more of the house?"

Emily stared at him, dumbfounded. "Surely, sir, you cannot mean you would conduct a tour just for me."

"I cannot think of anything I would rather do," he said earnestly. "The perceptive questions you've asked have shown you to be a highly intelligent young woman—something I rarely meet in my line of work." He studied her closely. "You would not by any chance be related to the noted scholar, Sir Farley Haliburton, would you?"

"He was my papa," Emily said, flushing with pleasure. "You know his work?"

"The duke and I have followed his research with great interest. In fact, two of his publications are in the library of the duke's London town house." He frowned. "But you referred to your father in the past tense. Could it be that the academic world has lost one of its most devoted researchers of ancient myths and legends?"

"Papa died three months ago," Emily managed in a choked voice. She looked away, avoiding Mr. Rankin's perceptive gaze, lest he see the sudden tears misting her eyes.

"My deepest sympathy, Miss Haliburton," he said gravely. "We are all the poorer for his passing." He cleared his throat self-consciously. "With your permission, I will forgo showing you the kitchens, the bakery, and the orangery, unless you particularly wish to see them."

Emily shook her head, still too moved by this stranger's sympathy to trust her voice.

"And I doubt you would find the shops which headquarter the carpenters, painters, roofers, and masons of much interest. Suffice it to say, it takes a small army of such people to maintain a place this size." He pulled a thin gold watch from his vest pocket. "I have an appointment with the duke in one hour, so we shall have to put off the stables until another day. Do you ride, Miss Haliburton?"

"I rode a great deal in the Cotswolds. The squire whose land adjoined my father's was happy to have someone take his nags for a gallop." Emily managed a smile. "But I haven't ridden in the two months I've spent in London."

"Ah! Then we shall have to do something about that." He offered her his arm. "But in the meantime, we have just enough time to see one of Brynhaven's most interesting rooms—the family portrait gallery. Unfortunately it is located in another wing of the house, but if you have no objections to a bit of a walk . . ."

"I don't mind a walk in the least."

"Capital! Then if you would care to take my arm, Miss Haliburton, we shall wend our way through the labyrinthine halls of Brynhaven . . . and hopefully become better acquainted in the process."

Emily couldn't remember when she'd met anyone as kind or as easy to converse with as the duke's mild-mannered man-of-affairs. One thing led to another and before they reached their destination, she found herself telling him about the disquisition on ancient Mesopotamian legends which her father had been working on at his death. She was in the process of confessing her intention to complete it for publication in his name when the footman who accompanied them opened the door to the vast, hall-like gallery. The words froze on her tongue when she found herself staring at a lifesize portrait of the first Duke of Montford.

"Handsome fellow," Mr. Rankin remarked. "And the present duke looks exactly like him. In fact, as you'll see as we progress from one generation to another, all the dukes of Montford bear a striking resemblance to one another."

Emily nodded. The frenzied thumping of her heart made speech impossible. She had recognized a similarity between the present Duke of Montford and her matutinal tormentor, but this portrait made her realize just *how* similar the two of them were. Her heart skipped a beat. If indeed there were two of them!

The inscrutable silver eyes staring down at her from the wall of the gallery looked frighteningly familiar, as did the raven hair and sensuous mouth, the powerful shoulders and lean hips. Except for his sixteenth century costume, this haughty aristocrat who had once representated the Montford dynasty could easily have been the mysterious stranger she'd encountered on her morning walk.

She closed her eyes and willed her heart to stop its thunderous pounding. But her mind flooded with memories—of a rich, cultured voice and strong, tapered fingers grasping her about the waist. And something else she hadn't registered at the time. A heavy gold signet ring on the third finger of the stranger's left hand.

She opened her eyes and stared in horror at the heavy gold signet ring on the third finger of the left hand of the first Duke of Montford.

* * *

Emily dressed for her first—and possibly last—dinner at Brynhaven with special care—as special as a limited wardrobe of ill-fitting, hand-me-down gowns would allow, that is. None of them were actually suitable for a paid companion, but Lady Hargrave had waved Emily's objections aside, declaring she would have to make do, as family finances were at too low tide to worry about outfitting someone with no social status and no hope of gaining any.

The dress Emily chose was a cream-colored silk with long sleeves to which Maggie Hawkes had added a burgundy overskirt. The color combination and fabric were more suited to December than May and the décolletage which had been modest on Lucinda's diminutive bosom barely managed to cover Emily's more generous endowments. The only thing to be said for Lucinda's castoffs was that they were of a more recent vintage than the threadbare garments she herself had brought from the West Country.

All things considered, Emily had fervently prayed she would not be expected to dine with the invited guests, but Mr. Rankin had insisted she was expected to join the duke's table. Interpreting her reluctance as dismay at being thrust into a level of society far above the one she normally moved in, he had assured her, "You have no need to be nervous, Miss Haliburton. I shall instruct the housekeeper to seat you next to me so we may continue this fascinating discussion on Mesopotamian legends."

Now, waiting for her aunt and cousin to complete their toilettes, she found herself hoping that Mr. Rankin would not be put in an embarrassing situation by befriending her if the handsome brigand she'd crossed swords with that morning did indeed turn out to be the Duke of Montford playing at being one of the common folk.

She could just imagine the cut direct such a man would give a little nobody who had dared call him a . . . a looby, for heaven's sake.

Her pulse was still fluttering wildly when thirty minutes later a footman led the earl and his bevy of females to the Grecian salon, where the guests had gathered before dinner. Emily immediately espied Mr. Rankin conversing with the Earl of Chillingham, a veritable peacock in orange-and-blue satin, and a handsome man in elegant black, whom she recognized as Beau Brummell—the commoner whose caustic wit and flair for fashion had made him a favorite of both the *ton* and the Prince Regent.

The three blond ladies who aspired to the duke's hand were dressed, like Lucinda, in virginal white. As a result, Lady Sudsley's red-haired daughter, in pale pink with tiny pink roses threaded through her auburn tresses, looked entirely unique. Lady Hargrave's ponderous bosom heaved with agitation. "We are undone by that shrew, Lady Sudsley, and her brazen offspring," she moaned to the earl.

"Never so, madam." The earl's eyes held a malicious gleam. "The chit has no chin. She may be appealing straight on; from the side, she looks like a chipmunk. Not at all the thing for a fellow as particular as Montford."

Emily barely had time to digest this enlightening bit of information when a footman opened the door and the Duke of Montford, flanked by his two elderly maiden aunts, made his entrance. Like Mr. Brummell, he was resplendent in black satin with pristine white linen, but even the elegant Beau paled before the imposing splendor of the tall, regal duke.

All conversation instantly ceased.

"Good evening. I trust you are all settled comfortably in your respective chambers." The duke's rich voice echoed in the silent room, and a chorus of eager assents rose from the people ringing its perimeter. How clever to hold this first reception here, Emily thought, noting the huge circular divan in the center of the room which forced the guests to line up along the walls for the duke's inspection.

She watched him progress from one group to the next,

chatting briefly with each and raising his quizzing glass to peruse each of the young ladies offered up to him with the same concentration she'd seen potential buyers inspect the horses for sale at a country fair. Any moment now, she expected the arrogant coxcomb to ask to see their teeth.

She was so incensed by this display of autocratic insensitivity she forgot her nervousness and before she knew it, he was approaching the Earl of Hargrave's party.

"I am going to faint, Mama," Lucinda protested in a strangled whisper.

"Do so and you will answer to me, miss," the earl hissed as Emily made a grab for one of Lucinda's arms, Lady Hargrave the other. Lucinda's eyes glazed over and her head rolled forward to her chest, but between the two of them, they managed to keep her upright.

"May I present the Earl and Countess of Hargrave, your grace," Lady Cloris cooed, "and their dear little daughter, Lady Lucinda." In concert, Emily and Lady Hargrave dipped Lucinda into a semblance of a curtsy.

"Charmed," the duke said in an apathetic monotone, and never blinking an eye, raised Lucinda's limp hand to his lips. "And . . ." His gaze swept Emily.

"My niece, Miss Emily Haliburton," Lady Hargrave supplied, wagging her eyebrows at Emily to signal her to curtsy. Emily curtsied, or at least came as close to it as her hold on Lucinda would permit.

"Charmed," the duke repeated, raising her left hand to his lips since her right was busy supporting Lucinda. Emily studied him closely, but not a sign of recognition did she see in his cold, silver eyes.

Surreptitiously, she glanced at his left hand. A massive signet ring adorned the third finger, but it was nothing like the plain gold ring the stranger had worn. This one was far more ornate and heavily encrusted with gem stones—

exactly the sort of ostentatious ornament she would expect
a foppish duke to wear.

She released the breath she hadn't known she was holding. Praise God. There *were* two of them! They might look
as alike as two fleas on a dog, but there the resemblance
ended. She could no more imagine this icy-eyed duke teas-
ing a simple country girl or hooting with laughter than she
could imagine that wicked-tongued tobyman disporting
himself in polite society. She was so relieved, she favored
the duke with a brilliant smile, which caused him to raise
his quizzing glass and give her a disapproving stare before
he moved on to inspect the pretty but vapid daughter of the
Earl of Pembrook.

Her first dinner at Brynhaven was an unqualified success
as far as Emily was concerned. Never mind that she was
pointedly snubbed by the young ladies and treated as if she
didn't exist by their mamas—or that she was generally ignored by the dashing Corinthians.

True to his word, Mr. Rankin had arranged to have her
seated next to him and they had such a marvelous conversation about Greek myths and Mesopotamian legends, she almost forgot to devote part of her time to the Earl of
Sudsley, who sat on her other side. But it scarcely mattered,
since he had imbibed so freely of the duke's excellent
Madeira at the reception he was already well and truly
foxed by the time the soup course was removed.

She didn't even have to worry about Lucinda, who had
recovered nicely from her swoon. She was seated next to
the Earl of Chillingham, who looked so pleased with himself Emily was certain he, too, had effected some last-
minute changes in the seating arrangements.

Except for one dreadful moment when the lamb was
served and she found herself thinking it could well be the
poor little nipper she had rescued early that morning, she

thoroughly enjoyed every bite of the most delicious meal she had ever consumed and every sip of the wines which accompanied each of the seven courses.

The balance of the evening was just as successful, albeit a bit more nerve-racking. Each of the young ladies, in turn, performed for the duke and his guests. Two of the young blond ladies sang quite prettily, one of them played a simple piece on the pianoforte and Lady Sudsley's daughter, staring directly into the duke's eyes all the while, recited a long and soulful rendition of Sir Walter Scott's popular poem "The Lady of the Lake."

"Lud, I hope she don't swoon," Lady Hargrave whispered when it came Lucinda's turn to perform. For one moment it looked as if that was exactly what she was going to do. After handing her music to Lady Sudsley, who had volunteered to accompany the young singers, Lucinda clutched the edge of the pianoforte in abject terror. But the Earl of Chillingham, his face a mask of concern, rushed forward to stand behind Lady Sudsley and turn the sheet music whilst he gazed at Lucinda with adoring eyes—and surprisingly enough, she sang her simple little country song in a clear, sweet voice that brought enthusiastic applause from all but the disgruntled mothers of the other two singers.

When the applause subsided, there was a brief moment of silence until the duke said, in that chilling way of his, "Your turn, I believe, Miss Haliburton."

"My niece does not perform," Lady Hargrave said quickly.

The duke scowled. "How odd. I was given to understand all well-bred young ladies performed." He raised his quizzing glass and surveyed Emily with a look of profound distaste, as if her very presence insulted his tender sensibilities.

Emily felt her hackles rise and ignoring her aunt's frown, returned the duke's haughty stare. "As a matter of fact, I do play the pianoforte . . . a bit," she said between gritted teeth.

"Any little thing will suffice," Mr. Rankin declared, taking her hand to lead her to the pianoforte. "It won't do to refuse the duke, you know."

Settling onto the bench already warmed by Lady Sudsley's ample posterior, Emily contemplated what she should play. She was tempted to perform an excerpt from Mr. Ludwig van Beethoven's wonderful "Eroica" Symphony, the music of which one of Papa's academic friends had brought back from the Continent, along with a case of French brandy he'd smuggled past the excisemen. But she decided it was a bit heavy for an informal occasion. Instead, she played a little-known piece by Mr. Mozart which had been one of Papa's favorites.

As always, once she began to play, she lost herself in the music and when the last note died away and the room burst into applause, she looked up in surprise and straight into the eyes of the duke. This time, they were not cold; they fairly glowed with appreciation for Mr. Mozart's unique genius—but only for a brief instant. Then once again, like a lake in winter, a film of ice hid the tiny fragment of human warmth she had glimpsed in their depths.

Mr. Rankin was not so loath to show his enthusiasm. He praised her effusively, and wonder of wonders, that notorious cynic, Mr. Brummell, did the same.

All in all, she decided as she discarded the despised dress and prepared for bed, it had been a remarkable day.

As was their habit, whenever circumstances brought the two of them together under one roof, the Duke of Montford and Edgar Rankin ended their day's activities with a quiet brandy in the library of whichever of the duke's houses they happened to be in at the time. Tonight they were joined by George Brummell, which meant that Edgar, proper fellow that he was, would adhere to the rigid proto-

col which was commonly observed between a duke and his
amanuensis.

The duke sighed. After an evening of being "your
graced" to death by the pack of ninnyhammers his aunts
had inflicted on him, he was in no mood to listen to Edgar
do the same. Edgar Rankin was the one man he counted as
a true and trusted friend. When they were alone, they
slipped into the easy camaraderie they'd formed as boys
growing up together and it was "Edgar" and "Jared." There
would be none of that tonight, and he found himself regret-
ting his spur-of-the-moment decision to invite the charming
Beau to join them in their nightcap.

On the other hand, Brummell's presence would save him
from one of Edgar's confounded lectures. The scurvy fellow had already managed an aside in the Grecian salon.
"Doing the ducal thing up a bit brown aren't you, your
grace?" he'd whispered as he'd passed on his way to escort
Miss Emily Haliburton in to dinner.

The duke poured the brandy, handed the snifters around,
and set the decanter on the table next to the leather armchair
that had once been his grandfather's. For some minutes the
three sat in comfortable contemplation of the fire crackling
in the stone fireplace. Finally, Brummell broke the silence.
"Interesting evening, your grace, although I suspect Rankin
had the best of it." He smiled lazily at the man sitting beside
him. "Dare I ask what subject you and the fascinating Miss
Haliburton found so engrossing during dinner?"

"Mesopotamian myths and legends; her father's research
into the God-King Gilgamesh to be precise." Edgar Rankin
sipped his brandy. "It turns out Miss Haliburton is the
daughter of Farley Haliburton, the scholar who wrote that
treatise on Orestes you liked so well, Jar . . . your grace.
She was most pleased to learn it was in the library of your
London town house."

"Unless my memory has failed me, I believe Orestes was
a Greek, not a Mesopotamian," the duke said dryly. He

couldn't remember when he'd seen Edgar so enthusiastic about any female. It was a little disconcerting.

"According to Miss Haliburton, her father spent the greater part of his life researching Greek and Roman mythology. It was only after the British Museum staged that exhibition of Ninevite tablets a few years ago that he became interested in Middle Eastern mythology. She hopes to complete the Gilgamesh work and publish it in his name."

"So Miss Haliburton is not only an accomplished pianist, but a bluestocking as well." Montford poured himself another brandy and handed the decanter to Rankin. "Has this original any other talents that you know of, or should I ask that question of you, Brummell? I noticed you spent a considerable time conversing with her later in the evening."

"That I did," the Beau admitted. "I was attempting to ascertain why a discerning fellow like Rankin was so drawn to a woman with such execrable taste in clothing—as well as one whose chief function appears to be bear-leading her lovely young cousin." He smiled his famous, caustic smile. "Although your heir presumptive appears to be relieving her of some of her duties in that quarter."

"And was your curiosity about Miss Haliburton satisfied?" the duke asked, pointedly ignoring the reference to the way that young fool Percival had ogled Lady Lucinda all evening.

"Entirely. The lady informed me both 'idiosyncracies' stem from necessity rather than choice." He chuckled. "When I complimented her on the originality of her dress, she flat out accused me of dealing her Spanish coin. I believe her exact words were 'It is one of Lady Lucinda's done over. It probably suited her admirably. I, however, resemble an overstuffed Christmas goose.' "

The duke stifled a laugh; he could well imagine the outspoken Miss Haliburton saying such a thing.

Brummell accepted the decanter from Edgar Rankin and

poured an inch of brandy into his glass. "The lady is no beauty, but she is as you say, your grace, an original. If I could take her in hand, starve off a few pounds, and dress her decently, I guarantee she would take London by storm."

"By all means a change of dress, but never suggest reducing the lady's measurements in the duke's presence," Rankin said with a chuckle. "It is well known his grace prefers his women plump."

"But Miss Haliburton is not one of my women," the duke pointed out. "Still, I admit I am amazed you both should be so intrigued by a lady of plain countenance with five beauties to choose from."

Edgar Rankin shrugged. "But the beauties had eyes only for you, your grace."

"Or for my title, at any rate," the duke said sourly. "But that is a subject best left unexplored." He raised a quizzical eyebrow. "However, do continue your discussion of the fascinating Miss Haliburton. Tell me, was her expertise limited to Mesopotamian legends or could she converse on other subjects as well?"

"She had a nauseating enthusiasm for horses," the Beau said with a shudder. "Informed me she loves to ride early in the morning, of all things. There we parted company. I myself cannot stand the beasts except to provide mobility for my carriage, and I consider any hour before noon fit only for such creatures as domestics and Hottentots."

"It appears Miss Haliburton and his grace have something in common besides an interest in ancient myths," Edgar Rankin commented.

"Mr. Rankin alludes to my own preference for an early-morning ride," the duke said, noting Brummell's puzzled expression. He smiled benignly at his helpful man-of-affairs. "If Miss Haliburton is such an ardent horsewoman, she must by all means avail herself of my stables whilst at Brynhaven. Send a footman to alert the head groom to have a mount ready for her at dawn—the dapple-gray mare sired by Windstorm, I think. And have a maid slip a note to that effect under the lady's chamber door."

Edgar Rankin's mouth dropped open. "Tonight, your grace?"

"Tonight, Mr. Rankin."

"Very well, your grace. And I shall request a groom be ready to accompany her, of course."

"I think not, Mr. Rankin. She is perfectly safe as long as she is on Brynhaven property and she would have to ride several hours to cross its boundaries." He idly twirled his brandy glass in his fingers. "And as I have recently been reminded, a companion for a companion is a bit superfluous."

The duke drained his brandy and set the glass on the table at his elbow. "And now, gentlemen, I bid you good night. The hour grows late and for those of us who are not confirmed lay-abeds, the morning comes early."

On his way to his suite after the tête-à-tête in the library, the Duke of Montford congratulated himself on managing two rather clever maneuvers which made an otherwise depressing evening worthwhile.

Firstly, he had gained a great deal of information from Edgar and Brummell about the unexpectedly intriguing Miss Haliburton, and then effectively silenced the questions he could see both those astute gentlemen were longing to ask about *his* interest in the lady.

And secondly, he had had the foresight, before he'd faced her as the Duke of Montford, to remove the plain gold signet ring he had worn since the day he'd removed it from his dead grandfather's finger. Replacing it with the gaudy bauble that had belonged to his tasteless, spendthrift of a father had truly been a stroke of genius.

Chapter Four

The dapple gray was the sweetest little goer Emily had ever ridden—swift as the wind with a stride so smooth, she found herself laughing aloud from the sheer joy of the ride. She would never be able to thank Mr. Rankin sufficiently for arranging this treat for her.

It had all been so unexpected. First the white envelope slipped beneath her chamber door during the night and then the footman standing by to escort her to the stables, where the gray stood saddled and waiting. Much as she hated to admit it, there were certain indisputable advantages to a life of privilege such as the duke's household enjoyed.

She had taken the gray into a glorious full gallop across an open meadow, then slowed to a canter in a sparsely wooded area when she suddenly became aware of someone watching her from atop a gentle rise. Her heart leapt in her breast when she saw the horseman's unruly black hair glistening in the morning sun, and an embarrassing rush of heat flooded her cheeks at the wicked gleam in his eyes when the magnificent stallion beneath him reared onto its hind legs at the sight of the little mare.

She urged the gray forward, but he edged his mount down the slope and cut her off. "You're a neck-or-nothing rider, I see, Miss Haliburton," he said conversationally. "May I compliment you on your excellent seat."

"I am a country woman, sir, and have ridden all my life," she replied, but she felt inordinately pleased at the unexpected praise.

"And now you are trying out one of the duke's nags."

"Yes. Isn't she a beauty! Mr. Rankin, the duke's man-of-affairs, arranged for me to ride her while I am at Brynhaven. The man is kindness itself. I cannot think how I shall ever be able to repay him."

One black eyebrow elevated slightly. "I am certain he will think of something. But be that as it may, I am happy to see you again, Miss Haliburton. May I join you in a ride?"

Emily surveyed him dubiously. He sounded entirely too polite to be trusted, considering his outrageous behavior of yesterday—and somehow this congenial mood made him appear even more dangerous than the mocking one he'd previously maintained. "I don't see how I can stop you," she said bluntly.

"Thank you, ma'am. Your graciousness is exceeded only by your sense of style." His silver gaze lingered on the moss green fabric straining across her bosom.

"This is not actually my riding habit, but rather one my cousin discarded," she explained self-consciously. Though why she should feel constrained to explain anything to this ratchety fellow, she had no idea.

He nodded. "I deduced as much. I take it the lady is somewhat less endowed than you." He smiled, as if the mere act of curving his well-formed lips would make his daring remark less offensive. "Oh well, at least it is an improvement over that schoolroom uniform you wore yesterday."

"Really, sir," Emily said, bristling with resentment at his untoward rudeness.

"It is an exceptionally fine morning," he remarked cheer-fully before she could make the cutting retort that sprang to mind. "And I am in the mood for a bit of sport. Are you game for a race, Miss Haliburton—say to the tallest oak at the far side of the meadow?"

He took her by surprise. She didn't know what to make of such a fellow. One minute he was insulting her; the next suggesting a friendly competition.

Obviously, the proper thing to do would be to give him the set-down he deserved and ride on. Still, she liked noth-ing better than a good race; the very thought of it heated her sporting blood to the boiling point.

She eyed the oak speculatively. The gray had speed but she could never match the stamina of the huge stallion. But then, at such a short distance stamina might not be a factor.

"Afraid to accept my challenge, Miss Haliburton?" he asked when she remained silent. "You surprise me. I would never have taken you for a pudding-hearted miss."

Emily's temper flared. "Done, sir!" she declared, throw-ing both propriety and caution to the winds.

"And for the prize, the winner may ask anything, within reason, of the loser."

Emily considered this carefully. "As long as I define 'within reason,' " she agreed finally, knowing full well that just being alone in this isolated spot with such a man was scandalous enough without the added iniquity of a provoca-tive wager. She wondered what her friend the village vicar would think if he could see her now.

For two-thirds of the sprint across the meadow, they rode neck and neck, although Emily could see that while the game little mare was pushed to her limits, the stallion merely loped along at his ease. He showed the gray his rump a safe distance from the goal, and the handsome rogue who rode him pulled him to and waited for Emily and the mare to catch up.

"A fool's bet wagered; a fool's game lost," Emily admitted breathlessly as she approached the devilish-looking pair. "I should have known the little mare had no chance against your stallion." Her cheeks were wind-blushed and her hair, loosened from its confining pins, fell like a mantle across her shoulders; she felt certain she must look a complete hoyden, but she couldn't remember when she had felt so wonderfully, vitally alive. For some reason she couldn't begin to understand, this annoying fellow had that effect on her. The truth was, she scarcely knew herself when she was in his presence.

"So, what is it you ask, sir?" she queried, twisting her hair into a coil and securing it at the back of her neck with her few remaining pins.

The duke couldn't tear his gaze from her luxuriant brown hair. Now that he knew how it looked tumbling like a lustrous, satin waterfall down her back, he found himself contemplating it fanned out across a pillow. His pillow.

He pulled himself up short. What was he thinking? Except for her glorious hair and the keen intelligence in her bright blue eyes, this was a plain-as-porridge spinster who was far more likely to give a man a tongue lashing than a sweet kiss-me-hello. Besides which, she was a commoner—too far beneath him to consider for a wife and too prim and prissy to be mistress to any man.

He must have attics-to-let to rise at dawn to clash verbal swords with this vinegary antidote when five milk-and-honey misses waited at the manor house to hang on his every word. Still, he had to admit he found an excitement in the challenge she offered—an excitement that had been noticeably lacking in his life of late.

"Please be good enough to tell me what forfeit you demand," she said when he failed to answer her question. "I cannot diddle away the entire morning you know. Mr. Rankin is organizing a picnic and has promised to take me rowing on the lake whilst the duke entertains his bevy of pretties. I should not wish to miss that, above all."

Edgar again. Hell and damnation! The fellow was becoming a nuisance. The duke swallowed his frustration. Changing tactics, he favored Miss Haliburton with a smile, the like of which his current mistress Lady Caroline Crawley had more than once declared could melt her bones at twenty paces. It appeared to have the opposite effect on the shrewish Miss Haliburton; she simply drew herself up straighter in the saddle and continued to stare at him with unconcealed impatience.

"I ask that we dispense with the tedious formalities, ma'am, and address each other by our given names," he said in a sugary tone that, even to his own ears, sounded a bit false. "Is that beyond reason?"

She cocked her head to the right while she considered his request, looking more than ever like the country sparrow he had named her. "It really is quite improper, you know, but then everything about someone like you is unthinkable for someone like me. So I suppose that, relatively speaking, your request could be considered within bounds." She frowned. "You already know my name, but how am I to call you by your Christian name when I have never heard it?"

"My name is Jared." He had intended to give her a false one in case she had occasion to hear the Duke of Montford's given name, but at the last moment, he couldn't bring himself to do so. She had a strangely husky little voice with a faint West Country accent, and he felt an undeniable compulsion to hear his name on her lips.

"Jared. It suits you. It has a wicked ring to it."

He laughed. "You see me as wicked? How so, Emily?"

"Dark and wicked and mysterious—quite unlike anyone I have ever before known."

"Except the duke, since we are peas in a pod."

"That cold fish!" Emily shook her head. "You are nothing alike. But speaking of the duke, are you not taking a great chance riding on his land? He strikes me as a man who would deal harshly with anyone who crossed him."

Jared leaned forward to stroke the restless stallion behind his twitching right ear. "I have always ridden Brynhaven as if it were my own. The duke cannot object to what he does not know—and the tenants are my friends; they pretend they do not see me when I pass."

Emily cocked her head again, her eyes thoughtful. "You are very bold, sir, as well as extraordinarily well spoken for the baseborn fellow you claim to be."

"As are you for the simple country woman you claim to be."

"I never purported to be a farmer's daughter. My father was a noted Oxford scholar who chose to pursue his research in the quiet countryside of the Cotswolds. He educated me himself."

Jared thought quickly. "And the local vicar saw to my education," he said, inventing the story as he spoke. "The poor fellow hoped I would someday succeed him, despite my unfortunate lineage. But I, of course, was much too wicked and mysterious to consider such a vocation."

"Now you are laughing at me, sir."

"Never, ma'am. I laugh at myself and my pretentions."

He watched her gaze drop to the signet ring adorning his left hand. "You wonder, no doubt, how someone of my lowly station should come by this expensive bauble." Lifting his hand, he let the sun glint off the rich gold. "The truth is, I took it off the finger of a dead man."

Emily's eyes widened; her cheeks paled. "You are even more nefarious than I had imagined." She gasped. "I cannot comprehend why I waste my time with you."

"Probably for the same reason I go to such lengths to

waste *my* time with you," he said, following close behind her. "Curiosity about a creature so different from myself."

She urged the gray forward into a canter. "Well, my curiosity is well and truly satisfied now."

"Is it? Mine is barely whetted." He slowed his mount and watched her take the little mare into a gallop, carrying her away from him. "Until tomorrow, Emily," he shouted. "I shall wait for you by the oak tree. Perhaps I may even carve your initials in the trunk."

"You shall wait in vain, sir," she called back over her shoulder.

"Oh I don't think so." He laughed to himself. "Somehow I don't think so, Emily." But by then she was too far away to hear him.

Dining alfresco was nothing new to Emily; picnicking had been her mother's favorite summer pastime. Even her reclusive father had found enjoyment in it since he could relax beneath a shady tree with one of his precious books after the meal. But the ostentatious luncheon the Duke of Montford hosted bore little resemblance to the simple basket of chicken, lemonade, and pastries Emily had carried across an open meadow to her favorite picnic spot.

The richly gowned ladies, complete with ornate fans and lacy parasols, traveled in open carriages to the chosen spot beside one of Brynhaven's lakes, where a massive table, complete with the finest linen, crystal, silver, and china had already been set up.

The gentlemen of the party rode escort on their blooded mounts, and behind them came wagons carrying covered serving platters of food and flagons of champagne, as well as three carriages conveying Pettigrew, the duke's butler, and twelve liveried footmen to serve the table.

Emily had been looking forward to a respite from the stifling formality of the duke's household and the sight of this opulence sent her spirits sinking to a new low. She turned to whisper as much to Lucinda but found her cousin gazing raptly at the Earl of Chillingham, who rode beside the Hargrave ladies' carriage. Lady Hargrave, who had apparently just noticed her daughter's overt flirtation with the earl, frowned disapprovingly, but to no avail. Lucinda was obviously besotted and had eyes for no one but the gauche young nobleman. Emily cringed, certain she would somehow be found to blame for her charge's defection.

Luckily, at that moment the duke diverted the countess's attention. Riding up beside his doltish heir, he tipped his hat, made a polite inquiry as to the ladies' comfort, then spurred his mount ahead to lead the procession to its destination.

Dressed in biscuit-colored buckskin trousers and a tawny velvet riding jacket the exact color of his gleaming chestnut stallion, he was the epitome of sartorial splendor. Sighing audibly, Lady Hargrave made a remark to that effect, but Emily couldn't help but compare him to his baseborn half brother—and she found the chilly duke sadly colorless beside that charming rogue.

"Take this silly chit for a stroll until luncheon is served," Lady Hargrave hissed, pushing Lucinda at Emily the moment they stepped from the carriage. "If she does anything to ruin her chances with the duke, I shall hold you responsible." Then, pasting a determined smile on her face, her ladyship proceeded to engage the earl in conversation before he could follow his heart's desire.

"Don't make a fuss," Emily warned as Lucinda balked at being led away like a naughty child. "Your mama always takes an afternoon nap after she lunches; you can walk with the earl then."

Lucinda's blue eyes puddled with tears. "Oh, Emily, whatever shall I do? Mama insists on tossing me at the duke as if I were a sweetmeat for him to consume, and I simply cannot abide the dreadful man. He terrifies me."

"He is a little off-putting," Emily agreed.

"Not at all like the Earl of Chillingham." Lucinda sighed. "I am never terrified of him."

"Of course you're not." Emily smiled to herself. She doubted a babe in leading strings could find anything terrifying about the earl.

"I will tell you a secret," Lucinda whispered furtively, although they were already too far away for the countess to hear their conversation. "I am certain the earl loves me to distraction; he has as much as admitted so. But naturally he cannot declare himself until he can make an offer, and that will be a whole year away when he reaches his majority. Of course, he is not nearly as plump in the pockets as the duke, but I do not care a fig. Nor do I care that he will no longer be heir to the silly old title once the duke sets up his own nursery."

"Well, there's your answer then," Emily declared. "If the duke offers for you, simply refuse him and wait for the earl. This is not the Dark Ages, after all. No one can force you to marry a man you dislike."

Lucinda shook her head. "You are wrong. Papa can and he will because he cannot afford to wait a year with all his creditors hounding him. If the duke should offer for me, I am lost; Mama says I am the only asset Papa has not yet gambled away."

She stifled a sob. "Oh, Emily, how lucky you are to be so ordinary-looking you will never come to the attention of a man like the Duke of Montford."

Emily was still mulling over her cousin's well-meant but somewhat unflattering observation when an hour later they sat down to the lavish picnic luncheon.

She looked up from her plate of salmon and asparagus pie, buttered lobster, and rechauffe of Veal Galatine to find the duke's stoic gaze leveled on her. Her breath caught in her throat, but he merely scowled darkly and looked away—leaving her with an odd feeling of deflation. Not that she cared the least for the man's opinion, she reminded herself. Still his obvious disgust of her somehow made Lucinda's thoughtless comment all the more cutting.

She watched him turn his attention to Lady Sudsley's daughter, who sat on his right. It was obvious someone had warned the poor girl of her profile problem, because she was so desperate to face the duke head-on, her chin appeared to have formed a permanent attachment to her left shoulder.

Emily stifled her urge to giggle and gladly abandoned the duke, and his opinions, to such silly fribbles as Esmerelda Sudsley. Evidently the dreary fellow could conveniently overlook one's physical shortcomings if one was born into the proper social status.

With a sigh of relief, she turned to Mr. Rankin, who sat beside her, and smiled so brilliantly at the kindly gentleman he blinked in surprise.

"I have two questions, Miss Haliburton," he said, pushing his spectacles onto the bridge of his nose and returning her smile with one of his own. "One—how soon do you think we can safely manage to slip away from this collection of boring aristocrats and go rowing on the lake? And two—since we have already discussed the first two tablets, what profound bits of wisdom do you conjecture the third tablet of Atrahasis contains?"

Emily laughed. "My answer to your first question, sir, is as soon as possible. My answer to your second is Papa believed that particular tablet most likely pertained to the great flood. He was working on the translation of the rubbings his friend at the British Museum sent him when he died."

"So we may never know for certain."

"Ah, but then again we may." Emily leaned closer to Mr. Rankin and lowered her voice. "Papa taught me everything he knew about cuneiform Akkadian which, of course, is composed of wedge-shaped characters quite unlike any of our modern written languages. As I mentioned before, I hope to continue his work once I reach my twenty-fifth birthday and receive my portion."

Mr. Rankin's eyes widened. "You are an heiress then, Miss Haliburton, as well as a scholar in your own right?"

"Hardly, sir, on either count. I have much to learn before I can be considered a scholar such as Papa, and my portion is a very small one willed me by my maternal grand-mother—but sufficient for my simple needs. I inherited Papa's cottage and all his books and papers, you see, but there was no money left and the sad truth is, one cannot survive long on myths and legends alone." She smiled. "But in exactly three months and twenty-two days, I shall be free to spend the rest of my life doing what Papa trained me to do."

"A worthy ambition, Miss Haliburton. One I sincerely hope you may attain."

"But why in the world should I not, Mr. Rankin?"

"Why indeed, Miss Haliburton?"

The Duke of Montford pushed aside his uneaten Banbury tart—normally his favorite dessert—and watched morosely as his man-of-affairs and Miss Emily Haliburton rowed away from the shore of the lake—undoubtedly to continue the lively conversation they had carried on during the pic-nic luncheon. The two of them had had their heads together for the past hour to the exclusion of everyone around them, and he fully intended to remind Edgar, when next he saw him, that he was expected to earn his remarkably generous salary by spreading his charm amongst *all* the guests cur-rently at Brynhaven.

He swiped angrily at a marauding fly that dared land on one of the raisins in his abandoned tart, and contemplated the boring afternoon stretching ahead of him. What sort of topsy-turvy world was this when his amanuensis was off happily punting about the lake with an exhilarating companion whilst he, the Duke of Montford, was left to entertain five insipid little misses recently released from the schoolroom?

He would most definitely have words with Edgar—and not just about his neglected duties. The cheeky fellow had as much as thrown down the gauntlet when he'd accosted him at the stables that morning and warned him against plotting to carry on an assignation with the innocent Miss Haliburton. He laughed to himself. As if even the boredom of choosing a wife could drive him to such extremes when he had a beautiful, sophisticated mistress waiting for him in London!

Still, he reminded himself as he signaled the nearest footman to refill his empty champagne glass, he deserved some diversion during this deadly fortnight his obligation to the title had thrust upon him—and his dual of wits with Emily Haliburton was diverting. Probably because she was the first woman he had ever dealt with as a common man—sans the title and wealth he suspected were a great part of what the women of his own social level found irresistible.

And, though she would never admit it, Emily Haliburton did find him intriguing, even though she believed him to be a wicked ne'er-do-well without a feather to fly with. The very air between them crackled like summer lightning whenever he drew near her, and the temptation to explore that potent force of nature was much too alluring to resist.

All at once, the despised Banbury tart looked appealing again, and he attacked it with his usual gusto. With each bite, his flagging spirits lifted. So Edgar thought to challenge him, did he? Very well! Let the prosy fellow try his best to win the sharp-tongued Miss Haliburton with his urbane charm and wit. For once he, as the penniless rogue Jared would compete with his clever man-of-affairs on his own level and best him at the game he played so well.

"Did you enjoy your morning ride, Miss Haliburton?" Edgar Rankin asked while plying the oars of the small boat effortlessly through the mirror-smooth water. His question seemed harmless enough, but Emily heard an intensity in his voice that immediately set up her guard.

"I enjoyed it very much," she said carefully. "The mare is an absolute joy."

"And did you see any other riders—for instance, the duke, who is also known to enjoy an early gallop?"

"No," Emily replied thankfully, raising the parasol Lucinda had loaned her. "I did not see the duke."

Mr. Rankin looked puzzled. "How odd. I am certain I saw him set out in the direction the groom mentioned you had taken." He studied her thoughtfully. "Then what about a scruffy-looking fellow in black trousers and a homespun shirt who bears a startling resemblance to his grace? Did you come across him?"

Emily had never knowingly told a lie in her life; she could not bring herself to do so now, although she felt she might well be treading perilous ground. "I did have words with someone of that general description who calls himself Jared," she said warily. "But only for a moment. I did not find him at all pleasant."

"I shouldn't think you would." Mr. Rankin sighed. "I feared the reprehensible fellow might accost you." He shipped the oars and sat back, smiling his charming smile. "I feel it my duty to warn you about him since I am certain you will encounter him again."

Emily's pulse quickened with sudden alarm. "Are you saying he is dangerous?"

"Not dangerous. Just annoying. The old duke gave him free run of Brynhaven, but he has a rather unsavory reputation with the locals."

"I suspected as much," Emily said primly, adjusting her skirt to make certain her ankles were properly covered. "One can always tell when someone is not quite a gentleman."

For some reason she couldn't fathom, Mr. Rankin's lips twitched suspiciously. She frowned. "Did I say something amusing?"

"Not at all, Miss Haliburton. You said precisely what I would have expected an intelligent woman like yourself to say." He paused. "I could arrange for a groom to accompany you if you would but request it."

"No." Emily shook her head vehemently. "I am accustomed to riding alone. I much prefer it."

"As you wish, ma'am." Mr. Rankin returned to his rowing while Emily trailed the fingers of her left hand in the cool water. She glanced up, her attention caught by a flurry of activity among the guests remaining on shore. "What do you suppose is transpiring?" she asked. "There appears to be a great deal of excitement."

Mr. Rankin glanced toward the spot from which they had launched the boat and his brow wrinkled in a frown. "I cannot imagine what it could be, but I had best investigate. The duke might need my assistance." He dipped the oars back into the water and minutes later the boat scraped bottom at the shallow shoreline. One of the footmen waiting at the water's edge hauled it far enough onto land to allow Emily and Mr. Rankin to disembark safely.

Puzzled, Emily joined the guests crowded around the duke, who had mounted his spirited chestnut and joined a portly, gray-haired gentleman on an equally spirited white stallion.

"Squire Bosley, how goes it with you, sir?" Mr. Rankin greeted the newcomer.

"Not well, Mr. Rankin. Not well at all. A most dreadful thing has occurred. My wife's carriage was waylaid last evening on the Pemberley Road, and she was relieved of some very expensive jewelry as well as the few guineas she had in her reticule. The poor woman was too overset to remember anything before she fainted dead away, but my coachman said the ruffian was dark-haired, armed with two pepperbox pistols, and riding a horse as black as his evil heart."

Emily gasped. The coachman's description sounded too familiar to mistake. Jared had already come by a costly signet ring through suspect means. Now this! The man must be a complete fool to court danger so close to home.

She kept her gaze carefully averted from Mr. Rankin's discerning eyes, lest he read her thoughts and realize the man he had already warned her about was the tobyman who had robbed the squire's lady. Much as she disapproved of the blackhearted villain, she could not bring herself to betray him.

The duke edged his horse around the crowd of excited guests and servants until he stood next to Mr. Rankin. "This thief grows too bold. I am leaving to collect some of my men to help hunt him down before he takes a life as well as a purse. I rely upon you to see my guests safely back to the manor house."

"Pettigrew and the footmen can handle that task quite admirably, your grace," Mr. Rankin declared. "I would ride with you . . . with your permission, of course."

A glint of something Emily could not quite identify shone briefly in the duke's eyes as he stared down at his man-of-affairs. "As you wish, Mr. Rankin. I shall see you at the manor in a few moments then."

He turned to Emily and acknowledged her with a brief

nod of his handsome, aristocratic head. "Your servant, ma'am," he said stiffly, and turning his horse, galloped off with the squire close behind.

Mr. Rankin directed a nearby groom to ready his horse, then turned to Emily with an apologetic smile. "It seems we must postpone our pleasant visit until later, ma'am." His eyes narrowed. "You are very pale, Miss Haliburton. Please be assured you have no reason to fear for your safety. The thief would not dare show his face with such stout men as Pettigrew and the footmen about. Neither the duke nor I would leave unless we were certain of that."

Emily hated the idea that Mr. Rankin should think her a missish creature, but she could scarcely tell him it was not for her own safety she feared. She cleared her throat. "What will you do with the thief if you catch him?"

"Not 'if' Miss Haliburton, but 'when,' and the answer is we shall see a noose about his scurvy neck. His grace is not a man to countenance such licentious behaviour close by one of his estates."

An icy chill traveled Emily's spine as a picture of Jared's lifeless body swinging from Tyburn's gallows tree suddenly flashed through her mind. "Perhaps circumstances have made the fellow desperate," she ventured.

Mr. Rankin's tight little smile did not reach his eyes. "You have too kind a heart, ma'am. There is no excuse for thievery—even in these desperate times. No man willing to put in a good day's work is turned away from Brynhaven, or any of the duke's other estates, with an empty belly. The brigand has made a calculated choice to live outside the law and for that mistake he will pay with his life."

Chapter Five

The rosy glow of dawn had barely tinged the horizon when Emily crept silently from the manor house and hurried to the stables the morning after the picnic.

She had watched by her chamber window until well after midnight when the duke and his men returned from hunting the outlaw. From their disgruntled remarks she'd concluded the hunt had been fruitless, and her relief had been so great she'd sunk to her knees and offered a prayer of thanks that the mocking silver eyes which haunted her every thought would see yet another day. Then, conscience-stricken, she had spent the balance of the sleepless night chastising herself for being so taken in by the wicked fellow she had lost all sense of right and wrong.

But all her soul-searching was to no avail. With the first light of day, devil take her conscience, here she was, scurrying to caution him to cover his tracks—like some witless chicken deserting the hen coop to give warning to a plundering fox.

As he had the day before, the head groom met her at the entrance to the stables. Today, however, he wore a scowl on his weathered face. "Gorblimey, ma'am," he exclaimed in a voice still rough with sleep, "what with all the commotion up at the manor house, I never thought to see you this morning."

Emily managed a shaky smile. "But, as you can see, I am here as usual." Feigning surprise, she looked about her. "Where is the little gray Mr. Rankin gave me permission to ride? Could you please have her saddled for me."

"I could, ma'am, but it's the should of it I don't know. It would be bellows-to-mend if I was to let one of his grace's lady guests ride off and get herself set upon by the gallows bird what robbed Squire Bosley's lady."

Panic welled in Emily at the thought that this well-meaning fellow might prevent her from warning Jared of the danger he faced. "I hardly think that is a serious concern as long as I stay within the boundaries of Brynhaven," she stated through lips whose trembling she could not quite control.

"Maybe not, ma'am. But then again, maybe so."

"Has the order to have the gray readied for me each morning been rescinded?" she demanded, gambling that with all he had on his plate Mr. Rankin wouldn't have given a second thought to her morning ride.

"No, ma'am, but that's not to say it shouldn't ha' been."

Emily drew herself up in her best imitation of Lady Hargrave. "That judgment is not yours to make," she declared haughtily. "Please be good enough to saddle my horse immediately."

"Yes, ma'am." The old fellow's bravado instantly wilted before her lady-of-the-manor posture. Moments later, to her relief, she watched him lead the gray through the stable door. Muttering a few well-chosen words about the cork-brained thinking of the gentry, he held the little mare steady while Emily availed herself of the handy mounting stair.

Jared Neville Tremayne, Eighth Duke of Montford was in a foul mood. Above everything, he hated cowards. They were the most unpredictable of creatures, tormented into rash acts by nameless fears that braver men steadfastly put aside. This thief who preyed upon helpless women traveling the roads near Brynhaven had to be just such a weakling. Sooner or later, unless he was caught and dealt with, he would likely be driven to murder some hapless coachman or traveler who challenged his demand to "stand and deliver."

They had set a careful trap for the brigand. Edgar, dressed as a woman and in the squire's coach, had been driven for hours on end down the countless highways and byways of the nearby countryside, while the rest of the party followed at a discreet distance waiting for the blackguard to strike.

The slippery devil had almost been lured in—had even been sighted waiting, pistols drawn, at one turn of the road. But at the last moment, he had smelled danger and turned tail before they could come within firing range.

Jared emitted a string of expletives that would have stood his aristocratic guests' hair on end had they heard him. It was a galling thing indeed to have to acknowledge defeat at the hands of such a blighter, yet here he stood with nothing to show for a long ride and a short night's sleep except a throbbing headache.

Desultorily, he tucked a clean, homespun shirt into his black trousers, then perching on the edge of his ornate canopied bed, pulled on the scuffed boots he habitually chose to wear for his first ride of the day, much to the disgust of his fastidious valet. Perhaps a brisk gallop in the cold morning air would set him right.

Minutes later, he exited the manor house by the private stairway leading to his suite and, much to his surprise, spied Edgar Rankin walking across the courtyard, apparently en route to the stables. "What brings you out at this hour?" he asked his somewhat bleary-looking man-of-affairs. "I've never known you to open your eyes before the morning was well and truly launched."

."Miss Haliburton," Edgar grumbled. "The head groom sent word she had persisted in her morning ride despite his protests that it wasn't safe until this blasted highwayman was apprehended. Though what he thinks I can do about the situation, I'm sure I don't know. Miss Haliburton strikes me as a woman who follows her own dictates."

"Amen to that," Jared said, more concerned than he wanted Edgar to know. He frowned. "I doubt our thief is bold enough to cross Brynhaven land, but still I would have expected Miss Haliburton, or any other sensible female, to stay safely within the walls of the manor house with such a fellow on the loose."

"I fear Miss Haliburton's good sense is overset by her zeal in this case," Edgar said morosely. "She is most likely hoping to encounter the thief so she can persuade him to give up his evil ways. I gained the impression yesterday that she held him in sympathy—claimed circumstances could have made him desperate—or some such rot."

"She said that?" Jared stopped in his tracks, struck by a sudden thought that brought an unconscious smile to his lips. He gave his close friend and man-of-affairs a hearty whack between the shoulder blades. "Go back to bed, Edgar. You're as useless as a duck in a thunderstorm before the hour of eleven. I'll search out Miss Haliburton. I feel certain I know where I can find her."

"How can you know that?"

"Because, dear fellow, I simply do. Leave it at that."

Edgar's sleep-glazed eyes narrowed to accusing slits. "Why, you unconscionable rake! You arranged an assignation with her yesterday morning, didn't you—and don't try to play the innocent. She's already told me she met up with some scruffy fellow named Jared on her ride." He gasped.

"Good God! Never say she thinks *you* are the highwayman!"

Jared shrugged, determinedly ignoring the twinge of conscience that made him avert his eyes from Edgar's shocked scrutiny. "It is possible I could have given her the impression that I plied some such lawless trade," he admitted, "but I shall tell her the straight of it when next I see her."

"I should certainly hope so." Edgar's voice held a quiet menace that set Jared's teeth on edge. "I have watched you play some havey-cavey games in the past with your demimondes and superficial ladies of the *ton*. But be assured Miss Haliburton is neither of those; she is, in fact, not at all the kind of woman a jaded aristocrat such as yourself could understand or appreciate. She could be deeply hurt by what you perceive as merely a clever jest."

"Cut line, Edgar; you overstep yourself," Jared snapped. "I'll tolerate no lectures on my behavior from any man, not even you. I said I would tell the lady the truth, and so I shall."

Edgar pulled himself up to his full height and stared Jared in the eye. "Be certain you do, your grace, or I swear by all that's holy, she will hear it from me."

Jared breathed a sigh of relief when he saw Emily had safely reached the oak tree before him. If the fool woman had come to harm at the hands of the outlaw because of him he would never have forgiven himself.

There she sat, stiff as buckram astride the gray, watching his approach, and only when he drew quite near could he see the shadows the long night had painted beneath her troubled eyes. The sight of those telltale shadows touched him as nothing else had in a long time.

"Good morning, Emily," he said softly. "I am pleased you changed your mind about joining me for a morning ride."

"I did nothing of the sort, sir. I am here only because I wish to . . . that is, I felt I should . . ."

"Should what, Emily?"

"Warn you, you fool. Whatever were you thinking of to rob a coach so close to Brynhaven? Now you have the Duke of Montford and Mr. Rankin and the local squire, and heaven knows who else, all determined to put a noose about your useless neck."

Jared smiled, moved by her sharp words of caution and by the concern he saw stamped on her pale, pinched face. "I take it you think I am the highwayman who is currently terrorizing the local gentry."

"I do not think so, sir. I know so. The description was far too accurate to mistake."

"It has been my observation, ma'am, that things are not always as they appear to be. However, I see you are not to be persuaded from your conviction." He raised a quizzical eyebrow. "Tell me then, how can a proper law-abiding citizen like yourself justify coming to the aid of a dangerous, hunted outlaw? For shame, Emily, I fear that beneath that prim country woman facade of yours lies a streak of larceny."

Emily's blue eyes sparked with anger. "Must you make a jest of everything—even your own impending death?" She leaned forward in the saddle, her neat but ordinary features taut with anxiety and some deeper emotion Jared couldn't quite name. "Heed me, sir, I beg of you," she cried. "You must give up this unlawful profession of yours before it is too late. You are an educated man; surely you can find an honest way to make a living."

The heat of her fervor washed over Jared's parched heart like warm rain. She hadn't the slightest idea who he was; she truly believed him a lawless renegade. Yet, every flash of her expressive eyes, every movement of her tense body spoke volumes. This sweet, gullible innocent honestly feared for his safety. He found himself wondering if she would be as passionate about making love to him as she was about saving his neck from the hangman's noose.

He pulled himself up short, remembering his promise to Edgar. Now was the perfect time to tell her the truth and end this ridiculous charade before he sank any deeper into the mire of his own falsehoods.

He opened his mouth, but his lips refused to form the words. Just a little longer, he told himself. What harm could come of a few more drafts of rich, heady country ale? Too soon he would be forced to settle for the insipid taste of champagne.

As if reading his mind, Emily raised her chin defiantly and stared him in the face. "I have done my best. If you refuse to acknowledge the danger you face, then so be it. I, for one, shall not weep over your grave."

"Liar," Jared said softly. "Even now your eyes are bright with unshed tears at the thought that I might reap my just desserts at the end of a rope." He leaned forward to tuck a windblown tendril of hair behind her ear. "Never be ashamed of your too-tender heart, sweet Emily. It is a commodity far more rare than any of the gemstones my 'unlawful profession' has yielded me."

His fingers grazed her cheek and instantly a hot rush of pleasure coursed through him. He stared at her, amazed by the intense, irrational desire he felt for this plain, unworldly woman—desire all the more poignant because it could never be fulfilled.

He'd become a master of seduction in the ten years he'd been on the town and he felt no regrets over his many conquests. His baser instincts told him this woman could be his for the taking, but some nobler aspect of his nature warned him that this was one seduction he would live to regret. For to seduce a woman like Emily Haliburton would be to destroy her.

His hungry gaze slid to her lips—her soft, unconsciously provocative lips. Hell and damnation. He might not be a complete scoundrel; but neither was he a saint. If nothing else, he owed it to himself to taste their sweetness just once before he took his leave of her.

"I will make you a bargain, Little Sparrow," he said. "One farewell kiss to remember you by and I will ride away, never again to ply my infamous trade near Brynhaven."

Emily stared into the silver eyes perusing her, expecting to see their usual glint of cynical mockery. She saw only a wistful sadness that twisted her heart and left it thumping painfully in her chest.

She frowned thoughtfully. "That is a most improper request, sir, and a frivolous one at that. I suspect you have kissed many women in your time and will kiss many more before you are through. Why you should wish to add a plain country spinster to that list, I cannot imagine."

"Nevertheless, that is what I wish. Is a kiss too much to pay for the satisfaction of knowing you have saved a man's life?"

"A very wicked life," Emily said severely. Still, to her everlasting shame she felt herself sorely tempted, as much by the rogue's bold, sensuous mouth as by the thought of how relieved she'd be to see him quit this part of England before the law caught up with him.

"Will you give me your solemn promise that you will never again rob a coach or stage?"

"I cannot promise you that, Emily. What self-respecting highwayman could? But I will promise never to accost another traveler within a hundred leagues of Brynhaven."

Emily studied his face with solemn eyes. "Will you take an oath on your honor?" She frowned. "No, for that is, I fear, suspect. On your mother's honor then."

Jared raised his right hand as if taking the oath she demanded. "On my mother's honor," he declared, a bitter note sharpening his voice. *My beautiful, fascinating mother whose "honor" did not prevent her from abandoning her only son when he was but six years old.*

"Very well then," Emily acceded, "you may have your kiss."

Before she could catch her breath, Jared dismounted, grasped her by the waist and lifted her to the ground. It was the first time she had stood next to him. He towered over her and the scent of him—musky, masculine, and faintly redolent of horse and leather—stirred her senses in a most disturbing way. Still, oddly enough, she felt none of the trepidation facing this lawless rogue that she'd felt in the presence of his half brother, the icy duke.

He cupped her face in his two hands and for one brief moment studied her upturned face with his remarkable eyes. Then drawing her gently into his arms, he brushed whisper-soft kisses across her eyelids, closing her into a dark cocoon in which nothing existed except the strange new sensations this man's touch evoked. As if in a dream, she felt his lips brush the shadowed hollows beneath her eyes, her fevered cheeks, the tip of her nose. Breathlessly, she waited for him to claim her lips.

Finally, when she thought her pounding heart must surely burst from her breast, his lips covered hers—firm, as she'd known they would be, yet softer than she had ever imagined—and so incredibly warm she felt their heat penetrate to the very core of her being.

She gasped, startled by the waves of pure exaltation undulating through her, by the heady feeling that she was detached from earth and only the strength of Jared's arms kept her from flying up into the boughs of the oak like the sparrow he had called her.

When those arms tightened inexorably around her, she wound her own about his neck and gave herself wholly to the strange and wonderful magic of his lips, his tongue, his very breath intermingling with hers.

Long moments later, he raised his head and grasping her shoulders in his strong fingers, put her from him. She felt instantly bereft, as if in severing his mouth from hers, he had stripped away some vital part of her and left her sadly empty and incomplete.

Dazed and trembling, she opened her eyes to meet his intense silver gaze. "So that is what it is like to be kissed," she murmured when she finally found her voice. "No wonder Mrs. Radcliffe makes such a to-do about it in her novels."

Jared drew a shaky breath, stunned by Emily's impassioned response to his kiss. He had expected her to be reticent, even a little frightened by what he'd felt certain was her first physical contact with the opposite sex. Instead, she had responded with such warmth, such pure, uninhibited pleasure, he had momentarily lost himself in the sheer joy of the experience.

He shook his head in disbelief. A strange reaction to a simple kiss from a man who had freely partaken of the endless sensual delights offered by London's most accomplished Cyprians. How ironic that an inexperienced little provincial from the Cotswolds should be the first to make him suspect there might be more to "making love" than mere physical gratification.

Studying her enraptured expression, he felt one brief moment of triumph that he had been the first man to awaken the passion lurking beneath her prim exterior until he remembered that some undeserving country bumpkin would likely warm himself at the fires he had banked.

With a groan, he pulled her to him and once again claimed her lips in a deeply passionate kiss. Then he lifted her into the sidesaddle atop the little gray, handed her the reins, and gave the mare a sharp slap on the rump.

"Ride for the manor house and safety, Emily, and don't look back," he commanded. "Ride as if Lucifer himself were at your heels—for he might well be."

Edgar was waiting for him at the stables when Jared rode in an hour later. The question in his troubled eyes begged an honest answer.

"No, I did not tell Miss Haliburton the truth of who I was," Jared said as they walked together through the walled courtyard leading to the duke's private stairway. "I could not bring myself to humiliate her—or myself by admitting how falsely I had played her."

He raised his hand to silence Edgar's objections before he could utter them. "But never fear, my friend, my days as a *soi-disant* highwayman are at an end. Regrettably so, since I suspect that in many ways my temperament lends itself more happily to that role than to the one I am forced to play."

Edgar removed his spectacles to polish the grime of the stables from them, and the dust motes circled his head like hundreds of tiny, glistening diamonds in the pale morning sun. "Then what *did* you tell her if not the truth?" he asked.

Jared shrugged noncommittally, grateful he'd had an hour to compose himself before he had to face his perceptive friend. "What else?" he asked, stopping before the door to his private suite. "I simply bid the lady farewell and promised to never again darken the Brynhaven countryside with my wicked presence."

"And what do you suggest I tell her to keep her from riding out alone until we capture the real highwayman?"

"Tell her the duke forbids it," Jared said wearily. "She already holds me in disregard. Such an edict will only add one more nail to my coffin."

"I will tell her. But I fear she will sorely miss her morning rides. I suspect that is the only real pleasure she derives from her stay at Brynhaven."

For a long moment, Jared massaged his aching temples, deep in thought. "Have a pianoforte moved into one of the small salons and make it available to her," he said at last. "It will help her pass the time. Anyone who plays with such skill must have a great love for music."

"Capital idea." Edgar hesitated just outside the door to the suite, an anxious look on his narrow, aristocratic face. "I take it your brief sojourn into the world of the common man is over, then?"

"Over and done with," Jared said, steadfastly ignoring the persistent ache deep in his chest.

"Then perhaps we should discuss the ball your aunts are proposing you give Saturday."

Jared groaned. "A ball! Good God, must we?"

"I am afraid so. Your guests expect it, as do your neighbors. It has, after all, been close to two years since you have been in residence at your ancestral home."

Jared grimaced. "I despise Brynhaven. It holds nothing but unhappy memories for me. If I had my way, I would never spend another night beneath its roof. But if you feel a ball is in order, then we must, by all means, have a ball." He beckoned Edgar to follow him into his suite.

A glimmer of understanding shone in Edgar's dark, myopic eyes but, as always, his advice was profoundly practical. "Bury those ugly memories as you buried the people who caused them, Jared. For here you must reside until you plant your seed in your future duchess. Every Duke of Montford, since the time of Charlemagne, has first seen the light of day at Brynhaven. Tradition dictates your son should do the same."

"My future duchess," Jared said grimly, "whom I am expected to choose from the five vapid creatures my aunts have decreed the most eligible candidates for the title."

Edgar raised a questioning eyebrow. "Need I remind you the method of choice was of your own devising."

"In other words, I am getting exactly what I deserve." Jared sighed deeply. "You are probably right, Edgar; you usually are. Certainly, this time you are on the side of the gods."

"The gods?" Edgar echoed with a puzzled frown.

Jared made a sweeping gesture which encompassed the luxurious room in which they stood. "Quite a clever balance actually. It appears they deem it only just that a man who enjoys such an embarrassment of riches should suffer a poverty of spirit."

Chapter Six

"Are you certain you are quite well, Miss Haliburton?" With Emily's permission, Mr. Rankin had joined her on the small divan in the blue salon where a late-afternoon tea was being served the duke's guests. He adjusted his spectacles and peered at her through the thick lenses. "You are very pale."

"It is nothing more than a slight headache, I assure you," Emily lied, squirming uncomfortably beneath his perusal.

"Another headache, ma'am? You have certainly been plagued with them this past se'nnight."

In reality, what she had been plagued with in the six days since her emotional parting from that scoundrel Jared was a deplorable tendency to moon over a man she should be grateful to never see again. Emily was thoroughly disgusted with herself. It was beyond her how any woman in her right mind could ache with longing for a man who had black-mailed her into allowing him to kiss her in a most improper fashion and then promptly dismissed her as if she were just another local dollymop he had tumbled behind a hedgerow.

Yet, ache she did and it didn't help that she must sit down to dinner each night with a man who looked enough like the cause of her insanity to be his twin. She could scarcely bear to look at the icy duke, yet she couldn't stop casting furtive glances at him—an added embarrassment since he invariably rewarded her with a scowl as black as the dreary rain clouds which darkened the skies above Brynhaven.

Of course, Mr. Rankin had noticed she had fallen into the doldrums. The man was entirely too perceptive, and too kind to be believed. He had even gone so far as to have a pianoforte moved into a small salon on the third floor so she could practice her music whenever Lucinda had no need of her services.

The duke's man-of-affairs was everything she could admire in a gentleman, guilty of neither the contemptuous, full-of-himself attitude of the stiff-necked duke nor the vulgarity of his baseborn half brother. A true middle-of-the-road man, as she was a middle-of-the-road woman. The solid backbone of England on whom king and country had depended throughout the nation's history.

Why couldn't she have developed a *tendre* for such a man as this? He made no secret of his admiration for her, and she half believed that given the least bit of encouragement he might even declare himself.

"Might I suggest a quiet lie-down before dinner." Mr. Rankin's soothing voice cut into her ruminations. "And I shall instruct Cook to prepare one of her excellent tisanes."

Emily smiled her gratitude for his concern. "I do believe a lie-down is exactly what I need."

"Just so. You will want to be at your best for the ball tonight." Mr. Rankin made his selection from the dainty cakes on the tea tray and placed two of the most delectable-looking on her plate. "The staff have been working round the clock and it is bound to be the social event of the season in these parts. Dare I hope you will save me the supper dance? It is, I believe, a waltz."

"Thank you for your kind offer, sir, but I have never learned to dance the waltz. It is still frowned upon outside London, you know."

"Then perhaps we could take a stroll on the terrace before supper."

"I should like that above all, but I cannot promise I shall be free. Lady Hargrave has instructed me to stay close by Lady Lucinda all evening, and I am at her command as long as I am in her employ."

"In other words, she has instructed you to keep the girl away from the Earl of Chillingham while there is still a chance to make a higher connection."

Emily flushed hotly, embarrassed that her aunt's deviousness should be so transparent.

Mr. Rankin pushed his spectacles higher onto the bridge of his nose—a gesture Emily was beginning to realize he often made when he had something on his mind. "Will you think me completely out of hand if I offer you some advice, Miss Haliburton?"

"Of course not, sir. I would welcome anything you have to say."

"Do not be too assiduous in your guarding of Lady Lucinda. She could do far worse than young Percival in choosing a husband. He may be an awkward colt right now, but he has the makings of a fine man—and an extremely rich one once he comes into his full inheritance."

"My observation exactly." Emily hesitated, wishing she could confide in this kindly gentleman, but she would only jeopardize Lucinda's chance for happiness if she let slip the fact that the Earl of Hargrave was so deep in dun territory he had to "sell" his only daughter to keep out of debtors' prison. "I take it you feel as I do, that the earl is a much more suitable *parti* for Lady Lucinda than the duke," she said finally.

Mr. Rankin nodded his agreement. "And she would appear to be the perfect wife for him. The earl's requirements for his future countess are relatively simple—a pretty face, a sweet nature, and a willingness to listen to an endless discourse on the merits of his prime cattle. The lad has, I am afraid, spent a great deal more of his young life with horses than with people . . . or books."

He made another minor adjustment to his spectacles and surveyed her with what could only be termed intense scrutiny. "The Duke of Montford, on the other hand, is endowed with both an exceptional intelligence and a depth of feeling. It will take a very special woman to make him a proper wife."

Emily choked on her tea. She found it difficult to believe a man of such obvious acuity could utter this drivel with a straight face. She had no way of measuring the arrogant duke's intelligence, but his method of choosing his duchess gave the lie to any pretense of depth of feeling. She could only assume the duke's man-of-affairs was blinded by his loyalty to his employer.

Mr. Rankin removed his spectacles, polished them on a linen handkerchief he drew from his waistcoat pocket, and returned them to his nose. "I can see by the expression on your face that you cannot envision the duke as anything but the haughty, inaccessible aristocrat he purports to be. I'm not surprised; it is a part he plays to perfection in his dealings with the *haut monde*. Why, I am not certain. Though I suspect it is a defense against the swarms of toadeaters who court him because of his title and wealth."

"I suppose that is possible," Emily said, though privately she considered the duke's standoffish ways a bit too convincing to be merely an act.

"In actual fact," Mr. Rankin continued, "his grace is one of England's most dedicated statesmen—was instrumental in the movement in Parliament to abolish the slave trade, and since the beginning of this fracas with Bonaparte has served both the War Office and the Board of Governors of The Duke of York Military Hospital." He paused thoughtfully. "Granted, he does tend to deal more easily with people en masse than with individuals, but many a man more reclusive than he has been drawn out of his shell by the right woman."

"It is plain to see you hold your employer in great respect," Emily said, for lack of something better to say. She found this idealistic portrayal of the duke almost as difficult to credit as the concept that one of the five empty-headed beauties who vied for his hand could be that "right woman" who would warm his frigid nature.

Mr. Rankin scowled, as if reading her thoughts. "The duke is more than my employer, Miss Haliburton," he said quietly. "He is, by blood, my second cousin, but we were raised like brothers from the time we were small boys. I owe him my life—but that is a story best told at another time. Suffice it to say, I would gladly give my life for him, should the need arise."

Emily gaped in astonishment. She felt certain Mr. Rankin was not a man given to idle chatter, but she found his amazing revelation about the powerful duke beyond belief. "Why are you telling *me* this?" she asked warily. "My opinion of the duke can scarcely matter a whit, and I cannot believe he would approve the telling."

"He would most likely be vexed all out of reason," Mr. Rankin agreed. "And I am undoubtedly the world's greatest fool for sinking my own ship before it ever leaves the harbor. But I have come to realize in the past few days that these are facts you should know, Miss Haliburton, and I am certain you will never hear them from the duke himself."

Her baffling conversation with the duke's man-of-affairs had left Emily so confused she'd lost all interest in a quiet lie-down. Now, just minutes before the gala preball dinner was to begin, she found herself wishing she had rested when she'd had the chance. The prospects for a peaceful evening ahead were not auspicious.

In a rare show of defiance toward her tyrannical parents, Lucinda had declared, while dressing for dinner, that she would rather die than dance with the "horrible duke" at the ball. This heresy immediately prompted Lady Hargrave to threaten Emily with the withdrawal of her yet unpaid stipend unless she made certain Lucinda behaved herself exactly as she ought.

Through no fault of her own, Emily found herself in the unenviable position of having to choose between promoting Lucinda's future happiness or insuring her own survival for the next few months. Her mind was in a turmoil, and the headache, which had originally been a convenient figment of her imagination, started throbbing in earnest.

She stared about her at the vast state dining room to which a footman had directed the earl's party. It was the first time she had seen this particular room and her initial glimpse of it was almost as overwhelming as her initial glimpse of the great entry hall had been.

The walls were covered with stretched-silk the color of rich cream, topped by an intricately carved rococo ceiling. A series of high, narrow windows draped in rich green velvet filled one entire wall, and the opposite wall was adorned with paintings which she recognized as the work of Holbein, Reynolds, and Constable, and even one she felt certain was by the great Dutch painter Rembrandt.

Masses of pale yellow and snowy white roses from the duke's orangery filled the series of tall silver epergnes marching down the center of the huge table—their fragrance almost overpowering in its sweetness. The service plates, goblets, and flatware, in the same beaten silver as the epergnes, bore the duke's coat of arms, and after her initial awe, Emily found herself contemplating the endless hours of polishing needed to present the dazzling display. Small wonder the Brynhaven staff had been working round the clock.

A number of strangers mingled with the usual house-guests waiting to take their seats at the table. "Who are all these people?" she asked Mr. Brummell when he stopped to pay his respects.

"The duke's neighbors, so I've been told. Twenty of them to be exact, and a more dowdy-looking lot of provincials I have never seen."

He raised his quizzing glass to study a stout silver-haired matron in a many-hued dress which gave her the appearance of a well-fed peacock. Beside her stood an equally stout gentleman in a long-tailed jacket of watered silk and purple satin knee britches. "Heaven help us, I do believe the fellow is wearing a bagwig," the Beau exclaimed in a hoarse whisper. "The ridiculous things went out of fashion fifty years ago."

He shuddered. "And these people are the cream of the local gentry. God only knows what we may expect from the sixty who've been invited for the ball and midnight supper. I begin to understand why Montford rarely visits this particular estate."

Emily was duly seated near the foot of the table between the Earl of Sudsley and Squire Bosley, neither of whom were the most inspiring of dinner companions. The earl, as usual, was so castaway he ended up facedown in a plate of roast venison and currant sauce, and was quietly carried to his chambers by two brawny young footmen.

The squire, on the other hand, belched his way through all nine courses, simultaneously reciting the pedigrees of the thirty-odd foxhounds, setters, and pointers that made up his excellent kennel. By the time dessert was served, Emily felt certain that if she never learned another thing about the breeding of hunting dogs, she would still know far more than she cared to.

Meanwhile across the table, Lady Lucinda flirted openly with the Earl of Chillingham despite her mama's fulminating looks and Lady Sudsley's pointed remarks that a certain young lady was obviously no better than she should be. Emily cringed, her premonition of impending disaster so strong, she patted her hair to make certain it wasn't standing on end.

Lady Hargrave's comment as the ladies adjourned to the gold salon, leaving the gentlemen to their brandy and cigars, only added to her presentiment. "Don't you dare let Lucinda out of your sight for one minute tonight, or so help me, my girl, you will live to regret it," she hissed in Emily's ear. "This is no time for the rattlepate to cut up smart. I have it on good authority the duke is planning to select his duchess tonight and I can tell, from the warm way he looks at her, Lucinda leads the pack."

Emily's blood ran cold at the thought, but she felt certain Lady Hargrave was simply indulging in her usual wishful thinking. As far as she could see, the duke's handsome face was still frozen in the same look of unremitting boredom he had worn since he'd arrived at Brynhaven.

Exactly thirty minutes from the time the ladies withdrew, the gentlemen joined them to repair to the ballroom. To Emily's surprise, Mr. Brummell offered her his arm. "Ah, Miss Haliburton, you are a sight for sore eyes," he murmured in his rich, cultured accents as they strolled the perimeter of the vast ballroom.

"Don't you mean a sight to make eyes sore, Mr. Brummell?" Emily quipped, glancing down at the only gown she owned which approximated a ball gown—the despised red and white.

Mr. Brummell laughed. "True, my dear, you do tend to embue one with a desire to hang mistletoe and light yule logs in the merry month of May, but your sparkling wit blinds me to the incongruity of your attire. I look forward to conversing with you with the same eagerness a starving man looks forward to a loaf of fresh baked bread. I have just endured two of the most dismal hours of my life listening to Lady Esmerelda Sudsley's chatter. I swear, the silly pea-goose could talk the hide off an Indian rhinoceros."

Emily couldn't help but smile at the ill-humored analogy, but she withheld comment. "You have traveled to India, Mr. Brummell?" she asked innocently.

"Not yet, but I may well be driven to such extremes before this deadly fortnight is over."

Brummell inclined his head in a brief nod of recognition as they passed Squire Bosley and his lady. "If t'were not for my devotion to the duke," he whispered once they were out of earshot, "and my deep appreciation for his fine cuisine, I should have instructed my valet to pack my bags days ago."

"You are a close friend of the duke?" Emily found the relationship hard to imagine. The duke did not strike her as a man who inspired affection, and Mr. Brummell was noted more for his caustic wit than his fidelity. Even his much-publicized friendship with the Prince Regent was reported to be a simple matter of social expediency on his part.

"No man is truly close to Montford," Brummell said. "Except Edgar Rankin, of course. But we enjoy a mutual respect." He paused. "Outstanding fellow, the duke. Brilliant mind and an infallible sense of style, though God knows he puts that to little use. Attends an occasional race at Newmarket and a mill now and then, but for the most part he tends to be something of a recluse." He shook his head. "How such a man could consider marrying one of the five pretty flea-brains his aunts have put forth is more than I can fathom."

Brummell sidestepped a group of local squires who had gathered at the edge of the dance floor, then led Emily to the row of chairs set up for the mothers and chaperons. "Too bad the poor devil is forced to choose his duchess from the daughters of the aristocracy. You would suit him most admirably, my dear."

"Me?" Emily laughed. "You are joking, of course."

"My dear lady, I never joke about something as serious as marriage."

Emily relinquished her hold on the Beau's arm and searched his face, expecting to encounter one of his famous cynical smiles. To her surprise, she found his expression strangely sober.

"Forgive my impertinence, sir, but I fear you must be mad," she declared. "I can think of no one in the entire world less suited to be a duchess."

Brummell nodded. "My point exactly. I sometimes think the last thing Montford would be, if he had the choice, is a duke. But more to the point, that clever tongue of yours might make him laugh—something he rarely does now and may never do again once he is leg-shackled."

His gaze shifted to the duke, who stood a short distance away, surrounded by a clutch of chattering females. "Look at the poor fellow. Have you ever seen a man more morose?"

Emily looked and found herself staring directly into the duke's stormy silver eyes. For one instant, their gazes locked, then he scowled darkly and turned away, leaving Emily to grit her teeth in anger. If this surly aristocrat was indeed Mr. Rankin's caring philanthropist and Mr. Brummell's hale-fellow-well-met, he was certainly adept at concealing his true nature.

Brummell raised Emily's hand briefly to his lips before taking his leave of her. "I see Lord Hargrave has inveigled one of the local landowners into a 'friendly' game of hazard," he murmured. "Quite a Captain Sharp, your uncle. He has already fleeced most of the duke's unsuspecting houseguests out of their pocket money—which does make one wonder how he has managed to get so deeply in debt to

London's gambling hells. Ah well, for lack of something better to do, I think I shall join the game and see if I can bend a few of the spokes in the ratchety fellow's wheels."

Sick at heart, Emily watched Mr. Brummell cross the room toward the alcove reserved for those who preferred cards to dancing. His admission that he was aware of the Earl of Hargrave's deplorable financial condition had been most revealing. If the scandal was such common knowledge, why had Lucinda been considered an eligible *parti* for the duke? Had his warped sense of humor led him to dangle a lifeline before her drowning relatives just so he could have the malicious pleasure of snatching it away at the last moment? Much as she disapproved of the Hargraves' manipulation of Lucinda, it at least was spawned by desperate need. There was no excuse for this depraved game the duke played.

The first set, consisting of the country dance Sir Roger de Coverley, was just ending, with the Duke of Montford partnering Esmerelda Sudsley and the Earl of Chillingham partnering Lucinda. Emily beckoned to her young cousin when the couples left the dance floor and watched the flushed and happy girl walk toward her on the earl's arm. "Oh, Emily," she gushed, casting a limpid gaze into the earl's bedazzled eyes, "I never dreamed dancing could be so exciting."

Out of the corner of her eye, Emily saw the duke deposit Lady Esmeralda with her mama, make his bow, and stride determinedly across the short space separating him from the spot where the three of them stood. He was apparently performing a duty dance with each of the five candidates for his hand—and Lucinda's turn was next. Emily had no time to warn her cousin before the duke was upon them.

"Lady Lucinda," the duke said, raising his ornate quizzing glass to his right eye, "may I have the pleasure of the next dance. It is, I believe, a waltz."

Lucinda gasped. Like a moth mesmerized by a candle flame, she stared, transfixed, at the magnified eye studying her. The color in her cheeks slowly faded until her taut, young face turned as pale as the virginal dress she wore, and before Emily could think to catch her, she crumpled into a heap of white lace and silver ribbons at the duke's feet.

"Dear God!" Emily exclaimed, kneeling down to cradle her cousin's golden head in her lap. She looked up to find the duke towering above her, the offensive quizzing glass still glued to his eye. "What a beastly thing to do," she cried. "How dare you leer at this poor child with that monstrous eye of yours when anyone can see your very presence fills her with terror!"

The duke lowered his quizzing glass, but he continued to stare at Emily in obvious astonishment. Beside her the distraught earl dropped to his knees, babbling something which sounded suspiciously like "my darling love."

"What is it? What has happened?" Lady Hargrave pushed her way through the crowd of onlookers to stare down at her daughter's prostrate form. "My stars and garters," she exclaimed, clutching her heaving bosom. "The little rattlebrain has done us in!"

"Calm yourself, madam," the duke said in a voice so cold Emily felt chilled to the bone. "Lady Lucinda has simply been temporarily overcome by the heat." This in a room so large and drafty, most of the ladies had already covered their bare shoulders with shawls.

He beckoned Mr. Rankin to his side. "Please see Lady Lucinda to her chamber while I attend to the rest of my guests."

"*I* will accompany Lady Lucinda," the earl declared, scrambling to his feet.

"*You* will accompany me," the duke corrected him, and turning his back on the pitiful little drama, stalked away.

The earl stood stock still—his fists clenched, his Adam's apple bobbing like a cork in a hurricane. "I swear I would call the man out if I didn't know he was such a crack shot."

"For raising a quizzing glass? Don't be absurd." Mr. Rankin's look of censure encompassed both the earl and Emily and she cringed, aware too late how ridiculous her rash accusation must have sounded.

"Your place is with your uncle, Percival. Join him at once." Mr. Rankin's use of the familiar address cut the young earl down to size as surely as the severity of his tone.

"Yes, sir. But Lady Lucinda . . ."

"I will see to Lady Lucinda, as the duke requested." Mr. Rankin leaned forward and with a strength surprising in such a slender man, lifted Lucinda in his arms and strode toward the nearest door, with Lady Hargrave and Emily trailing behind. Every eye turned away as they passed, as if the very act of looking at them would somehow tar the viewer with the same brush as the social outcasts.

"What happened? What dreadful thing did Lucinda do?" Lady Hargrave whimpered, obviously cowed by the cuts direct she was receiving from people who just minutes before had professed to be her friends.

"I will tell you everything, Aunt Hortense, just as soon as we reach our chambers," Emily promised, knowing full well the most "dreadful thing" she would have to relate would be the ill-chosen words that had tripped off her own precipitate tongue.

Chapter Seven

Brandy in hand, Jared settled into the old leather chair before the blazing library fireplace and fit his weary body into the depression shaped by his father and grandfather before him.

The hour was one-and-twenty, and for the first time in the interminable evening, he had a few moments to himself, moments gained by leaving Edgar to see the local gentry to their carriages and failing to issue his usual invitation to Brummell to join him for a late-night discussion. His mood was black enough without listening to the cynical Beau's view of the bizarre happenings of the last few hours.

The door behind him opened; then shut. Without looking up, he knew who it was. No one but Edgar would dare intrude on his sanctuary. "Your ball guests have departed, your grace, and your houseguests have taken to their beds—all except your lady aunts, who are hoping to have a word with you."

Jared groaned. Leave it to Edgar to get right to the point, and the obsequious "your grace" portended another of his tedious lectures. "I will deal with my aunts tomorrow," he muttered. "Tonight I want a little peace and quiet. It has been a very long, very tiresome day."

"As you wish, your grace. I shall instruct Pettigrew to convey your message to them," Edgar said and disappeared through the same door he had just entered.

Moments later, he returned to stand in front of the fireplace. With his face in the shadows and the bright flames
leaping behind his slender, black-clad figure, he put Jared
in mind of some dark angel from the nether world come to
pass judgment on him.

Edgar removed his glasses to polish them on the handkerchief he withdrew from his jacket pocket and in so
doing, glanced down at the quizzing glass Jared had tossed
into the fireplace ashes. "A rather drastic reaction to Miss
Haliburton's outburst, wouldn't you say?" he inquired, with
a short bark of laughter.

Jared squirmed uncomfortably. "I never did like the
blasted thing," he grumbled, tempted to exercise his ducal
privilege and dismiss his man-of-affairs as peremptorily as
he had his aunts, before the cheeky fellow started in on
him. But it was a little late in the game to begin playing
lord and master with Edgar.

"I see. Well, no loss then." Edgar lifted the poker and
gave a sharp jab to the log Jared had earlier tossed onto the
glowing embers. Instantly, it burst into flames.

"Your aunts are quite put out with you, you know," he
said offhandedly. "As they understood it, and I must say so
did I, you were supposed to choose your future wife and
make an offer to her papa before the evening was out."

Jared slumped deeper in his chair, hoping his silence
would discourage any further discourse on the painful subject, but Edgar was not to be deterred.

"Imagine, if you can, their humiliation when you disappeared without a word after they had promised the mamas
of the five incomparables your decision was imminent."
Edgar shook his head slowly back and forth. "Rather mean-
spirited of you, old fellow, when they had gone to so much
trouble to ferret out the cream of this season's crop. I doubt
either of them will ever forgive you."

"Oh, do shut up, Edgar, and pour me another brandy."

Jared leaned his head back against the soft, old leather of the chair and stretched out his long legs. By rights he should be awash with guilt over his cavalier treatment of his venerable relatives, not to mention the five anxious mamas. He felt nothing but a vast sense of relief that he'd escaped parson's mousetrap with a whole skin.

"In case it has slipped your mind," he remarked coldly, "I am the Eighth Duke of Montford. I do not have to explain my actions to anyone."

"It would never occur to me to suggest anything so presumptuous, your grace."

Silently, Jared watched the flames Edgar had stirred to life lick hungrily along the log which spanned the fireplace cavity. "I simply couldn't do it," he said finally. "I took a long look at those five simpering ninnyhammers—four actually, since I must count Lady Lucinda out unless I'm willing to put a bullet in young Percival—and I couldn't envision spending the rest of my life leg-shackled to any one of them. For God's sake, I could scarcely tell them apart, except for the redheaded chipmunk. How Percival has managed to weed one out of the herd, I cannot imagine."

Edgar shrugged noncommittally and crossed to the sideboard for the brandy. "Tell me the truth," Jared said, "can you see yourself bedding one of those pretty little innocents fresh from the schoolroom?"

"Heaven forbid," Edgar demurred. "I have no desire to rob the cradle. But luckily it is not up to me to perpetuate one of England's oldest and noblest titles."

He raised the sparkling crystal decanter and surveyed its amber contents against the glow of the firelight. "On the other hand, I could easily imagine bedding a warm, compassionate woman like Emily Haliburton; but then I am not restricted to the daughters of peers of the realm." He removed the stopper from the decanter. "As a matter of fact, I

have been so taken with the lady this past fortnight, I have
seriously considered making her an offer."

Jared shot upright, instantly alert. "The devil you say."

"But not unless she comes to realize the folly of her in-
fatuation over that annoying highwayman . . . and my
hopes on that score are dimming." He grimaced. "I have no
desire to take a wife who is wearing the willow for another
man."

Jared's pulse skipped a beat. "What makes you think that
Em . . . Miss Haliburton is wearing the willow. She strikes
me as too sensible for such folly."

"Sensible? Miss Haliburton? You jest. The woman is obviously a hopeless romantic. Good heavens, haven't you
noticed her pallor, her loss of appetite, her lack of spirit
these past six days? Any reader of Mrs. Radcliffe's novels
could tell you the lady is suffering from unrequited love."

Jared recalled Emily's glowing eyes when she'd said,
"So that is what it is like to be kissed." Could Edgar be
right? Did the sharp-tongued innocent imagine herself in
love with the wicked brigand who'd given her her first taste
of passion? Now that he thought about it, it would be just
the sort of thing a woman who dedicated her life to deci-
phering ancient myths and legends might do. An odd combination of guilt and triumph swept through him at the
thought.

Edgar poured a generous amount of brandy into Jared's
empty glass and an equally generous glass for himself. "I
can well understand why you failed to note Miss Haliburton's megrims," he mused. "You have, after all, been busy
licking your own wounds. More than one of your guests
has remarked how closely you've resembled a lion with a
thorn in its paw these past few days. Strange how differently men and women show their emotions."

Jared slumped back down in his chair. "I am not infatu-
ated with Miss Haliburton, if that is what you are hinting."

"Heaven forbid, your grace! I never considered such a thing."

A picture of Emily's troubled blue eyes and trembling lips when she'd begged him to give up his wicked ways passed before Jared's eyes, sending a flood of liquid warmth into certain regions of his body. He pulled himself up short. What was he thinking of? He had already ascertained that she could be neither wife nor mistress to him.

"The woman is nothing to me," he said glumly. "Why, she is as plain as a . . ."

"A church mouse, your grace." Edgar nodded. "I quite agree. And, as Brummell pointed out, she is entirely too plump to do justice to the current fashions. Not that that would matter. A common little nobody from the Cotswolds would never be accepted in London society anyway, not even if she were slender as a wraith and a raving beauty as well."

He sighed. "I think I must have been quite mad to consider offering for her. The woman has little to recommend her, and a caustic tongue to boot. What man would be fool enough to take such a creature to wife?"

"What man indeed!" Jared agreed, his lips twisting in an unbidden smile.

He took a healthy swallow of brandy. "Still, did you see how her eyes flashed when she chastised me for 'leering' at her missish cousin? I swear, for a moment there, I couldn't decide if I wanted to throttle her or . . ."

"Kiss her, your grace? Now that would have provided the cats of the *ton* with the prime *on dit* of the season. Besides, I suspect you have already tasted that forbidden fruit. I happened to encounter Miss Haliburton when she returned from her ride Monday last. She had the look of a woman well and thoroughly kissed."

Jared flushed—something he hadn't done since he was a mere stripling. "Damn you, Edgar, one of these days you'll go too far!"

"Not to worry, your grace. I have set aside sufficient quid to book passage to the Americas should such an eventuality occur."

Edgar settled in the chair opposite Jared and crossed one elegant leg over the other. "Come to think of it, that might be the solution to Miss Haliburton's problems—the Americas, that is. She is certainly finished here, what with publicly insulting someone as exalted as yourself. In fact, I wouldn't be a bit surprised if she, and her relatives, were packing this minute to leave Brynhaven in disgrace."

"As well they should. A more pawky lot I've never seen," Jared grumbled, but the ache he had carried in his heart for the past six days sharply intensified at the thought that Emily might disappear from his sight.

"That 'pawky lot' will be your cousins by marriage within the year unless I mistake young Percival's intentions—and what a deucedly awkward situation that will be, unless . . ."

"Unless what?" Jared asked cautiously.

"Unless you make some gesture to show you found the little contretemps this evening more amusing than offensive."

"Which I did, actually. I could hardly take the actions of two emotional females seriously."

"Hardly, your grace." Edgar took a thoughtful sip of his brandy. "I suppose, if you wish me to, I could instruct the head gardener to prepare posies to deliver in your name to the ladies involved. Roses, I think, would be most appropriate."

"Do you think that would make things right?"

"Without a doubt. A posy from the Duke of Montford! They would swoon with gratitude. Well, at least one of them might."

"I'll do it then," Jared declared, feeling as if someone had just lifted an anvil off his shoulders. "I'd hate to cause

Lady Lucinda any more trouble than she already has with that gambling fool Hargrave for a father."

Edgar's lip twitched. "I felt certain you would feel that way, your grace . . . about Lady Lucinda."

"And so I should," Jared declared. "She is the daughter of an earl, after all." He smiled to himself as an idea crossed his mind. "But, no need for you to bother with the tedious business, Edgar. I'll handle it myself. I've been planning to visit the orangery anyway. I used to be rather close to old Ben when I was a child, and I understand he's still in charge there."

For the first time Jared could remember, Edgar looked honestly surprised, but being Edgar, he quickly recovered. "Good idea, your grace," he said, something that sounded suspiciously like humor coloring his voice. "I am certain *Lady Lucinda* will appreciate the gesture all the more because of your personal touch."

Jared rose at dawn after the first good night's sleep he'd had in a se'nnight. Dressing quickly, he slipped silently into the hall and hurried through the maze of connecting passages to the stairs leading to the old nursery. Since none of his guests had small children, he felt certain that wing of the house would be empty.

He opened the door to the cosy room where he had spent so many hours the first seven years of his life and found himself gripped by memories, both poignant and painful.

Everything was just as he remembered it. His toy soldiers, in their bright red uniforms and black shakos, still marched across the ornately carved dresser; the same blue coverlet still adorned the narrow bed; the same blue draperies still framed the recessed window seat—and unless it had been removed sometime during the past twenty-three years, the object he sought would still be on the floor of the old clothespress.

He opened the heavy doors and peered inside. There it was, his wooden toy chest, exactly where he had placed it the day he'd been whisked off to live with his grandfather after his drunken father broke his neck escaping through a neighbor's bedchamber window when her husband returned home unexpectedly.

That had been a momentous day in his young life—almost as momentous as the day, one year earlier, when his lovely, young mother, whom he'd adored, had kissed him tenderly, promised she would always love him, and promptly run off with the French dancing master.

It was as if all the joy and laughter in his young life had gone with her, leaving only a dark cloud of gloom hovering over Brynhaven. For weeks, nay months, he had watched in vain from his nursery window for her return. Many years later, when the pain of her desertion was nothing but a bitter memory, he had learned that Madame Guillotine had claimed both her and her dandified Frenchman shortly after they'd reached the Continent.

He'd never felt a minute's grief over the loss of his father—only bewilderment at being wrenched from the only home he knew. The marquess had never visited the nursery and on the one occasion Jared had dared seek him out, he'd found him stark naked and tumbling one of the chambermaids. His father had looked up just long enough to laugh at Jared's wide-eyed confusion. Then, muttering an obscenity, had gone back to pumping the squealing maid, and Jared had run to the comforting arms of his nanny as fast as his stumpy little legs could carry him.

A few months later, he had stood beside his tutor at the entrance to the great hall and watched his father's lifeless body lifted from a carriage and carried up the long flight of stairs. Remembering, he felt a shudder ripple through him. Even now, he could feel the freshening breeze that had lifted the cloth covering the broken body, could see the copper pieces covering the once mocking eyes—the chalky skin and purple bruises on that bloated, mud-spattered face. Even now, he could smell the onions on his tutor's breath when he'd murmured, "Now *you* are the Marquess of Staffield, my lord, and *you* will be the Eighth Duke of Montford when your grandfather dies."

He had wriggled free of the bony fingers gripping his shoulder and with the first show of the chilling arrogance for which he would one day become famous, declared, "Then I shall have sausage and eggs and muffins for my breakfast this morning and I shall never again eat porridge."

With a determined shrug, he relegated his depressing memories back to that dark chamber of his soul where they'd lain hidden so many years. Pulling the chest from the clothespress, he traced his finger across the childish scrawl scratched into the scarred lid:

Propity of the futur Duk of Montford. Open on pane of deth.

Lifting the lid, he surveyed the hoard of treasures a seven-year-old had hastily squirreled away on that long-ago spring morning. He hadn't thought of them in years. Yet now, viewing them like this, he remembered how precious each one had been to him and how fearful he'd been that some chambermaid might find them irresistible.

One by one, he lifted them out: a leather sack containing a pearl-handled knife with a nicked blade and five crudely whittled mumbletypegs, a glossy black crow's feather and an equally glossy black curl he'd once purloined when his mother's maid had trimmed her glorious hair, a red top that still whistled when he gave it a spin, a shell from the beach near his old nanny's home at Bournemouth, the set of jack-straws with which he'd entertained himself by the hour on rainy afternoons—all items a lonely boy, without any play-mates, had methodically collected.

At the very bottom of the chest, he found the thing for which he searched—a birch bark basket with a handle formed of two twisted twigs. Inside it lay a short length of satin ribbon—once white, now yellowed with age. Gently, he lifted the crude little basket; then closing the chest, he shoved it back into its hiding place deep inside the clothespress.

Ben Pippin, Brynhaven's head gardener, had long ago seen his seventieth birthday—how long ago no one was certain, but it was generally agreed he had outlived two Dukes of Montford and a great many of their progeny in the years he'd overseen the care of the estate's gardens. Jared had spent many an hour in the old man's company when he was a small boy, and he never failed to visit him when he was in residence at Brynhaven.

This morning, he found the gardener watering the few roses that had escaped the housekeeper's shears when she'd decorated for the previous night's ball. "Good morning, Ben," he said. "I hope I find you well."

A warm smile lighted the old man's face. Relinquishing his hold on the watering can, he clasped Jared's outstretched hand. "Good mornin' to you, your grace. I was wonderin' if ye'd remember old Ben, what with it bein' near two year since last we seen ye at Brynhaven."

"Remember you, Ben?" Jared scoffed, deeply shocked by how fragile and wrinkled his old friend had become since last he'd seen him. "Hell's fire, man, the only happy memories I have of this place are of you and Nanny Partridge."

"Aye. A fine woman that. Sad I was to 'ere of 'er passin', but many's a good year she 'ad in that cottage in Bournemouth you set 'er up with."

Jared smiled. "And what of you, Ben? Do you want me to set you up somewhere? You've earned it, you know."

"Me, your grace? And who would see to me flowers or provide Cook with all the fancy fruits and vegetables she's forever demandin' when your relatives descends on her unannounced?" He shook his head and a wisp of thin, gray hair fell across his forehead. "If it's all the same to you, your grace, 'ere's where I've lived and 'ere's where I'll die." His sharp old eyes made an anxious search of Jared's face. "Is that what you come to tell me—that you're plannin' to put me out to pasture?"

"Good God, no." Jared frowned. "Brynhaven is your home as long as you want it. I just came to say hello . . . and to ask a favor of you." He looked about him questioningly. "Did the housekeeper leave you enough roses to make up a bouquet for a lady?"

"Not if she's partial to yellow or white," Ben said drily. "And the red 'ave pretty much finished their bloomin'. But I've a few pink ones wot's still middlin' fair."

"Pink is just the color for Lady Lucinda. If you'll make up the bouquet, I'll send a footman to deliver it to her maid." Jared hesitated, twisting the small basket round and round in his hands. Finally he thrust it at Ben. "There's another lady, Miss Emily Haliburton—a country woman from the Cotswolds. I thought violets might suit her better, if that patch at the edge of the wood still blooms this time of year."

"It blooms same as ever," Ben said, staring at the small basket. "Wot's this you 'ave 'ere, your grace? Sink me if it don't look like one o' them May baskets you and me used to make for your mama when you was no bigger'n a tadpole. Violets was always her favorite. Funny too, with all the grand flowers she could 'ave chose."

He raised his head. "Do you want me to line it with moss like we used to?"

"I had that in mind," Jared said quietly.

"And I suppose this 'ere ribbon is to tie the bunch of violets with, same as before." Ben looked thoughtful. "So it's true then. Cook said you was choosin' yourself a duchess. I wish you happy, your grace. Miss Emily must be a most particular lady."

Jared cleared his throat. "You mistake my motives, Ben. It's nothing like that. Nothing at all." Strangely embarrassed, he dropped his gaze to make a serious study of Ben's well-worn boots.

"Miss Haliburton is merely a friend," he said stiffly. "Hardly even that. A chance acquaintance actually, whom I met up with on a morning's ride. It's just that we had a slight misunderstanding which, as her host, I feel obliged to rectify." Though why he should feel compelled to explain himself to one of his gardeners, he couldn't imagine.

Ben nodded his head sagely. "Aye, your grace. I heard about the lady wot trimmed your sails, so to speak, at the ball last night. T'was all the staff could talk of when I stopped at the kitchen for my mornin' cuppa."

His wise old eyes regarded Jared with twinkling humor. "Like I said, Miss Emily must be a most particular lady."

Emily was in Lucinda's chamber listening to yet another of Lady Hargrave's tirades when Maggie Hawkes entered with a bouquet of long-stemmed pink rosebuds in a tall crystal vase. "One of the footmen give 'em to me for Lady Lucinda," Hawkes said, setting the vase on a nearby chest of drawers.

Lucinda, who had been weeping steadily for the past hour as Emily and she suffered the countess's vicious tongue lashing, leapt to her feet and snatched the accompanying card from Hawkes's gnarled fingers. "They must be from the earl," she said, then broke into a fresh bout of weeping when she read the card.

"They're not from the earl," she wailed, throwing herself onto the bed, a picture of abject misery. "They're from the duke."

"The duke!" Lady Hargrave shot from her chair, circumvented a half-packed portmanteau, and pried the card from Lucinda's fingers—a remarkable feat considering her impressive bulk. "My deepest apologies," she read in an awestruck voice. "Oh, my, can you believe it! The man is so besotted with the silly widgeon he will excuse anything."

She glanced about the untidy room. "Put Lady Lucinda's dresses back in the clothespress immediately before they become hopelessly wrinkled," she directed Hawkes. "Then come to my chamber. I shall need repairs to my coiffure before I make my appearance downstairs."

Her eyes gleamed with malicious triumph. "Wait until I tell Lady Sudsley about *this*. I'll make that harpy regret the snub she gave me last night if it is the last thing I ever do."

She stared down at her daughter's prostrate form. "Listen to me, Lucinda, and heed what I say. I absolutely forbid you to invite that woman or her chinless brat to any of the routs we shall give once you become the Duchess of Montford."

So saying, she sailed from the room with all the majesty of a four-masted schooner putting out to sea.

Lucinda's sobs reached a new crescendo as Emily looked on, feeling utterly helpless and bewildered. All through the long, miserable night she had consoled herself with the thought that the drubbing she would take from the irate countess over her social gaffe would be worth the agony because she had unwittingly saved Lucinda from the clutches of the dreadful duke. Now this!

"Pssst." Maggie Hawkes caught her attention. "There's one for you too, miss," she whispered.

"One what, Hawkes?"

"A posy, miss. Though not so elegant as Lady Lucinda's. But still, what with her ladyship bein' so touchy and all, I thought I'd best put it in your chamber, if you know what I mean."

"You can't be serious. A posy for me. From the duke."

"The very same, I'd say. There was just the one card, but the footman was carrying both together—Lady Lucinda's roses in one hand and your little posy in the other."

More bewildered than ever, Emily mumbled her excuses to Lucinda and, with Hawkes at her heels, repaired to her own chamber.

She had never before received a posy from a gentleman, and receiving her first from the icy duke somehow made her feel a bit sad . . . until she saw the little birch bark basket and the bunch of violets nestled on the damp, velvety moss.

Tears misted her eyes. How could he have known? How could a jaded aristocrat like the Duke of Montford have known she had made baskets just like this for her dear mama and lined them with moss and placed bunches of May violets in them? How could he have known that of all the flowers on God's green earth, violets were her favorite?

"Kind of a piddling thing next to all them roses," Hawkes said, looking over her shoulder. "And I'd swear that bit of ribbon is a scrap what's been lying around here for years. But then you're not a highborn lady, are you, miss? Bein' a duke and all, I guess he took that into account."

"They're lovely," Emily said, fingering the yellowed ribbon securing the violets. "I shall press them in my Bible and keep them forever."

"You do that, miss. I guess, considerin' how his dukeship feels about women, it's a rare thing at that."

"What do you mean, 'how he feels about women'?"

Hawkes darted a glance around the room, as if to make certain they were alone. "Cook says he don't like 'em much, and one of the upstairs maids told me she heard him and Mr. Rankin talkin' a while back and it don't matter who the duke marries, he'll have nothing to do with her once he gets her with child."

She wagged her head, setting her white cotton cap askew. "Cook says it's no wonder he feels like he does, all things considered. Them what remembers her says the old duchess, his grandmama, was the worst jade in the old king's court. Died of the French pox she did and took four of his ministers with her. And his mama wasn't much better. Ran off with some smooth-tongued Frenchie when the duke was scarce out of leading strings."

"That is enough, Hawkes," Emily said severely. "I do not care to hear any more such gossip. The duke's family is none of our business."

"That it isn't, miss. Unless he marries our poor little lady . . . and her nibs is right, you know. It's beginnin' to look like he favors Lady Lucinda."

A trickle of fear traveled Emily's spine, and she shivered despite the warm sun pouring through the chamber window. She looked down at the little basket she held in her hands and her heart felt like a great, heavy stone in her breast. Heavy with worry over Lucinda's uncertain future. Heavy with sorrow for the Duke of Montford's unhappy past.

Chapter Eight

His guests were already assembled in the salon adjoining
the dining room when Jared joined them the evening after
the ill-fated ball. All except Brummell, who had left for
London at ten o'clock that morning, an unheard of hour for
the Beau to be stirring about. But, as he remarked when
taking his leave of his host, after a fortnight of the excellent
cuisine at Brynhaven, nothing short of Watiers would do
for his next meal. He intended to drive straight through to
London rather than partake of the miserable fare offered at
the posting inns along the way.

With the Beau's leaving, a pall had fallen over the gathering. Jared sensed it the minute he walked into the salon,
and two hours later, with dinner complete, the mood was, if
anything, yet more subdued. Even Lord Sudsley was still
on his feet and relatively sober.

It was as if the departure of the first guest signaled the
beginning of the end of what had turned out to be a most
frustrating fortnight. Looking back on it now, Jared found
himself wondering how he could ever have thought such a
cork-brained idea could produce anything but disaster.

The rest of the houseguests were scheduled to leave on
the morrow and the mamas of the incomparables made no
effort to hide their distress over his failure to announce his

choice of his duchess—all except Lady Hargrave, who apparently took the peace offering he had sent Lady Lucinda as a sign that he had already made that choice.

He would certainly think twice before agreeing to one of Edgar's schemes again. If the countess had thanked him once, she had thanked him a dozen times—even gone so far as to whisper behind her fan that the earl was at his disposal whenever he wished to "have their little talk."

In the meantime, he could only be grateful that by the time the virago discovered her error she would be back in London and he would be safely ensconced at Staffield, his estate on the most remote stretch of the Northumberland coast.

Lady Lucinda had mumbled a perfunctory "Thank you for the pretty roses" as they'd all trooped into dinner, but only after her mother had pushed her forward and given her a sharp jab in the back. Even then, the unhappy child had regarded him with such obvious loathing, he had been hard-pressed to keep from telling her she had nothing to fear from him.

Emily had said nothing about the posy he had sent her, but twice he had seen her gazing at him with a highly speculative look—and no wonder. In a moment of painful soul-searching, he had faced the fact that the crude little basket with its bunch of wild violets must have seemed an odd offering indeed from a peer of the realm . . . even in the eyes of a country woman from the Cotswolds.

His only hope was that he could manage to avoid her the rest of the evening so he would not have to witness her attempt to express her gratitude. Emily did not strike him as a woman who took easily to lying.

"I see the Hargraves are still with us and both the countess and Lady Lucinda have thanked you prettily for your roses." Edgar Rankin approached him, a smug smile on his face. "Apparently our strategy was successful."

"*Your* strategy, my friend," Jared said bitterly, "and I am firmly convinced that all we would have needed to turn Trafalgar into a monumental defeat was to appoint *you* Lord Nelson's strategist."

"Is there a problem of which I am unaware, your grace?"

"Nothing my leaving for Staffield tomorrow at dawn won't solve." Jared's gaze traveled to where the Countess of Hargrave was holding court with the disgruntled mamas of the four other incomparables. "If you must know, Lady Hargrave has been eyeing me all evening with a view toward measuring me for a wedding suit, and I strongly suspect the gentle Lady Lucinda is, at this very moment, plotting my murder—probably with my heir presumptive's help."

Edgar chuckled. "Well, that should enliven an otherwise dreary house party. And what of Miss Haliburton? Has she properly expressed her gratitude for her roses?"

"Not yet," Jared said, deeply grateful Edgar had no inkling of the actual "posy" he had sent to Emily. He glanced across the room to where she stood beside her cousin and inadvertently caught her eye. "But heaven help us, I think she is about to," he groaned as she excused herself and started toward him.

"Your grace." She curtsied gracefully. "I cannot thank you enough for the violets. They are my favorite flower."

I somehow knew they were. Maybe because your eyes deepened to violet when I kissed you, sweet Emily.

Jared drew his brows together in the scowl that had terrorized more than one *ton* hostess in the years since he'd acquired the title. "Violets, Miss Haliburton? Is this your doing, Mr. Rankin?"

Emily's bewildered gaze darted from one to the other. "In the little birch bark basket," she stammered. "Lined with moss." Vivid color flooded her pale cheeks. She looked rattled and embarrassed at his silence, and he wanted desperately to say something to ease her discomfiture, but out of the corner of his eye he caught a glimpse of Edgar's face, blank with amazement.

"It was your card, your grace, so naturally I assumed . . . and it was exactly like the May baskets I made my mama when I was a little girl. Violets were Mama's favorite flower, too," she ended lamely. She was chattering now, out of sheer nervousness, he could tell.

Then we have one thing in common, little country sparrow, and Edgar be damned. I'll not regret my impulse—for it is all I shall ever be able to give you.

"My head gardener is apparently a fanciful fellow," Jared said coldly. "But if you are pleased, Miss Haliburton, then I cannot fault him."

He caught her hand in his and raising it to his lips, briefly touched her fingers.

This is the last time I shall ever touch you, but I shall always remember you. When I am an old man, grizzled and stooped with age, I shall remember how once long years before Miss Emily Haliburton, late of the Cotswolds, berated me for my sins.

"Your servant, ma'am," he said curtly, "And now if you will excuse me, I must see to my guests."

Emily blinked back the tears of humiliation stinging her eyes. "I have made such a fool of myself," she said, accepting the linen handkerchief Mr. Rankin offered. "I should have known it was you who sent me the violets in the duke's name. It was not at all the sort of thing *he* would do."

She wiped her eyes and blew her nose. "Even after two months among them, I am still quite ignorant of the ways of the *haut monde*, you see. In fact, I find I do not understand them at all."

Edgar Rankin's gaze followed the imposing figure of the black-clad duke as he made his way toward the group of chattering women surrounding the Countess of Hargrave. "Think nothing of it, Miss Haliburton," he said in that soothing way he had of talking. "I have spent a lifetime studying the strange species, and I still find them beyond belief."

The evening progressed from bad to worse from then on, in Emily's opinion. She was sorely tempted to make her excuses and have an early night. But sheer stubbornness made her ignore the humiliation she had suffered and soldier on.

It soon became apparent she was not the only one sunk in the doldrums. Lady Hargrave's stern edict against conversing with the earl had sent Lucinda into the sulks and she flatly refused to contribute one of her plaintive little country songs to the evening's entertainment. For once, Lady Hargrave did not press the issue. The reason was obvious; in her eyes, the important issue was already settled.

Two of the blond incomparables had already retired to their chambers, pleading headaches, and the third claimed she had misplaced her music. Only Esmerelda Sudsley felt up to performing, and she gave such a lengthy and depressing rendition of a section of Edmund Spencer's *Cantos of Mutabilitie* that two of the titled papas drowned out the last few verses with their snores.

"It appears it is left to you to provide the musical entertainment this evening, Miss Haliburton," the duke said, removing a small silver snuffbox from his waistcoat pocket. He took a pinch and inhaled first through one nostril, then the other. "I hope you have something spirited in your repertoire. I find I am sadly in need of stimulation."

Emily rose from her chair. Head high and back straight as a ramrod, she walked to the pianoforte. He wanted stimulation, did he? Well, she had just the thing for him. She raised her hands, poised her fingers over the keys for the opening bar of Joseph Hayden's Second Symphony . . . and

the door to the salon burst open. The duke's butler Pettigrew, usually the model of stoic decorum, rushed in, and
behind him, without waiting to be announced, so did Squire
Bosley.

"Forgive this untimely interruption, your grace," the
squire panted, "but I have such splendid news, I could not
wait till the morrow to convey it."

He pulled a large square of white linen from the pocket
of his greatcoat and mopped the perspiration from his florid
face. "We have him, your grace, and it was just as you said
it would be. He finally made the mistake of being too sure
of himself."

The duke shot to his feet. "You've caught the highwayman?"

"The very same." The squire gloated. "And the blighter
has robbed his last coach this side of hell. Dead as a door-
nail, he is. Shot through the heart by old Lord Epsley, of all
people, when he waylaid the lord's coach on that lonely
stretch of the Mayburn Road."

Emily's fingers crashed onto the keys in a wild, cacoph-
ony of sound. She closed her eyes, but the grisly pictures the
squire's words evoked danced across her eyelids. Jared's
warm, red blood oozing from the hole in his chest and
spreading across his white shirt—Jared's strong body limp
and lifeless, his beautiful, wicked eyes glazed in death.

Great, shattering waves of shock and grief swept over her,
pushing her ever deeper into the black abyss that was opening up beneath her. She felt strong hands grip her arms and
for one shining moment she thought she saw Jared's face
poised above her, thought she heard his voice call her name.

But it could not be. Jared was dead, and the pain inside
her was too great to bear. It sapped her strength and dulled
her mind until, helpless, she plunged down, down, down
into blissful, mindless nothingness.

* * *

Slowly, the gray fog swimming before Emily's eyes parted and the splotches of paler, muted color hovering above it evolved into eyes and noses and mouths and finally entire faces she recognized as Mr. Rankin and Lady Hargrave . . . and good heavens, the Duke of Montford.

"Ah, she is coming around." Mr. Rankin leaned over her, his eyes anxious behind his spectacles, and Emily realized she was lying flat out on one of the loveseats in the Brynhaven music room.

She tried to push herself upright, but Mr. Rankin caught her shoulders in his two hands and gently pressed her back down. "Not so fast. Give yourself time to get your wits about you," he said kindly.

"What happened? How did I get here?" Emily asked, feeling utterly foolish and disoriented.

Lady Hargrave shoved Mr. Rankin aside. "You had an attack of the vapors and draped yourself all over the pianoforte. That's what happened. And the poor duke was obliged to carry you across the room."

The duke! Emily darted an embarrassed glance in his direction. The color had washed from his face, leaving him ghastly pale, and there was a strange, almost haunted expression in his silver eyes. Swooning women were obviously not his grace's cup of tea.

"Whatever could you have been thinking of, girl?" Lady Hargrave continued her tirade. "No sooner had Squire Bosley announced that dastardly outlaw had reaped his just reward than over you keeled."

Emily gasped as once again the horror of the squire's words washed over her.

"Miss Haliburton has a gentle nature. Talk of such violence would naturally upset her," Mr. Rankin said quickly, searching her face with the same troubled expression he'd worn since she'd recovered consciousness.

"By Jove, I surely didn't mean to shock you with my blunt talk, ma'am," Squire Bosley boomed behind him. "Don't know what possessed me to rush in here like I did. Should have known it would upset the ladies."

"Humpf!" Lady Sudsley gave a disgusted snort. "Most *ladies* would rejoice in the news you conveyed. It appears to me there's a missish streak throughout the entire family." She gave the duke a meaningful glance. "Such things are known to run in families, if you know what I mean." Even in her dazed state, Emily could tell Lady Sudsley was implying the "something" running in the Hargrave family could be far more serious than a tendency toward vapors.

"Nonsense. A great, healthy girl like Emily. She's no more given to swooning than the kitchen cat," Lady Hargrave said indignantly. "It must have been something she ate at dinner. Probably the lobster. I have a cousin, once removed, who swells up like a toad with the first bite; likely Emily has the same problem."

"She ate lobster all right; I saw her do it." This from Lord Sudsley.

Emily sank back onto the pillow of the loveseat, grateful Lady Hargrave had come up with an explanation, no matter how erroneous, for her fainting spell. At the moment, she felt incapable of speaking on her own behalf.

Her relief was short-lived. No sooner had her head touched the pillow than she heard her aunt give a surprised gasp. Glancing up, she saw the duke clearing a path through the assembled spectators. Without a word, he bent over and scooped Emily up in his arms as easily as if she had been a rag doll.

"The cause of Miss Haliburton's indisposition is irrelevant," he declared firmly. "The fact remains she should be taken to her chamber at once."

"Your grace! Whatever are you thinking of? I beg of you, let me summon a footman to carry the young lady." Pettigrew sounded shocked beyond belief.

"Miss Haliburton is *my* guest and, therefore, *my* responsibility. I shall see her to her chamber," the duke replied in a voice that brooked no opposition.

Emily cringed at the thought of being carried like an invalid—and by the duke at that—but she was still too numb with shock and grief to protest.

Across the vast hall and up the massive staircase he carried her, a grim expression darkening his handsome features. Because she had no choice, Emily relaxed and he instantly tightened his grip, making her all the more aware of the muscles rippling in his strong arms and the hard, male feel of his chest.

"Which is your door?" he asked, and when Emily pointed it out, he set her on her feet in front of it, retaining a firm hold on her upper arms.

"There is something I must say to you," he said, gazing down at her from his great height. He cleared his throat. "Something for which I am most heartily sorry."

Emily stared at him in dismay. His exertions had rumpled his precisely tied cravat and a lock of jet black hair had fallen over his forehead. For the first time, the stiff-necked duke looked almost human, and his resemblance to Jared was so strong, Emily was hard-put to keep from bursting into tears.

He appeared to be trying to apologize for something. What, she couldn't imagine. Unless. Good heavens, did he think that demanding she perform had upset her to the point of bringing on her vapors?

Emily blinked back her tears. "Thank you for your concern, your grace, but you have no cause to blame yourself in the least," she said wearily. She gazed longingly at the door to her chamber. Her head was still spinning and her stomach felt as queasy as if it had in fact developed an antipathy to the innocent lobster Lady Hargrave had impugned.

She reached for the doorknob, desperate to escape the duke's presence before the full impact of the squire's dreadful news hit her and she made an even greater fool of herself than she already had.

"No, wait." He put out a hand to stop her. "Please, you must listen to me. I . . . "

But before he could finish his sentence or Emily could turn the knob, the door burst open, revealing Maggie Hawkes's formidable figure and behind her a frightened-looking Lucinda. "There you are, my poor miss," Hawkes exclaimed. "Lady Lucinda came looking for me all in a pother—said you was ailing something awful."

She wrapped a protective arm around Emily's shoulders. "Now don't you fret, miss. I've turned down your bed nice and comfy and sent a footman to the kitchen for peppermint tea with a drop or two of laudanum in it. Nothing like it to sweeten a sour stomach and make you sleep like a babe."

Without a backward glance at the duke, Emily relinquished herself to Hawkes's motherly care. She could feel the tears she could no longer control welling at the corners of her eyes and she knew she was just seconds away from turning into the worst kind of watering pot—something she didn't relish doing in front of the duke. In truth, all she wanted was to be left alone with her own despair.

Vaguely, she heard the duke utter a protest, heard Hawkes's brief, no-nonsense reply and the decisive click of the door as the elderly maidservant closed and locked it. Then she heard no more. She sprawled across the bed, buried her face in the cool freshness of the lavender-scented pillow, and gave herself up to her grief over the untimely death of the charming scoundrel, who along with all his other thefts, had stolen her heart.

In the darkened hallway, Jared stood alone in stunned silence, rooted to the spot where a mere servant had relegated him, the Eighth Duke of Montford, and then slammed the door in his face. Had the world gone mad? It surely must have, he decided, as he stood outside Emily's door, feeling more like a green stripling who'd been put in his place than a powerful peer of the realm.

His first inclination was to kick the damned door down and toss Lady Lucinda and her officious maidservant into the hall. He needed to be alone with Emily, needed to take her in his arms and confess his shameful duplicity so he could beg her forgiveness.

His booted foot was raised and ready to strike when he thought better of it. He had already wounded Emily's generous heart; he could not risk ruining her reputation as well. And it would indeed be ruined if even the faintest hint of the havey-cavey game he had played with her this past fortnight became public knowledge. Such a scandal could be so titillating to the gossip mongers it could even follow his little country sparrow to her village in the Cotswolds.

He pressed his fingers to his aching temples. But now he must face the long night ahead, knowing Emily was grieving needlessly and he was powerless to keep her from shedding a single tear. He only hoped Cook would have the sense to put enough laudanum in the tea to sink Emily into a deep and dreamless sleep.

He was not surprised to find Edgar waiting for him when he made his way to the library a few minutes later. "No, I did not get the chance to tell her the truth," he said before Edgar could ask. "Some ancient she-devil in a mobcap snatched her away and tucked her into bed before I could get a word out. I had to choose between saving her from a night of unnecessary grief and protecting her reputation. Under the circumstances, the latter seemed the wisest choice. But come what may, I will speak to her first thing in the morning."

Edgar crossed to the sideboard and poured two stout

brandies. "I should hope so, your grace," he said in that tight-lipped way Jared had come to think of as Edgar's voice of disapproval. "Because rightly or wrongly, Miss Haliburton believes she is in love with you—or I should say with your alter ego."

Jared cringed as if Edgar's barbed words had drawn blood. "I have come to realize that," he said quietly. "I doubt I shall ever forget the look on her face when Squire Bosley declared that I . . . that the highwayman was dead."

"Nor I, your grace. Nor I."

Jared downed a healthy swig of brandy. "Fool's courage" he had heard it called, and if ever a man needed the courage to say what should be said, he was that man. "As you well know, my friend," he began, "I have not always led the life of a saint in the thirty years I've walked this earth."

Edgar said nothing, but the look in his dark, myopic eyes spoke volumes.

"And strange though it may seem to an upstanding fellow like you, I have few regrets."

"To feel regret over one's actions can be rather humbling, and humility is not a trait one normally associates with a duke," Edgar remarked dryly.

Jared gritted his teeth. Edgar wasn't making this easy. He finished his brandy, set the glass on the table beside his chair, and took a deep breath. "But I confess I deeply regret deceiving Emily Haliburton about my identity. She deserved better treatment than that from me."

Edgar raised his glass in a brief salute. "There may be hope for you yet, my friend." He eyed Jared speculatively. "Miss Haliburton is an extraordinary woman. One who would make any man, even a duke, a fine wife."

"A Duke of Montford marry a commoner? You cannot be serious. My blue-blooded relatives would never recover from the shock. Nor, I think, would the Regent and the rest of the Royals. Why, even *you* once remarked that she would never be accepted in polite society."

"Is that so important, Jared?"

"To another man—possibly not. But I hold a title which is nearly as old as England itself. I have no choice but to take such a consideration into account when I choose my duchess."

Jared stared morosely into the bleak, soot-coated interior of the cold fireplace. "You are the family historian, Edgar. Tell me, has any Duke of Montford ever taken less than an earl's daughter to wife?"

"No. Nor, to the best of my knowledge, has any Duke of Montford ever married for love. But that is not to say it cannot be done."

"Love?" Jared laughed bitterly. "A fairy tale spun by the Brothers Grimm to entertain the common folk. Such gullibility was bred out of my genes long before the first Tremayne crossed the Channel."

Edgar pushed his spectacles higher onto the bridge of his nose. "Good!" he declared. "Then you can have no objection to my pleading my cause with the lady in question once she recovers from her present insanity."

A picture of Emily's lush, warm body pressed into Edgar's mattress, Edgar's hands on her full breasts, his mouth tasting the sweetness of her soft lips flashed before Jared's eyes, and a stab of fierce, hot jealousy shot through him.

"Do so," he snarled, "and though I look on you as the brother I never had, I swear I will see her a widow before I see you take her to the marriage bed."

"As I thought," Edgar chortled, and his laughter still rang in Jared's ears long after the annoying fellow had taken his leave to wish the houseguests a peaceful sleep on their last night at Brynhaven.

Chapter Nine

The black, storm-tossed night had finally come to an end, giving way to a dawn as bleak and dismal as Jared's mood.

He had stood for hours by his bedchamber window staring into the inky darkness and listening to the wind howl through the ancient oaks for which Brynhaven was famous. For a brief time, hours earlier, he had watched jagged streaks of lightning slash across the sky so close to the manor house the answering thunder rattled the window-panes in their leaded casements—and all the while his jumbled thoughts chased each other around his brain like so many befuddled rats in a cage.

All was quiet now at Brynhaven except for an occasional rumble of distant thunder, but it was a strangely expectant quiet, as if nature were simply gathering her forces for another spectacular assault on the ancient estate.

Jared's gaze lingered on the banks of dirty gray clouds gathering on the horizon and he frowned darkly. For the last hour or two, brief spits of rain had lashed the window like carelessly tossed pebbles—forewarnings of the coming deluge destined to turn the nearby roads into seas of mud that would bog down the strongest of horses and sturdiest of carriages.

This was more the weather of early March than late May, and as a proper host he would be expected to extend his hospitality until such time as his guests could safely travel back to London. He groaned. From the looks of things, this infernal house party he'd foolishly initiated could drag on indefinitely. Well, that would be Edgar's problem, because weather be damned, he fully intended to leave for Staffield the minute he finished his talk with Emily. He could stay there until autumn, and hopefully by the time he returned to London Emily would be safely back in the Cotswolds and Lady Lucinda safely betrothed to young Percival.

But that was all in the future; right now he faced the unpleasant task of divulging the truth of his duplicity to Emily. The very thought made his blood run cold. She already held the aristocracy, and him in particular, in disgust; she would probably thoroughly despise him once she learned the true identity of the highwayman she had championed. But the task was one which must be done. He was first and foremost a man of honor, and he could think of nothing less honorable than letting a woman mourn needlessly.

Still, sound as the reasoning might be, the very idea of confessing his sins rankled him. He was not accustomed to being held accountable for his actions; he was the Duke of Montford and no man in England dared raise a voice against him. Even his cheeky man-of-affairs knew enough to tread lightly when expressing disapproval. Yet here he was, a peer of the realm, deferring his travel plans so he could bare his soul to a country spinster he would probably never see again—and feeling every bit as guilty as when he'd been caught in a schoolboy prank at Eton. The world had indeed gone mad and he with it.

He had half a mind to order Edgar to handle the miserable business for him—a coward's way out, he knew, but smacking of reason just the same. Emily already thought him a snobbish prig; what did it matter if she thought him a coward as well? Besides, Edgar had a rare talent for smoothing ruffled feathers—something he himself had never needed to cultivate.

Restless, he paced the floor, debating with his conscience the wisdom of this simple solution to his problem. The more he thought about it, the more he realized what a mistake it would be to confront her himself. The poor woman would likely have another attack of the vapors from sheer embarrassment. Why, he wondered, had he lost sleep over the matter when all he had to do was leave the necessary instructions for Edgar and then depart for Northumberland posthaste.

Feeling very pleased with himself indeed, Jared stopped his pacing long enough to change from his evening clothes into the rough shirt, britches, and well-worn boots he always wore when traveling alone and on horseback. Out of deference to his fastidious valet's tender sensibilities, he would dispatch him to his London town house along with all the elegant clothing so unsuitable for the monastic life at Staffordshire.

He packed his razor and a few other necessities, including a container of that miserable shaving soap his valet insisted on preparing for him, in his leather travel pouch, then crossed to the window to make a final check on the weather.

The usual flurry of morning activity was in progress in the courtyard below. Stable boys rushed to and fro like ants tending their ant hill—some hauling barrows of manure and stale hay out through the wide-flung doors of the vast stable, others carrying bales of fresh hay in.

As Jared watched, the elderly head groom appeared, leading a horse already saddled, and headed toward the mounting block. Jared shook his head in disbelief. Which of his guests was such an avid rider he would choose to pursue the activity on a morning like this? Couldn't he hear the ominous rumble of thunder in the distance?

He looked again. Hell and damnation! He might have known! It was the dapple gray, and there was Emily in her ill-fitting green riding habit and a foolish little hat that would afford her no protection whatsoever from the inclement weather.

What was the fool woman thinking of? Didn't she know how dangerous it was to ride during a thunderstorm? And what business did his head groom have putting her to mount without permission from either Edgar or himself?

Moments later, after a mad scramble down his private stairwell, he reached the stables on the run. It was too late; Emily had already ridden off. Without even stopping to give the groom the tongue-lashing he deserved, Jared saddled the black stallion himself and took off after her.

He knew instinctively where she was heading—the great oak tree that had been their trysting place—the worst possible place to be if lightning struck. The sentimental little fool probably had some crazy idea of bidding a last goodbye to the scoundrel who had stirred her virginal passions.

He felt another of the painful jabs of conscience that had plagued him ever since he'd had the misfortune to lay eyes on Miss Emily Haliburton. Never again would he make the mistake of fixing his interest, even temporarily, on a woman who was ruled by her emotions. A man might as well commit himself to Bedlam because she would drive him there eventually anyway. Give him a vacuous little debutante any day, or better yet, a jaded aristocrat or demimonde who knew the rules of the game.

A flash of lightning split the stormy sky and the stallion reared in protest. With a firm grip on the reins, Jared calmed the frightened beast and once again urged him forward.

His thoughts returned to the woman he pursued. If the testy little gray had been spooked as well, Emily could have been taken unawares and thrown from the saddle. She could this very minute be lying crumpled and broken in the meadow or the patch of woods that lay between him and the oak tree.

He was not normally given to panic, but a rushing tide of it welled in him now, and his chest heaved with the effort of drawing a breath past the great lump filling his throat.

Anxiously, he studied the landscape ahead but could see no sign of the gray or her rider. What if he had guessed wrong about Emily's destination? It would be just like her to be heading nowhere in particular, but simply riding willy-nilly, numb with grief. In such a state, she could fail to note her surroundings and become hopelessly lost for hours. At the very least, she was certain to get herself soaked to the skin.

The wind was blowing in earnest by the time the giant oak came into view, whipping the thick branches about as if they were slender twigs. He instantly spotted Emily and expelled the breath he hadn't realized he'd been holding. She was standing with her forehead pressed against the trunk and God help him, she was tracing her fingers over the ridiculous heart and initials he'd foolishly carved the day he'd bid her farewell. What, he wondered now, could have possessed him to do such a thing?

He dismounted and walked toward her. He might have known she would be crying, and Emily crying was not a pretty sight. He'd seen ladies cry; they sniffed daintily into lace handkerchiefs. He'd witnessed the apocryphal wailing and moaning of his various mistresses when he'd given them their congés. Emily followed neither of these patterns. She emitted great, loud, racking sobs that seemed to be ripped from the very depths of her soul.

He had never heard a woman cry like that; he had certainly never thought to hear one cry like that over him. The sound ripped through his heart and left him feeling both humbled and sickened by the thought that he had unwittingly brought her to this.

He found himself despising the fictitious alter ego he'd so conveniently created, yet envying the scoundrel as well. He seriously doubted any woman would ever cry over Jared, the Eighth Duke of Montford with the same heart-rending passion Emily cried over Jared, the highwayman.

It was obvious she hadn't heard him approach. He stepped closer, eager to speak yet afraid he might shock her if he did so.

"Emily," His voice cracked and he cleared his throat. "Emily," he repeated when she failed to answer him.

She turned around and instantly every drop of color leached from her face. Staggering backward until she was pressed against the tree trunk, she stared at him with a look akin to horror. "Jared?" she mouthed, but no sound came out.

She rubbed fiercely at her puffy, tear-drenched eyes. "Jared?" she squeaked and rubbed her eyes again. "But it cannot be. Am I hallucinating or are . . . are you a ghost?"

"Neither, Emily." He took a step toward her and held out his hand. "Touch me and you'll see I'm every bit as real and alive as you."

Emily shrank back against the tree trunk, gripping it with both hands as if to keep herself from falling to her knees. Her eyes widened to two red-rimmed circles of disbelief. "But the squire said . . . How could he have been mistaken? He said you were lying dead in the road."

"The highwayman who has been robbing the locals was lying dead in the road," Jared said gravely. "But I am not that highwayman. I told you as much but you refused to believe me."

"Dear God, it is true, then. You really are alive." Emily pressed her hand to heart. "I can scarcely credit it."

"I am very much alive, little sparrow, and I swear if I'd

had any suspicion that witless thatchgallows would be so careless as to get himself killed, I'd have made you listen to the truth. I would never have let you grieve needlessly."

Emily swiped the last of her tears from her cheek. "Of course you wouldn't. No one could be that cruel. It is all my own fault. I should never have distrusted you."

Guilt, sharp as a knife, stabbed Jared and every word Emily said twisted the blade a little deeper. Once again she was leaping to a wrong conclusion, assuming she was the one at fault in the sorry business. He swallowed hard, "You misunderstand me, Emily. The blame is mine and mine alone. There is something I must tell you. Something for which I am deeply sorry."

"No more sorry than I, I'm sure," Emily declared. "If only I had listened to you. If only I had trusted you. I have always been much too quick to make judgments, you see. Much too sure of my own opinion. It is a grievous fault and one for which I paid dearly this time." She pressed her fingers to her trembling lips. "Because when the squire described the dead highwayman, I was so sure . . . and I just couldn't bear to think . . . but you're not . . . and you really are alive!"

Jared squirmed uneasily. He could never remember feeling guilty about anything before he met Emily, but then Emily made him feel a great many things he had never felt before. He stared at her, wondering what there was about this woman that made him see her differently from all other women. At that moment, her hair was wildly disheveled and hung from beneath her bedraggled little hat in an untidy braid, her face was swollen and blotched from crying, her eyelids red and puffy, and she'd evidently been in such a hurry to dress, she had most of the buttons on her riding habit in the wrong buttonholes, which made her look oddly lopsided. She was the closest thing to a complete disaster

Jared had ever seen . . . and so unbelievably desirable, she took his breath away.

"Hell and damnation," he said, holding out his arms. He told himself he merely wanted to give her a bit of friendly comfort, but she launched herself at him like a ball from a cannon, and the next thing he knew, they were tangled together, body pressed to body, mouth pressed to mouth.

"Emily, sweet impossible Emily," he murmured, tasting the warm, salty residue of the tears she'd shed for him—yet not really for him. A hot rush of desire swept through him and he tightened his hold, trapping her soft, womanly curves between the unyielding tree trunk and the hard evidence of his own maleness.

She gave a small, startled gasp and color flooded her pale cheeks. With a groan, he deepened the kiss, exploring the secret sweetness behind her parted lips with all the hunger of a man on the brink of starvation. He felt her arms slide around his neck and her hands in his hair, and forgetting everything but this moment and this woman, abandoned himself to the passion she stirred in him—a passion as wild and dangerous as the storm breaking above them.

Lost in Jared's embrace, Emily was dimly aware she was acting like the worst kind of wanton. She didn't care. Her joy was too great to contain. He was alive, and if only for a moment his strong arms were wrapped around her, his warm lips pressed to hers. She had no illusions about the depth of his feelings for her, but wonder of wonders, he had cared enough to seek her out so she would not grieve needlessly.

Tears puddled in her eyes and slid down her cheeks, but this time they were tears of gratitude. She had thought never to see him again when last they'd parted and she could live with that as long as she knew he was safe, but the thought that this beautiful, vital man could be hunted down and disposed of like a rabid dog had been more than she could bear.

A jagged shaft of lightning flashed across the sky and seconds later a stentorious clap of thunder rumbled all around them. Jared ended their kiss and raised his head toward the heavens. "That was too close for comfort, little love," he said, tracing the path of a tear with a gentle finger before putting her from him. "And this is not the ideal spot to be in when the gods start tossing their thunderbolts."

He looked about him. "As I recall, there is a gardener's cottage over the next rise that has been empty since old Ben moved into the servants' quarters at the manor house. We can shelter there until the storm passes . . . and we can talk. I have much I need to say to you."

"Talk?" Emily echoed, unable to tear her gaze from the firm lips that had the power to give such unimaginable pleasure.

Jared's laugh was deep and throaty and his silver eyes held a wicked twinkle. "We need not talk all the time," he teased, pressing a kiss to his fingertip and planting it on her lips. "And think how much more comfortable we will be in a warm, dry cottage once those dark clouds overhead spill their rain."

So saying, he lifted her into her saddle and bolted into his own. "It is not far. Follow close behind me and keep your head down. The wind has grown quite fierce," he instructed and set off in the direction of the nearest hill.

The wind was indeed fierce, but with none of the chill of a winter storm. The little gray kept her nose close to the stallion's tail and trailed along behind him trustingly. In no time at all, Emily spied the cottage they sought standing just beyond an oak that was almost as tall as the one they had just abandoned. She felt the first drops of rain splash against her cheeks as they came to a stop at the foot of the shallow stairs fronting the small structure.

"Go inside," Jared said, dismounting and taking her reins after he helped her from the saddle. "I'll tether the horses behind the cottage where they'll be protected from the worst of the storm."

He watched Emily climb the stairs and push open the door. Then leading both horses, he started around the corner of the cottage. The wind had reached near gale force and the rain it drove before it, pricked his face like dozens of sharp needles. Unable to see ahead of him, he stumbled over a fallen branch, and the reins slipped from his fingers.

"Good lad," he praised the stallion, who stood stock still despite his momentary freedom from restraint. "Where would we be if you and the little mare deserted us?"

Jared stared at the reins once again resting in his hand. "Where would we be indeed?" he asked again, slapping the reins against the palm of his other hand.

Stranded in this cottage until someone from the manor came searching for us after the two horses returned to the stable. That is where. And what then? Emily's virtue would be hopelessly compromised, of course, and I would be honorbound to offer for her despite our disparity of social station. She may be a commoner, but she is a lady and the niece of a countess, albeit one who, according to Edgar's research, had acquired the title under questionable circumstances. Not even a high stickler like Aunt Sophia could fault me for doing the gentlemanly thing.

He pulled his hat farther down on his forehead to keep the driving rain out of his eyes and felt his soggy shirt billow out behind him when the wind whipped through it. Absentmindedly, he reached up to rub the stallion behind his ear, and wondered if he dared drop the reins and give him a sharp slap to send the restless black back to the stable.

Why not? He wanted Emily Haliburton more than he had ever wanted any other woman he had ever known. She had no idea how passionate she was, nor how deeply sensuous. He longed with all his heart to teach her.

Moreover, he liked and respected her and found her keen mind and sharp tongue so challenging, he could even imagine spending the rest of his life with her—something he could say of no other woman he knew. He would not tire of her as his father had tired of his pretty, addlepated mother, nor drive her to the arms of another man—nor be driven himself to take mistresses and servant girls to satisfy his physical needs. Emily would satisfy all his needs quite adequately.

He had no desire to marry but if marry he must, then Emily Haliburton would be the ideal choice of a wife—in all respects except one. She was a commoner with blood as red as that which flowed in the veins of the lowliest cottager who worked his estates, and red blood was not meant to mix with blue—at least not blood as blue as Montford blood. And therein lay the rub, for his sole reason for marrying was to produce strong sons with noble blood in their veins who would be a credit to his ancient line.

The marriage of a Duke of Montford to a commoner would create scandal in the hallowed ranks of the *ton*—to say nothing of the upheaval it would cause in a certain hallowed churchyard when his grandfather and all the dukes of Montford before him turned over in their graves at such desecration of their noble lineage.

"No, my old friend," he declared, running his fingers across the sleek, dripping back of the stallion. "Emily Haliburton is not the woman destined to be my duchess. I have known that from the first moment I saw her and no amount of rationalization will make it otherwise. So I had best get this blasted confession of mine over and done with and be on my way before I create any more heartache for either of us."

As if to punctuate his statement, a bolt of lightning split the sky above him, sending both horses into a panic. The little gray simply made soft, whimpering noises and nuzzled herself against Jared. But the huge stallion reared onto his hind legs, and eyes wild and nostrils flaring, whinnied his terror at the top of his lungs.

Jared took a tighter grip on the reins and at the same time sidestepped out of the way of the frantic horse, but it was all he could do to hold on to the reins and at the same time manage to avoid the lethal hooves flailing the air.

Which was why he failed to hear the wind-tortured branch directly above his head snap in two before it plunged toward the earth.

Chapter Ten

Emily made a dash for the cottage, only to find herself further drenched by the curtain of murky water spilling from the roof as she struggled with the rain-warped door. In desperation, she put her shoulder to the heavy panel, gave a mighty heave and finally managed to pry it open and stumble inside. But the sudden draft of damp air across her back told her that more than the door had given in that last push—namely the overtaxed seams of Lucinda's riding habit. She gave a deep sigh—something she hadn't been able to manage since she'd buttoned herself into the constricting garment—and turned to watch Jared.

He appeared to be having his problems. At least, he'd made little progress toward tethering the nervous horses; in fact, he was still standing a short distance from the foot of the stairs apparently deep in conversation with his wild-eyed stallion.

Emily watched the driving rain plaster his jet black hair to his head and run rivulets down the finely chiseled contours of his face. She smiled, wondering how many men would stand in such a downpour calmly conversing with a horse. But then, in the short time she had known him, she'd come to the conclusion this free spirited half brother of the icy duke had little in common with more conventional men.

The wind was intensifying by the minute, whining through the treetops like a thousand frenzied banshees. The very sound sent shivers down Emily's spine, and she raised apprehensive eyes to the boiling clouds just as a shaft of lightning split the sky directly overhead. Her heart leapt into her throat and at the same instant the terrified stallion reared onto his hind legs, striking a glancing blow off the little mare's withers.

She saw Jared lunge for the reins, which had slipped from his fingers, and realized he was unaware that a branch high above his head had ripped loose from the great oak and was plunging toward him. She screamed, but it was too late. To her horror, she watched it crash down upon his head, burying him facedown in the mud beneath a tangle of leaves and splintered wood.

Numb with fear, she rushed forward, slipping and sliding in the ankle-deep muck until she reached the spot where he lay. With pounding heart, she pushed aside the muddy debris and turned him over. His eyes were closed, his face deathly pale and caked with dirt, and blood oozed from a deep gash above his right temple. Frantically, she lifted her skirt, ripped a length of ruffle from her petticoat and bound the ugly wound.

"Wake up, Jared," she pleaded, dropping into the mud to hold his head in her lap. She tore off another section of ruffle and aided by the driving rain, wiped the worst of the mud from his face.

Something crashed behind her and glancing around, she saw the door of the cottage swinging wildly on its hinges in the gusting wind. Never had anything looked so inviting as that open doorway—or so remote. But somehow she had to get Jared through that doorway and into shelter. He had suffered a dreadful shock and he was soaked to the skin; he could be taken with lung fever if he lay much longer in the rain and mud.

Methodically, she ran her hands across his ribs and down his long legs the way she'd seen the village doctor do when she'd helped him tend a carriage accident victim. As far as she could tell, nothing was broken. Only his poor head had suffered in the accident and she doubted moving him would worsen that.

Scrambling to her feet, she bent over and slipped her hands beneath his armpits and dragged him slowly toward the stairs behind her. He was dead weight and heavy as an anvil. His chin lolled forward onto his chest and the boots encasing his long legs dug two tracks in the ever-deepening mud—and with each step Emily took, the seam of Lucinda's riding jacket ripped another inch or two until she could feel the rain pelting her back and shoulders through the flimsy fabric of her chemisette.

Finally she reached the stairs, and with the last of her strength hauled his limp body up stair by stair until she reached the open doorway—an effort which completed the demolition of Lucinda's jacket, leaving the right sleeve attached to the armhole by nothing more substantial than a few threads. Impatiently, she yanked it from her arm and tossed it to the floor.

Peering about the dim interior of the single room, she spied a high, narrow bed with two blankets folded across the foot. "Well I'll never be able to hoist a great hulking fellow like you onto that," she declared to her silent burden. "The floor will have to do, but I suspect you've slept on many a floor during your colorful career."

With trembling fingers, she stripped Jared of his soggy shirt and wrapped one of the blankets around his powerful shoulders and across his chest. His was not the first male torso she had seen; the field laborers back home often stripped to the waist in the heat of summer. Still, something about the sight of this particular bare, muscular chest left her feeling strangely weak of limb and flushed of cheek.

"Act your age, Emily Haliburton," she chided herself. "You are no green girl and this is an injured man who needs your help, not your maidenly vapors." Ignoring her pounding heart, she wrapped the other blanket around her own bare shoulders, sat down on the floor, and cradled Jared in her arms.

He moaned softly and turned his face into her breast like a babe nestling against his mother, and a surge of tenderness swept through her, so intense it felt almost like pain. Gently, she brushed a lock of blood-matted hair from his forehead.

With his eyes closed and his sensuous mouth twisted in pain, he looked so much younger, so much more vulnerable then the wicked tease who had ridden into her life a fortnight before. So young, so vulnerable . . . so infinitely dear. Tears misted her eyes. Had she foolishly lost her heart to this impossible man? Was this terrible ache deep inside her that emotion the poets described with such fervor? If so, she found love a far more painful thing than their glowing words portrayed.

For long, terror-filled hours, she held Jared—watching with anxious eyes every expression that flitted across his face as he slipped in and out of consciousness. Sometimes his inky brows drew together in a scowl; sometimes a faint smile lingered at the corners of his mouth as if he were only asleep and dreaming pleasant dreams.

Once when he opened his eyes and stared at her, he grimaced in pain and mumbled, "I must tell you the truth, little sparrow." But almost instantly, his eyelids closed and his breathing deepened, and Emily was left to ponder what mysterious truth he felt impelled to tell her.

With anxious heart, she waited for the raging storm to abate so she could find her way back to the manor for help. Much as she dreaded the thought of exposing Jared to the

tender mercies of his arrogant half brother, she had no alternative—and she clung desperately to the belief that not
even the icy duke could refuse to aid an injured man.

Eventually the hours took their toll. Emily's arms began
to ache and her legs felt as stiff as two broomsticks. She
stirred cautiously, hoping to bring the circulation back into
her tortured limbs without disturbing Jared, but the slight
movement set him to moaning restlessly.

"Hush, my love," she crooned, tightening her hold until
his cheek once again rested against her breast. Jared nuzzled against her but this time, when he opened his eyes, the
expression in their silver depths looked vacant and disoriented, and she felt a new wave of fear engulf her.

A powerful gust of wind rattled the cottage door and
splattered rain against the windows. Emily groaned. Rather
than lessening, the storm appeared to be gathering momen-
tum by the minute.

Tenderly, she pressed her lips to Jared's feverish brow
and murmured a desperate prayer. "Please tell me what
to do, dear God, for I am at my wit's end." Tears welled
in her eyes and splashed onto his pale cheek—and as if
in answer to her supplication, the door burst open, revealing Mr. Rankin and one of the duke's grooms. They
stopped dead just inside the doorway, their faces blank
with shock.

"Thank heavens you've come," Emily cried, so relieved
to see them she failed to register their stupefied expres-
sions. "But however did you find us?"

Mr. Rankin ignored her question. Dropping to his knees
beside her, he lifted Jared from her arms. "Your grace," he
muttered in a choked voice, "what in God's name have you
done to yourself?"

Jared's fingers closed on Mr. Rankin's neatly tied cravat,
sending it askew. "Is that you, Edgar?" he asked in a voice
barely audible.

"It's I, Jared . . . your grace. We've come to take you home. I swear to God I lost ten years off my life when that devil stallion of yours returned to the stables without you. Every man at Brynhaven, including old Ben, is out looking for you. It was just luck I remembered this cottage."

Your grace! Emily stared dumbfounded, first at Jared, then at the man who bent over him so anxiously. Shock and disbelief warred in her muddled brain, turning the terror that had gripped her just moments before into bitter, chilling anger. "Are you saying this man is the Duke of Montford?" she managed between gritted teeth.

"Of course 'e's the duke. 'Oo'd you think 'e was, ma'am?" The groom knelt beside Mr. Rankin. "Lucky we come in a carriage, sir. 'Is grace don't look up to makin' it back to the manor anyways but flat on 'is back."

"Right you are, John Groom, and the sooner we get him there the better." Mr. Rankin lifted the bloody bandage to check his employer's injury. "Fetch the coachman, lad. Tell him we need his help to lift the duke," he ordered, and the young groom immediately pulled himself to his feet and disappeared through the door, shutting it behind him.

Mr. Rankin raised his head and fixed Emily with an assessing stare that made her humiliatingly aware she was not only muddy and disheveled, but missing part of her clothing as well. From the look on his face, she suspected he thought she'd been thoroughly ravished.

His gaze dropped to where the blanket had slipped aside to show her sleeveless arm. "Please be good enough to explain what happened here, Miss Haliburton," he demanded with a chilling politeness that confirmed her suspicions of how he viewed her state of dishabille. "In particular, how his grace sustained such a lethal blow to the head?"

"I didn't hit him, if that is what you're asking," Emily replied caustically. "*His grace* was hit by a falling tree limb and I dragged him in out of the storm—an act of mercy I now heartily regret. I should have left the villain lying in the mud where he belonged."

"Oh, Emily . . . " the injured man protested without opening his eyes.

Emily clutched her blanket tighter around her and rose to her feet. "Don't you, 'Oh, Emily' me, you blackhearted rogue," she snapped, embracing her rage as if it were a shield with which she could momentarily fend off reality. Later, when she was alone, she would face the paralyzing hurt and humiliation of this bewildering betrayal.

"And don't *you* say a word either," she added, leveling an accusing look on the duke's bespectacled man-of-affairs. "It is plain to see you were part and parcel of this havey-cavey game your depraved employer was playing." To her everlasting shame, her voice broke in a sob. "My God, I cannot credit to what lengths you shallow creatures will go to find amusement."

Turning her back on the two men, Emily marched out the door and into the raging storm, nearly bowling over the young groom and the coachman in the process.

"Damn your eyes, Jared, you promised me you'd tell Miss Haliburton the truth," Edgar muttered before the groom and coachman drew close enough to hear.

Edgar's voice sounded far away, as if he were deep inside a cave, but Jared had no trouble understanding his words. Nor, even in his befuddled state, could he mistake the disgust with which those words were uttered.

He struggled to gather his wits sufficiently to defend himself against the accusation. "I tried," he murmured thickly, but his head ached so abominably he couldn't for the life of him remember what it was he had tried or what had prevented him from succeeding.

Through half-closed eyes, he watched the groom and coachman cross the room to stand over him and moments later felt himself lifted and carried through the rain to a covered carriage.

The last thing he heard before someone closed the carriage door was Emily declaring she would rather ride up beside the coachman through a full-blown hurricane than share a carriage with the despicable duke and his mealy-mouthed minion.

The decision to ride outside the carriage on the coachman's seat had been a grievous mistake—one of those dangerous impulses her dear mama had often proclaimed would one day land her in the soup. If Mama were looking down from heaven now, she must surely be shaking her head and saying, "I told you so."

Emily had been so shocked, so angry, so devastated by the perfidy of the man she had thought a common highwayman, she had made her stubborn stand without considering how strongly she would be buffeted by the wind and rain or how difficult it would be to keep the blanket clutched about her while she clung to the seat for support. Nor had she stopped to think how she would appear to onlookers when she arrived at the manor house with her hair whipped from its pins and her clothes looking as if they'd been forcibly ripped from her body.

She thought about it now, alone in her bedchamber. She thought about the crowd of anxious houseguests and servants waiting outside the manor house to greet the duke's carriage. She thought about the horror and disbelief in Lady Hargrave's and Lucinda's eyes and the earl's beefy face mottled with rage. She thought about the giggling housemaids and the stoic butler and the disapproving looks on the faces of the duke's two aunts . . . and Lady Sudsley's look of smug satisfaction that said she had not only brought disgrace upon herself but on everyone related to her.

No one had spoken a word. The entire assemblage had

appeared stunned into absolute silence. Everyone, that is, except Mr. Rankin, who very curtly ordered her to stay seated while he arranged to have the duke carried to his suite—then personally handed her down from her elevated perch. With his hand firmly gripping her elbow, he led her through the group of gaping spectators, up the stairs, across the great entry hall, and finally to the door of her bedchamber.

"You showed your colors, Miss Haliburton, and very dramatically, too," he remarked as he raised her hand to his lips in farewell. "I cannot speak for the duke, but I know I feel quite properly chastised."

Gravely, he searched her face, "But, all things considered, would it not have been wiser to make your point a bit more discreetly?"

Emily gave him a scathing look, stalked into her bedchamber, and slammed the door in his face—but in her heart she knew he was right. She had had good reason to hate the man who had played her for a fool, but in letting that hatred drive her to such extremes, she had made an even greater fool of herself. In one reckless moment, she had branded herself a hoyden—probably worse—in the eyes of all who had witnessed her ignominious return to the manor.

She slumped onto the bed, a bundle of abject misery. Had it been only an hour ago that she had gazed at a man's face and felt warmth and tenderness? Now the very thought of that cruelly handsome face turned her blood to ice and her heart to stone.

Behind her, the door opened and then closed. "Emily?" Lucinda's voice sounded even more tentative than usual.

Emily turned to face her wide-eyed young cousin and forced her rigid lips into a semblance of a smile.

"Dear Emily, whatever have you done?" Lucinda wailed, crossing the room to sit beside her on the bed. "I have never seen Mama so distraught nor Papa so furious. They have forbidden me to ever speak to you again or even to mention your name in their presence. I could not be here now if Hawkes were not standing watch by your door."

She took Emily's cold hand in her small, warm one. "Papa says you have brought such disgrace upon our family the duke will never offer for me now. I cannot say I am sorry for that, but it breaks my heart to know you are a fallen woman and Papa will never allow you to darken our door again." Her eyes grew wide as saucers. "Oh, Emily, where will you go? What will you do?"

What indeed? Emily felt gripped by absolute terror at the thought of being left alone and penniless, and she had not the slightest doubt that Lord Hargrave would cast her out without a farthing now that she had ruined his grand scheme to refill his empty pockets.

"Hurry, Miss Lucinda." Hawkes poked her head in the door. "Her nibs wants to leave for London afore Lady Sudsley has another go at her. She said to tell Miss Emily she's to ride in the luggage carrier and stay out of sight of the earl 'cause he's hoppin' mad."

Lucinda's eyes puddled with tears. "Oh, Emily, will I ever see you again?"

"Of course you will, and you must not worry your head about me for I shall be quite all right. I am very good at taking care of myself, you know." Emily gave Lucinda a hug and even managed a genuine smile, but everything inside her felt as if it were cracked and crumbling as she watched her tearful cousin leave the room. For all her addlepated ways, Lucinda was a love, and she would miss her dreadfully.

"You'd best hurry and change into a traveling dress, miss, whilst I pack the rest of your things," Hawkes said in her best no-nonsense voice. "As browned-off as the earl is, he'd likely leave you here at Brynhaven if you was to keep him waitin'. And you wouldn't want that now, would you, miss?"

Emily instantly leapt to her feet and tossed aside her blanket. Facing the great, inhospitable city of London alone and without funds might be terrifying; remaining at Brynhaven was unthinkable.

"Oh, my poor miss, what has that blackhearted rake done to you?" Hawkes commiserated, her eyes wide with horror at the sight of Emily's torn and sleeveless garment.

She gave Emily a sympathetic pat on her bare shoulder. "If it's any comfort, you're not the first woman what's had her good name ruined by such as the duke. Nor will you be the last. It's how the gentry takes their pleasure. Many's the tweeney and chambermaid I've hidden behind the linen stacks when the earl come home drunk as a wheelbarrow and lookin' to drop his britches."

Maggie Hawkes's favorite subject of conversation was the depravity of the English aristocracy. Emily had often thought that if Madame Guillotine were ever to hold sway in London, Hawkes would be the first to embrace the sans culottes and shout, "Off with their heads." She had to admit she was sorely tempted to do a little shouting of her own at the moment, but for the sake of her self-respect, she felt honorbound to set the record straight.

"The duke never touched me," she said quietly, trusting she'd be forgiven for stretching the truth to exclude some highly improper kisses. She explained in careful detail how she came to rip the seams of Lucinda's riding habit, ending with, "You know how tight it was across my chest."

Hawkes surveyed her with dubious eyes. "So you says, miss, but there's no use bamming me. I knows there's more to the story than that, because I knows the duke's kind and knows 'em well."

Emily ignored Hawkes's obvious attempt to draw her out. The woman had a heart of gold but gossip was her meat and Emily had no intention of giving her any more choice bits to chew on. With shaking fingers, she buttoned herself into one of the ill-fitting cotton frocks Lucinda had abandoned once she left the schoolroom.

Hawkes folded the last item of Emily's scant wardrobe and placed it in her portmanteau. "I hopes for your sake, miss, you're not so foolish as to think the muckworm gives a fig what's to become of you now he's had his fun," she said sourly.

Emily shook her head. "No, Hawkes. Even *I* am not *that* foolish."

"And if you're thinkin' the earl will change his mind about throwin' you into the street, you can forget that, too. The old curmudgeon is gettin' boskier by the minute on the duke's brandy and if he don't fall off his fine new horse and kill himself, he'll be meaner than a snake by the time we reaches London."

Hawkes warmed to her subject. "Why, even her nibs, fatched as she was at what you done, spoke against him taking his revenge. Said no matter what, you was still her only sister's daughter and he should at least give you coach fare back to the Cotswolds. But she might as well have saved her breath, for all the good it done. Though to give the devil his due, I doubt the earl had it to give. One of the duke's footmen told me Mr. Brummell picked him clean in a game of hazard the night of the ball."

She reached into the pocket of her apron and withdrew a handful of coins. "Take this, miss. It's only a few shillings but it will get you a bit of bread and a place to lay your head until you can figure what to do."

Emily raised her hand in protest. "I can't take your money, Hawkes. I know for a fact you've not been paid for months and chances are you'll need it yourself before long the way things are going with your employers."

She donned her serviceable pelisse and tied the ribbons

of her chip straw bonnet. "Not to worry. I'll just nip around to my grandmother's solicitor and ask him to give me an advance on the monies due me," she said cheerfully.

"He can do that, miss?"

"Of course he can and I feel positive he will once he hears of the change in my situation," she declared with a great deal more certainty than she felt. The last time she'd made such a petition, she'd been told no funds could be released before she was five-and-twenty.

But that was a problem she would face when she came to it. In the meantime, all that stood between her and starvation was the five shillings she had hidden in the lining of her reticule the day she left the Cotswolds.

Chapter Eleven

Jared awoke to a room deep in the shadows of early evening. Somewhere a window was open; he could feel the breeze on his face, see it ripple the canopy above him. Gingerly he turned his head on the pillow, expecting the searing pain he'd experienced the last time he'd attempted such movement. To his surprise, he felt only a dull throbbing in his temples.

Edgar was sprawled in a wingback chair stationed near the bed. His spectacles had fallen down his nose and his mouth hung open. He was snoring gently, but the minute the bed squeaked as Jared shifted his cramped legs to a more comfortable position, Edgar's eyes flew open.

"Jared?" he inquired anxiously, rising to stand beside the bed.

Even in the dim light, Jared could see his man-of-affairs looked nothing like his usual dapper self. Dark smudges underlined his bloodshot eyes and there were unfamiliar hollows beneath his cheekbones. His cravat was missing, as were his coat and waistcoat, and his linen shirt looked as if he'd slept in it for a se'nnight. "Curse me if you don't look like the one with the headache," Jared murmured and was rewarded with a smile that spread across Edgar's taut features like a ray of sunshine brightening a stretch of bleak, gray moor.

Edgar drew a long-barreled pepperbox pistol from the waistband of his pantaloons and laid it on the table beside the candle. "Thank God I'll have no more need for this."

"Since when have you needed to arm yourself at Brynhaven?" Jared asked, scowling at the wicked-looking weapon.

"Since your lady aunts called in the local doctor. The quack insisted you'd expire unless I let him bleed you, and the only way I could change his mind was to threaten to blow a hole in him if he so much as stepped through the door."

Jared chuckled. "Good thinking, old friend. I know the man well. He buries more patients than he cures." He swallowed the lump in his throat, touched by Edgar's loyalty, but certain he would embarrass him mightily if he tried to express his gratitude. "So, you've been standing guard while I slept," he said simply.

"Exactly. Even as you stood guard over me under similar circumstances a few years back," Edgar replied gravely. Then, lightening the mood, he gave Jared a gentle punch on the shoulder, "Though why I've wasted my time worrying about you these past two days, I'll never know. I should have realized a mere tree limb couldn't crack that thick skull of yours."

"A tree limb. Is that what struck me?" Jared asked, fingering the bandage covering the tender spot above his left temple.

"So I was told by Miss Haliburton. After which she dragged you into the gameskeeper's cottage, removed your wet shirt, and wrapped you in a blanket. Good thing too, since it was several hours after your riderless stallion returned to the stables that one of the grooms and I found you."

Several hours. Jared hated the thought that he'd lain helpless for so long while Emily was left to cope on her own. But Emily Haliburton struck him as a woman used to coping with difficult situations. "Miss Haliburton is an extraordinary woman," he said quietly. "The sort a man can count on in an emergency."

"Miss Haliburton is a stubborn, opinionated female who is ruled entirely by her emotions," Edgar said, his voice strangely bitter. "And you, my friend, are an unprincipled autocrat so taken with your foolish games-playing you have lost all sense of propriety. Between the two of you, you have managed to rock society to its very foundations."

Jared jerked to attention—an action which caused him to wince with pain. "What the bloody hell are you talking about?"

"I am talking about the fact that Miss Haliburton was still unaware of your true identity when we found her in a remote cottage weeping copiously over your unconscious form."

"Oh, that," Jared said, shifting uncomfortably beneath Edgar's accusing stare. He grimaced. "But I'll wager you set her straight forthwith."

"I had no choice. I could scarcely pretend I thought you a local thatchgallows with one of your grooms looking on, could I?"

"I suppose not." Jared lay back against his pillows and closed his eyes, gripped by a sudden premonition of disaster. "How did she take it?"

"The same way General Graham took Barrosa. I am still picking grapeshot out of my eyebrows. The lady was so incensed once she realized how shabbily she'd been treated, she flatly refused to ride in the carriage with 'the despicable duke and his mealymouthed minion.'"

"The devil you say. I'm almost afraid to ask how she got back to the manor."

"She opted to ride on the coachman's bench through the worst rainstorm this part of England has seen in years. Made quite an impression on your guests and staff when we arrived at the manor, let me tell you."

Jared pressed his fingers to his temples, which for some reason had begun throbbing again. "The stubborn little fool," he muttered. "I suppose that, combined with the hours we'd spent alone in that blasted cottage, created quite a scandal."

"I'm afraid so. But we might still have carried it off, with you unconscious and all, if she'd managed to hang on to her blanket when I handed her down—or if her clothes hadn't been torn to shreds."

Jared stared open-mouthed at his grim-looking man-of-affairs, too startled by his bizarre recitation to utter a word.

"Personally, I believe her story that she split her seams while dragging you to shelter," Edgar continued. "One could hardly fail to notice she is a bit too amply endowed to fit comfortably into Lady Lucinda's hand-me-downs."

He shrugged. "But naturally my opinion counts for little. I am afraid that despite my efforts to convince them otherwise, most of your guests set off for London this morning firmly convinced you had ravished the lady and received a crack on the skull in return. In fact, I can almost guarantee that, even as we speak, that titillating *on-dit* is being discussed behind every door in London, including Carlton House."

Jared groaned. "Hell and damnation, what possessed the woman to make such a cake of herself? And why in the name of God didn't you stop her?"

Edgar pushed his spectacles higher onto the bridge of his nose. "In answer to your first question, I believe Miss Haliburton was so deeply hurt and so profoundly shocked by what she termed your 'havey-cavey game' that she was beyond thinking reasonably.

"And as for my stopping her from making such a public spectacle of herself, I would have sooner thrown myself in front of a team of runaway horses than face down a woman as angry as Miss Haliburton was when last I saw her. It was never *my* game after all, your grace."

Jared shrank beneath the contempt he read in Edgar's eyes—contempt he knew he deserved. His head was throbbing in earnest now and more than anything, he wanted to turn away from those accusing eyes and find the sweet oblivion of sleep. But first he must make his peace with Emily.

He raised himself up on his elbows. "A favor, Edgar, before you retire to a well-earned rest. Would you please locate Miss Haliburton and ask her to join me here in half an hour. I would prefer meeting her in a more proper setting, but I have a feeling my legs would buckle under me if I tried to rise."

"But—"

"Spare me your objections, my friend. My mind is made up. Granted I would not normally consider a woman of her social station a suitable candidate for the role of my duchess, but she is a good woman, despite her humble background, and I have been the instrument of her ruination. I feel honorbound to offer her my name and my protection, and I cannot believe that under the circumstances, even such high sticklers as my aunts will dare speak against it."

"I have no intention of objecting," Edgar said dryly. "In fact, I would be obliged to tender my resignation as your general factotum and offer for her myself if you failed to do the honorable thing where Miss Haliburton is concerned."

Jared's heart skipped a beat. "Are you mad? You would not suit at all. Emily is much too . . . entirely too . . . Take my word for it, Edgar, you would not suit."

Edgar smiled—something Jared realized he had done little of since this business with Emily began. "You are absolutely right; we wouldn't suit. Much as I enjoy the mental stimulation Miss Haliburton offers, I have come to the conclusion I would be more comfortable with a gentle, biddable sort of woman as my life's companion. But that is not to say a volatile woman such as Miss Haliburton would not suit *you*."

Drawing a linen handkerchief from his pocket, Edgar polished his already spotless glasses. "As for her being beneath you, that is pure claptrap in my opinion. She is a remarkable woman in all ways and just what you need, my stuffy friend. She will give you such a merry chase, you may even become quite human in time."

Jared drew himself up to a sitting position. "Enough," he said, raising his hand imperiously. "I weary of your everlasting sermonizing. Hand me my dressing gown and fetch the lady. Let us be done with this tiresome business once and for all."

"Here is your dressing gown," Edgar said, tossing the wine velvet robe across Jared's knees. "But I fear you will have to wait until you are well enough to travel to London to make your honorable offer. Miss Haliburton, and the Hargraves were the first of your guests to depart."

"She is gone?" Jared slid back down on his pillows, feeling a strange combination of relief and deflation. "Ah, well, perhaps it is for the best. Emily in a rage would not be a pretty sight."

"I can vouch for that," Edgar agreed, folding the dressing gown and returning it to the foot of the bed.

"Perhaps it would be wise to let her temper cool a bit before I make her an offer," Jared said, more to himself than to Edgar. "A fortnight should do it, I think."

So saying, he dismissed Edgar, closed his eyes, and dropped off to sleep to dream of Emily's sensuous mouth begging for a kiss, Emily's lush body tangled with his in the marriage bed.

He could not remember when he had had such a satisfying dream.

"I don't like it, miss. Don't like it one bit—leavin' you alone like this with night comin' on. You don't strike me as the kind of female wot would last long on the streets of London." Numbly, Emily watched the wiry young driver of the hired carriage set her portmanteau beside her on the cobblestone walk and climb back onto his perch.

"But I got no choice," he continued. "I've me mum and the nippers waitin' with empty bellies, and the old sod's a payin' customer. 'Drop the trollop at the 'aymarket 'e says, and give me no guff or you'll not see a brass farthing from me, my lad.'"

Emily thought it would be a miracle if the boy managed to wring a brass farthing, or anything else, out of the impecunious Earl of Hargrave, but she held her counsel. That was his problem; she had plenty of her own.

The boy stared down at her, his pinched young face gray from the dust of the road. "Drunk on 'is arse, 'e was, so maybe 'e'll come round when 'e sobers up, miss, dependin' on wot you done wot turned 'im up waxy." He shrugged his thin shoulders. "But I wouldn't count on it if I was you. Them old ones is touchylike. Seems like when everythin' else starts shrivelin' up, if you gets my meanin', their bloomin' pride gets bigger'n ever."

His pale gaze strayed beyond Emily to a bright pink curricle with an inset of black cane which had pulled up behind the luggage carrier. "Or maybe you already got a young buck to take 'is place. For unless me eyes 'as gone bad, this is the same bloke wot's been followin' us since we changed the nags at Croyden."

He doffed his cap. "If so, I says God bless you, miss, for such as you and me needs any 'and up we can get, and I feels easier in me mind knowin' you got somethin' goin' for you." With a snap of the reins, he urged the horses forward and joined the stream of carriages circling the King's Theatre.

Emily picked up her portmanteau and started walking as rapidly and as purposefully as her legs would carry her, though she'd no idea where she was going. She had heard tales of the libertines who frequented this area looking to arrange their night's sport, and she felt certain any man who drove a gaudy pink curricle must surely be such a creature.

With grim determination, she plowed ahead through the crush of gaily dressed people strolling the walk, never looking into the curious faces which turned her way as she passed. Her heart pounded wildly in her breast and beads of perspiration dotted her brow. Out of the corner of her eye, she saw the pink curricle pull up alongside her.

"Wait up, Miss Haliburton. I am here to help you. Lady Lucinda sent me."

Emily stopped in her tracks, colliding with a dapper gray-haired gentleman walking in the opposite direction. She dared a glance toward the pink curricle and found herself staring into the earnest face of the young Earl of Chillingham.

"My lord," she breathed as he raised his stylish highcrowned beaver in greeting and directed his tiger to take the reins while he alighted to join Emily on the walk.

"She told me of your plight, ma'am," he said, brushing the dust of travel from his bottle green topcoat. "And she assured me you were merely an innocent victim in that dreadful affair at Brynhaven."

He stared at the toes of his highly polished Hessians, avoiding Emily's eyes. "I swear I cannot credit what came over Montford; he is the last man in the world I would expect to involve a decent young woman in a scandal. No need, you see." The earl's blush spread into the roots of his straw-colored hair. "I mean no offense, ma'am, but with his blunt, the duke has his pick of the brightest birds-of-paradise London has to offer."

Emily assured him she took no offense whatsoever, though in truth his insensitive words sent a new flood of pain and humiliation coursing through her. For she understood all too well why he found it difficult to believe the titillating gossip about the duke and her. She had seen the beautiful woman all London knew was Montford's current mistress. Why would a man with such sophisticated taste waste his time with a plain-faced provincial from the Cotswolds?

But he had. The wealthy and powerful Duke of Montford had chosen to amuse himself for one brief fortnight by playing the part of a common highwayman, and now she was left to pay the bill for his cruel farce. It was all so unfair and her aching heart cried out for revenge.

"I promised Lady Lucinda I would see to your safety and I will. I would walk through fire if she asked me to," the Earl of Chillingham continued fervently, his bobbing Adam's apple punctuating every word. "But the thing is, ma'am, I cannot think what to do with you."

It was too much. The young earl meant well, but he made Emily feel like a piece of refuse he'd been asked to dispose of, and the tears she had held at bay through the long, tortuous ride from Brynhaven spilled from her eyes and trailed down her cheeks.

A horrified expression crossed the earl's face. "Don't worry, ma'am, I'll think of something," he declared, pulling a linen handkerchief from his pocket and pressing it into her hand. "It's just that it would never do to put you up at my bachelor quarters in St. James Street. No women allowed, you see. And my mama moved to Bath two years ago when Papa died, so that's out."

He stared into space, apparently racking his brain for a

solution to the problem Lucinda had saddled him with, and Emily was moved to assure the kindly young gentleman that she had no need of his assistance. But she looked about her at the street hawkers and the newsboys, the flower girls with their pathetic little nosegays, and the beggars with their tin cups, the elegant dandies and the painted prostitutes who vied for their attention—and she realized the young coachman had been right. She had not the slightest idea how to survive on the streets of London. The time had come to swallow her pride and admit she was in desperate need of help.

"I shall not need accommodations beyond tonight," she stammered, hoping against hope there was some truth to her claim. "For tomorrow I shall seek out my grandmother's solicitor, and I am certain he will provide for me from then on."

The earl looked as if the weight of the world had been lifted from his thin shoulders. "One night! Well then that's no problem at all, ma'am," he declared cheerfully. "I shall simply take you to my aunts' town house in Grosvenor Square."

Grosvenor Square. Emily found it hard to believe that anyone residing at such an elegant address would welcome a homeless woman tainted by scandal into her home. She cleared her throat self-consciously. "Are you certain your aunts will not object to such an intrusion?"

"They won't know a thing about it—leastwise not until after you're gone. Staying in the country for a few days, don't you know." He held out a hand to help her into the curricle. "You'll be no trouble at all, ma'am. Why, I wager the staff will be happy as pigeons to have someone to do for. Must be a dead bore when the old dears are away."

It was obvious to Emily the minute the butler opened the door that the staff of the elegant Grosvenor Square town house was not the least bit happy about having "someone to do for."

The stiff-necked butler greeted the earl with the deference due a titled member of his employer's family, but both he and the housekeeper let Emily know, by the sour looks they cast her way whenever the earl's back was turned, that they considered her a common interloper and utterly beneath their contempt. Emily straightened her back and elevated her nose in her best imitation of Lady Hargrave, but never had she been more painfully aware of her shabby appearance, or her lack of the proper chaperon required by a single lady of impeccable reputation.

Oblivious to the repressive undertones, the earl ordered a bedchamber prepared for Emily and a light repast of cold chicken and fruit served in the small but ornate dining room. Emily had little appetite, but she forced herself to eat a hearty supper. There was every chance it might be her last good meal for some time if the solicitor was still as hard-nosed as she remembered him.

She had just quartered a luscious-looking red apple and popped a slice into her mouth when the butler announced the arrival of Mr. George Brummell.

"Percival! I did not expect to see you here." Mr. Brummell swept through the door, a picture of sartorial splendor in his usual black evening clothes. "I just stopped by to hear your lady aunts' version of the bumblebroth at Brynhaven, but I see they've not yet returned. Tell me all about it, lad. There's talk of nothing else at White's and Watiers, and I am devastated that I left a day too early and missed it all.

His gaze traveled to Emily, who had instinctively risen the minute she saw him, and his eyes widened to two startled question marks. "Good Lord! Can it be?" He raised his quizzing glass and peered at Emily. "By Jove, it is . . . my little friend from the Cotswolds."

He stepped forward, caught Emily's hand in his, and raised her fingers to his lips. "My dear Miss Haliburton, what is this foolishness I hear about you and the duke? What an unlikely pair to be involved in the scandal of the season. I am quite green with envy."

Emily didn't know whether to laugh or cry at the Beau's frivolous reaction to the miserable situation she found herself in. "It is not humorous, Mr. Brummell," she said primly.

"Nonsense. Of course it is. Scandal is always humorous and always entertaining. It is only when one takes it seriously that it becomes tedious. But pray tell, dear lady, whatever are you doing in the camp of the enemy, so to speak?"

The camp of the enemy. Emily stared wide-eyed, first at the Beau, then at the earl, whose face was a study in shock and guilt. All at once phrases like "my lady aunts" and "not yet returned" took on a new meaning. How could she have forgotten that young Chillingham was the Duke of Montford's heir presumptive, as well as his cousin?

She pressed her hand to the spot where her poor, thundering heart threatened to leap from her chest. "Dear God in heaven," she murmured, "Never say this is Lady Cloris and Lady Sophia's house."

"Of course it is our house. Whose house did you think it was, Miss Haliburton?" The voice was strident and unmistakably feminine. Emily, the earl, and Beau Brummell turned as one to find Lady Cloris Tremayne fluttering like a small, anxious bird in the open doorway—and behind her, leaning on a stout, ivory-headed cane, stood the imposing figure of Lady Sophia.

Chapter Twelve

"Aunt Cloris! Aunt Sophia!" The earl's face turned paper white and the freckles dusting his bloodless cheeks stood out like pebbles on a sun-bleached beach. "I didn't expect you to return so soon."

Lady Sophia limped forward, leaning heavily on her cane. "That is rather obvious, Percival. What is this my housekeeper tells me about your turning our home into a hotel? And do stop slouching. Poor posture will only result in a crooked spine; it will not make you one whit less visible."

The earl drew himself up to his full height, his face flushed with indignation. "Your housekeeper is too full of herself and should be sacked forthwith, if you want my opinion. I have merely offered one night's shelter to a lady who has been turned out of her home through no fault of her own."

"No fault of her own! Is it possible you are even more witless than you appear, nephew? Or is this a different Miss Haliburton from the creature who arrived at Brynhaven Manor just yesterday with half her clothing missing and relegated to the coachman's bench like a common lightskirt once the duke had had his way with her?"

Emily watched her gentle knight-errant wilt before Lady

Sophia's attack—and a terrible, cold anger filled her. She laid a hand on the earl's arm. "I will speak for myself, my lord."

She faced the she-dragon squarely. "The duke did not relegate me to the coachman's bench—I chose it myself rather than spend one more minute in the hateful man's presence. Nor did he ravish me, as you would like to believe. Apparently you do not know your nephew well, ma'am. An arrogant, selfish hedonist he might be, but he is no rapist—and that he would have to be to have had his way with me. I have too much sense of my own worth to submit to any man without the sanctity of the marriage vows."

"Bravo, Miss Haliburton. Well said." Beau Brummell raised his hand in salute.

"Do shut up, George. This is none of your affair," Lady Sophia snapped. "So, miss," she said, turning back to Emily, "I take it you expect me to believe the cock-and-bull story you related to Edgar Rankin about falling tree limbs and split seams."

"Believe what you will, Lady Sophia. I care not. But it is the truth." Emily snatched up her reticule, ready to march out of the town house pride intact. But without warning, her knees buckled beneath her and she sank onto the nearest chair.

Lady Sophia's chin elevated imperiously. "I do not recall giving you permission to sit in my presence, Miss Haliburton."

Emily clenched her fists in frustration. "You are not the Queen, my lady, and I am not a green schoolgirl standing reprimand." She pressed her fingers to her trembling lips. "And I am so angry I fear I have developed the ague."

"Impertinent chit!" Lady Sophia glared at Emily, but there was an odd light in her hooded eyes, which, under different circumstances might have been thought a twinkle.

"Very much like yourself at that age, sister," Lady Cloris said in her soft, whispery voice. She fluttered to the sideboard, poured a glass of amber liquid, and handed it to Emily. "Try a sip of this, my dear. There is nothing like a good sherry to calm the nerves. I keep it on hand for just such occasions as this."

She smiled sweetly at Emily. "You must not mind my sister's curt way of speaking. She is just so anxious to sort things out, you see, now that dear Jared is on the mend."

"He is going to be all right?" Despite herself, Emily felt a profound relief.

"Of course." Lady Cloris glanced pointedly at her sister. "Montfords are noted for their hard heads."

"For heaven's sake, Cloris, stop fluttering about and light somewhere." Lady Sophia switched her hawklike gaze to the earl, "And you, nephew, where are your manners? Fetch me a chair at once."

The earl leapt to do her bidding, then stood behind the chair as she settled her considerable bulk. "Cloris is right, for once," she said. "This unfortunate bumblebroth wants sorting out, but first I must demand of all present that nothing of our discussion will leave this room—and that includes you, George," she said to Brummell.

The Beau, who had been watching the proceedings with avid curiosity, drew forth a chair and joined the circle. "Devil take it, my lady, you ask a lot of a man. You know gossip is my life's blood." He sighed deeply. "Very well, I swear not a word will pass my lips."

Lady Sophia acknowledged his solemn oath with a brief nod, then turned to Emily. All eyes followed suit. "So, miss, what do you have to say for yourself?" she demanded.

Totally confused by the turn of events, Emily gaped at her tormenter, unable to think of a single word.

"Out with it, my girl. You deny that the duke ravished

you. Do you also deny he flummoxed you into believing he was a common highwayman and then, as Edgar Rankin so delicately put it, 'engaged your interest'?"

Emily felt her cheeks flame. She raised her chin defiantly. "No, my lady, that I cannot deny."

"Which, I assume, is why you swooned dead away when Squire Bosley delivered his news of the local footpad's demise."

Emily's cheeks flushed even hotter.

"A highwayman? How romantic. But how unlike dear Jared who, sad to say, has always been rather stuffy and unimaginative." Lady Cloris looked thoughtful. "It must be in the blood. Some of our ancestors were quite notorious rips, you know."

"For heaven's sake, Cloris, be still. We are trying to settle a serious matter here." Lady Sophia fixed Emily with a basilisk stare. "So, how do you plan to take your revenge, my girl? And do not bother to deny revenge has been uppermost in your mind, for only a saint would forgive the rogue who conceived such a hoax and I see no halo round your head."

"I would dearly love to make your arrogant nephew pay for his sins, my lady," Emily said bitterly, "if you would be good enough to tell me how a penniless commoner can revenge herself against the Duke of Montford."

A crafty smile spread across Lady Sophia's face. "I shall be happy to, Miss Haliburton. I have a score to settle with the jackanapes myself over a little matter of marriage brokering gone sour, which left my sister and me in a most embarrassing position. I do believe we may both have our satisfaction if we join forces, but that is something we shall discuss further in the morning. In the meantime, I bid you good night."

She tapped her cane on the highly polished hardwood floor with all the authority of a judge wielding a gavel. "Ring for a footman, Percival," she ordered, "and have

Miss Haliburton escorted to that bedchamber you have already had prepared for her."

"But, your ladyship . . . " Emily's protest was cut short as she felt her arm grasped with surprising force by Lady Cloris. "No use objecting, my dear," the lady whispered as she hurried her out the door and into the vestibule. "You will only upset Sophia, and you wouldn't want to do that. She is the dearest of souls, but she can be quite dreadful if she fails to have her way."

Her softly wrinkled face dimpled in a smile. "It runs in the family, you know."

Beau Brummell offered his arm to Lady Sophia and escorted her to the door of the salon which had been converted into a bedchamber once she could no longer navigate the stairs to the upper floor.

"The girl has spirit; I'll say that for her," Lady Sophia remarked after a moment of silence.

"Miss Haliburton does have that, ma'am."

"Edgar Rankin seems quite taken with her. Says she is smart as any bluestocking but with none of the silly airs such creatures usually put on."

"I share his enthusiasm, my lady. In fact when the two of us discussed Miss Haliburton at Brynhaven, we agreed she would make the duke an admirable *parti* . . . were it not for her inauspicious background."

"An obstacle, I agree, but not an insurmountable one," Lady Sophia said, stopping at the entrance to her chamber. "Though I suspect the duke might consider it so; he is insufferably high in the instep, you know."

She chuckled. "But then, I never thought to see the day the sly boots would carry on in such a shameful fashion as he has this past fortnight. A highwayman. Can you imagine, George? I didn't think the lad had it in him."

"He is a deep one, ma'am."

Lady Sophia scowled thoughtfully. "The truth, George. I know you and the duke are friends. Has he, by any chance, confided his feelings concerning Miss Haliburton?"

"Not to me, my lady. I believe Edgar Rankin is his only confidant."

"And I would have more success milking a duck than prying any of my nephew's secrets out of *that* young man. The fellow is disgustingly loyal. I am surprised he divulged as much as he did of the sorry affair."

Brummell patted the hand clutching his arm. "If I know Rankin, he had his reasons."

"You think he was championing the chit's cause with me?"

"I think he would champion any cause he thought would make the duke happy, ma'am."

"As would I, George. As would I. The duke and I do not often see eye to eye, and I suspect he considers me an irascible old busybody whose sole purpose in life is to nag him into producing an heir to the title. This I cannot deny, for it is imperative that he secure the title with his own issue, and not leave it to a nodcock like Percival.

"Still, I have always had a soft spot in my heart for the duke. He was such a sweet-natured little boy, but far too serious. More like a little old man than a child. The only person who could draw a smile from him was his care-for-nothing mother and the strumpet abandoned him when he was still a babe."

She gave a heartfelt sigh. "He absolutely adored that mindless bit of fluff—which was why Lady Cloris and I thought another mindless bit of fluff would be just what he would want for his duchess. I see now we were wrong. The duke wears his wealth and title like a suit of armor, and it will take a very strong and very compassionate woman to reach the lonely man inside. I would do anything in my power to help him find that woman."

"And you think she may be Miss Haliburton?"

"I wasn't certain until Lady Cloris mentioned the duke was recovering. Did you see how the girl's face lighted up? After all that rascal's naughtiness, she still cares for him. I find that quite remarkable."

"Then why did you spin that tale about joining forces to take your revenge?"

"Because I doubt her pride would allow her to admit how she feels about him. I know mine wouldn't if he had treated me so abominably. But any woman worth her salt would be aching to even the score."

"And you will pretend to help her?" Brummell shook his head. "How will you carry that off, my lady? For I know you too well to credit you actually mean to do the duke harm."

Lady Sophia's eyes sparkled with mischief, and for one brief instant, Brummell caught a glimpse of the legendary beauty who had taken London by storm half a century earlier. "On the contrary, I have every bit as much desire to take my arrogant nephew down a peg as does Miss Haliburton. No man ever deserved it more. Nothing drastic, you understand—just a little of the same kind of public humiliation he so thoughtlessly caused us."

She glanced about her as if to make certain there was no one within hearing distance. "But unbeknownst to Miss Haliburton," she continued in a sibilant whisper, "all the while we two plot our little revenge, I shall be playing another game—one in which I have need of your help, my friend, because while Lady Cloris is pluck to the bone, she is not at all devious."

Brummell raised a quizzical eyebrow. "I am at your command, my lady. But am I allowed to know the name of this game in which I am to be involved?"

"Of course, George," she said, and once again a crafty smile played across her austere features. "But surely you've already guessed. It is called matchmaking."

* * *

The Tremayne ladies were early risers by *ton* standards. Emily had expected to have to wait out the entire morning for her discussion with Lady Sophia. Instead, promptly at eight o'clock a maid tapped on her chamber door and entered with a pitcher of hot water, fresh linen towels, and a steaming cup of rich, delicious chocolate. "Breakfast will be served at nine o'clock in the morning room, miss," she announced shyly, "and I am to be your abigail. My name is Martha."

Emily stared at the pretty dark-haired girl. "Thank you, Martha, but as you see, I am already dressed and have no need of an abigail. Indeed, since I have never had one, I shouldn't know what to do with you."

The girl looked stricken. "Please, miss. I could be ever so much help if you'd let me. Especially with your hair. I am very good with hair, if I do say so myself and yours is such a pretty brown; it just needs a bit of fancying up like."

Tears pooled in her soft brown eyes. "My sister, Lucy— she's Lady Cloris's maid—taught me everything else I need to know. It's a rare step up from the kitchen, you see, and I'm ever so tired of peeling potatoes and plucking chickens."

"I can well imagine." Emily removed the handkerchief she'd earlier tucked in her sleeve and handed it to the girl. "I've done enough of both in my day and hated them with a passion." She smiled sympathetically. "But I shall only be here a few hours, so I'm afraid your promotion is a temporary one."

"Oh no, miss. How can that be? For I heard Mr. Finster, the butler, tell the housekeeper to air the bed in the yellow bedchamber as that was where you'd be sleeping from now on, and it's ever so much nicer than this little room—and I'm to have my own bed in the dressing closet."

Emily's heart gave a leap. The thought of finding a safe haven to carry her over until she received her portion was tantalizing . . . but with the duke's eccentric relatives? The idea was too preposterous to credit.

She was still pondering the little maid's bizarre claim when she descended the stairs to the lower floor promptly at nine o'clock. Straightening her shoulders with an air of confidence she was far from feeling, she followed a footman to the morning room. Both Lady Cloris and Lady Sophia were there before her.

"Sit down, Miss Haliburton," Lady Sophia said, tucking into a plate of ham and coddled eggs. "You've no time to be standing about looking hangdog. We have a busy day ahead of us. I have sent word to Madame Fanchon to be here at eleven o'clock and there are any number of things we must settle before then, as you'll be of no earthly use once she starts fitting you."

"Fitting me for what?" Emily stammered.

Lady Sophia frowned. "What is one usually fitted for, my girl? And don't play dense with me, for it won't fadge. Edgar Rankin warned me you were far too quick-witted for your own good."

She paused as if waiting for a comment. When none was forthcoming, she continued. "You are being fitted for a new wardrobe, of course." She surveyed Emily with obvious distaste. "And I must say, I have never seen a young woman who needed one more."

"I cannot afford a new wardrobe, my lady, as you well know," Emily declared. "And I am not a charity case to be dressed by strangers." *Certainly not strangers related to the Duke of Montford.*

"I have no intention of offering you charity, Miss Haliburton. Do I look like a woman easily parted from her money? But your present mode of dress offends my delicate sensibilities." She dabbed at her lips with a lace-edged linen serviette. "We will deduct it from your wages."

Emily laughed in spite of herself. "What wages, my lady?"

"The wages Lady Cloris will pay you for acting as her companion, you silly chit. Did you judge my sister such a pinch-penny she would expect you to perform your duties free of charge?"

Emily darted a quick look at Lady Cloris, whose faded blue eyes had widened with surprise. "I think there has been some misunderstanding, my lady," Emily said quietly.

Lady Sophia switched her baleful gaze to her sister. "Don't tell me you have neglected to make the proper arrangements with Miss Haliburton, sister. I distinctly remember requesting you to settle the matter immediately so we could move on to more important business."

"I must have forgotten," Lady Cloris said, breaking a small piece off a scone and spreading it with marmalade. "I haven't the memory of a flea lately."

She smiled sweetly at Emily. "Do say you'll accept the position, my dear. I've no one to visit the shops with now that sister is unable to get about—and we have this lovely pianoforte in the drawing room and no one to play it unless . . . but then, *he* rarely visits anymore. You could play for us each evening after dinner, as you did at Brynhaven."

"Exactly," Lady Sophia agreed. "And now that we have that bit of business out of the way . . . "

"One moment, Lady Sophia," Emily interjected, smitten with a bout of conscience at the thought of taking advantage of these two rather dotty old tabbies who seemed bent on taking in the stray kitten their toplofty nephew had abused. "I thank you for your kind offer, but I cannot but think I am the last person you should be hiring as a companion. You yourself made reference to my rather unsavory reputation last evening. Think what a heyday the gossips of the *ton* would have if they sniffed out such an arrangement between

you and the women your nephew·is reported. to have ravished. It would prolong the life of the tittle-tattle tenfold."

"Does that bother you, Miss Haliburton?"

"Not on my own account, my lady. I care nothing for the
opinions of members of the *ton*. From what I have observed
in the short time I've lived amongst them, they are all too
shallow and worthless to be taken seriously."

- 'They toil not, neither do they spin.' Matthew 6:28,"
Lady Cloris quoted in her sweet singsong voice. "You must
try one of these scones, Miss Haliburton. Cook has outdone
herself this morning."

"Oh for heaven's sake, Cloris, do be quiet." Lady Sophia
fixed her piercing silver gaze, so like the duke's, on Emily.
"If you take no stock in the gossip, what then is your objection to the proposed arrangement?"

"In less than two months, I shall return to the
Cotswolds," Emily said. "I doubt the reputation with which
I have been branded will reach that far and if it does the
few people I care about will never believe it. But London is
your milieu; you will have to live with the gossip long after
I am gone."

Lady Sophia blinked in astonishment. "With all that is on
your plate you are worried about *our* reputations? Well, I
never." She extracted a handkerchief from the pocket of her
severe black gown and blew her nose. "I begin to see how
the duke came to hoodwink you so successfully—for you
are quite obviously a silly chit who is given to maudlin
flights of fancy. A dangerous trait, Miss Haliburton, and
one you should endeavor to control."

Emily stared open-mouthed as Lady Sophia wiped her
eyes and·blew her nose again. She could not believe the old
virago could be so moved by a simple expression of concern.

"Save your solicitude for those who need it," Lady
Sophia said brusquely, obviously embarrassed by her show

of sentiment. "For your information, there is no one in London, with the possible exception of George Brummell, who is more adept at twisting the tails of the *haut monde* than I, and luckily the Beau is eager to join forces with us in this little endeavor."

She returned the square of linen to her pocket. "I learned long ago that to be timid in the face of scandal is to invite the vicious quidnuncs of the *ton* to crush one like a bug. As Brummell has so often noted—the more outrageous one is, the more fools will grovel at one's feet. And, pray tell, what could be more outré than for the Duke of Montford's aunts to sponsor the very woman he has ruined?"

Despite herself, Emily began to warm to the idea. What did she have to lose? Her reputation couldn't be any more tarnished than it already was, and the idea of two old ladies and a simple country woman getting back some of their own from the powerful Duke of Montford was almost too intriguing to resist. "Do you honestly think we could pull it off?" she asked.

"Frankly, I do not know," Lady Sophia replied. "But I cannot remember when I have looked forward to anything with such anticipation. There is nothing which stirs one's blood like taking a risk—and in this endeavor we risk everything.

"If all goes as planned, you will become the toast of London society and Lady Cloris and I will once again be its leading arbiters. If we fail, we shall be forced to retire to some spot in the country and live out our days in obscurity. But either way, we shall have a wealth of memories to warm our hearts on cold winter nights."

"But you must promise me you will not be too severe with dear Jared, sister, for I could not bear to see him deeply wounded." Lady Cloris folded and unfolded her serviette with quick, nervous movements. "A little rap on the knuckles, figuratively speaking, should suffice, I think.

He is not a cruel man, after all. Only one who is so isolated by his wealth and power, he tends to be a bit careless with the feelings of lesser mortals."

Emily closed her ears to Lady Cloris's anxious plea and to her sister's mumbled assurances. She did not want to think of the duke as lonely and isolated; nor did she care to hear any excuses for his reprehensible behavior. It was easier to hate the cruel, unfeeling man she believed him to be.

And hate him she must—or else face the utter despair of admitting the unprincipled devil still held her foolish heart in his hands.

Chapter Thirteen

There were times during the ensuing fortnight when Emily felt as if she had wandered into one of the Drury Lane farces where all of the characters disguised their true identity behind clever masks. For she had instantly deduced that Lady Sophia's haughty demeanor and sharp tongue hid a heart as big as Westminster Abbey and while Lady Cloris might claim to have the memory of a flea, she was anything but a flea-brain. Even that notorious cynic and avowed misogynist Beau Brummell turned out to be a true and caring friend once he committed himself.

In truth, she herself was the greatest change-artist of all, for it scarcely seemed possible the elegant lady of fashion she encountered each time she peered into a mirror could be plain Emily Haliburton. The vivid colors Madame Fanchon had chosen for her exquisite gowns made her skin look fresh and glowing, and the delicate fabrics draped her body in such a way that even Beau Brummell had clapped his hands and declared, "Magnificent!"

Just this morning, she had finally agreed to let Martha try her hand at arranging her hair and the result had been truly miraculous. The little maid had swept her heavy locks into a coronet which added inches of height and with a couple of snips of the manicure scissors had created two soft ten-

drils that curled along her cheek line to create a provoca-
tively feminine look. Emily had to admit that no one seeing
her for the first time would ever guess she was a simple
country woman from the Cotswolds.

The problem was that the more she listened to Brummell
and Lady Sophia map out the strategy of "the plan," as they
called the proposed revenge on the duke, the more certain
she was that this particular farce would soon turn into a
comedy of errors.

Even now, on the morning of the fourteenth day Emily
had been in residence at Grosvenor Square, Lady Sophia
was eagerly awaiting Brummell's daily visit with yet another of her outrageous ideas. Not even Lady Cloris's persistent objections could dampen the spirit of her militant
sister.

Meanwhile, Emily was enduring another of Madame
Fanchon's interminable fittings—this time for a riding
habit in a luscious periwinkle blue.

"Please reconsider," she begged Lady Sophia. "This is
such a ridiculous waste of money. I shall not be in London
long enough to get any wear out of a riding habit—and
there will be the added expense of hiring a nag." She
groaned. "I shall be in debt the rest of my life at this rate."

Lady Sophia looked up from the copy of *La Belle Assem-
blée* over which she and Lady Cloris were poring, and
scowled fiercely at Emily. "I cannot credit what a selfish,
ungrateful girl you are, Miss Haliburton. Can you not see
how much Lady Cloris and I are enjoying being back in the
swim of fashion, if only vicariously. Are you so engrossed
in your own concerns, you begrudge two helpless old ladies
a few moments of pleasure?"

"Helpless old ladies!" Emily burst into laughter and was
rewarded with a jab of one of the fitter's pins. "If Wellington had an army of such 'helpless old ladies' as you, Lady
Sophia, he would have defeated Bonaparte long ago."

"I'm afraid she has your measure, sister," Lady Cloris said with a chuckle.

"She has an impertinence that is beyond anything I have ever encountered," Lady Sophia grumbled. "I've half a mind to abandon 'the plan' entirely and let the thankless chit go on her way."

Emily turned, as the fitter directed, which put her back to the two onlookers and gave her the courage to speak her mind. "Then do so, my lady, for I fear the scheme is doomed to failure anyhow. I've little interest in and even less aptitude for playing the role of 'the toast of London society.'"

"Thinking of doing a *volte-face*, are you, Miss Haliburton? You disappoint me. I thought you were made of sterner stuff."

Emily gritted her teeth in frustration. Lady Sophia had a way of turning one's words to suit her needs which was absolutely infuriating. "I am made of as strong a fabric as you, my lady, and shall live up to our agreement as long. But I tell you this: I have stood for the last fitting. What clothes I do not now have, I shall do without. You have already ordered more gowns and shifts and slippers and fans than most ladies buy for their trousseau, for heaven's sake."

The fitter turned Emily again and out of the corner of her eye she caught an odd look that passed between the two sisters. It was not the first such look she had espied in the past fourteen days, and it made her vastly uneasy.

She had, in fact, been growing more uneasy about her involvement in "the plan" as each day passed. Fond as she had grown of the two old ladies, she felt as much a square peg in a round hole here in Grosvenor Square as she had under the Hargraves' roof. The sad truth was, the useless way of life of the *haut monde* bored her to flinders, and she could not imagine how she could carry off the charade they had in mind.

To top it all, the idea of revenging herself on the duke was rapidly losing its appeal. She should have realized it would, for she was not by nature a vindictive person. Nor was she a grudge-keeper. Hers was the kind of temper which instantly flared white hot, but quickly burned itself out when no new fuel was added to the fire—and right now she stood knee deep in cold, gray ashes.

In short, she was ready to beg off, but she was trapped by her mounting indebtedness to the duke's aunts—another instance where she had jumped her fences before thinking about what was on the other side. Mama must be tearing her hair out up in heaven.

Emily's moment of introspection was cut short by the arrival of George Brummell, but this time he was not alone. Behind him, flapping about like a frenetic crow, hovered a tiny man, all in black from the top of his well-oiled black curls to his highly polished black boots. Monsieur Pierre Lafitte, as Brummell introduced him, had small black beady eyes, a tiny, black stiffly waxed moustache, and a pair of very large, very shiny silver shears.

He took one look at Emily and screeched at the top of his lungs. "*Mais non, c'est impossible!* Mademoiselle must have the hair cut." He brandished the shears within inches of Emily's head. "Curls—*beaucoup de* curls to enhance the so beautiful eyes."

Despite the fitter's protests, Emily stepped back as far from Monsieur Lafitte and his treacherous shears as she could get. "Never!" she declared firmly. "There I draw the line. I cannot return to the Cotswolds with my hair cropped like that of a London demirep. What would my vicar say?"

"Don't be ridiculous, my girl. Of course you must have your hair cut. It is all the crack this season." Lady Sophia waved her hand in a gesture which signified Monsieur Lafitte should proceed. "And what, may I ask, would a country vicar know of fashion anyhow?"

Emily took another step backward, ready to do battle if necessary to save her precious locks, but to her surprise, Brummell intervened on her behalf. "Now that I reflect further on it, I do believe Miss Haliburton is right," he said, studying the softer hairstyle Martha had created with the same absorption he had studied Madame Fanchon's samples of fabric earlier in the week.

"I agree Miss Haliburton's eyes are one of her best features," he said thoughtfully. "But let us be honest, she has another notable asset, which we have already discussed."

Remembering the heated debate they had indulged in each time she'd complained of the shocking décolletage of her new gowns, Emily felt her cheeks flame with mortification.

Brummell smiled at her embarrassment. "Let us simply say I have come to the conclusion that Miss Haliburton's most outstanding asset is best accented by the more classic hairstyle she has already adopted."

Hours later, with a paisley shawl draped discreetly over her "most outstanding asset," Emily sat at dinner, listening despondently to the never-ending discussion of how "the plan" should be carried out. Lady Cloris had just lowered her forkful of salsify pie to raise a mild objection to Mr. Brummell's latest proposal when the butler announced the arrival of the Earl of Chillingham.

"He's back!" the earl declared as soon as Finster had withdrawn from the dining room. "Montford is back in London. Freddie Fabersham told me he saw him at Tattersall's just yesterday and looking fit as fivepence."

Emily's heart took such a leap her "most outstanding asset" nearly burst from the daring neckline of her pale green spider-gauze dinner gown.

"Finally!" Lady Sophia cast a triumphant look at Brummell. "Now we can set a definite date for Miss Haliburton's entrance into society. Friday next, I think. As I recall, that is the night Catalani has agreed to sing the role of Konstanz in a special performance of *Seraglio* to raise money for the new wing of the Duke of York Hospital. Montford will be there, of course, since he is on the hospital board—as will everyone else who is still in town."

"Oh no! Surely not the opera!" Lady Cloris gasped. "I cannot think you mean to embarrass poor Jared in such a public place as that, sister."

"Don't be a ninny. Nowhere else would be half as effective."

"But Mozart is his favorite composer, and I am certain 'the plan' will quite spoil the performance for him. You know what an intensely private man he is." Tears glistened in Lady Cloris's eyes. "I will not be a part of such cruelty."

Emily cleared her throat. "I have to agree with Lady Cloris. When I consented to help put the duke in his place, I had no idea you intended to do so with all of London looking on."

"*Et tu*, Miss Haliburton." Lady Sophia glared down the table at Emily and Lady Cloris, who sat beside her. "I take it since you two pansy-hearts have lost your thirst for revenge, you have also abandoned the nobler cause of 'the plan' as well."

"Nobler cause?" Emily and Lady Cloris asked in unison.

"As I understood it," Lady Sophia said, "we all agreed that the duke was sorely in need of a lesson which would teach him to consider the feelings of others. Am I correct?"

Emily nodded halfheartedly and out of the corner of her eye saw Lady Cloris do the same.

"Very well then. In light of the news Brummell brought me yesterday, this lesson assumes a far greater importance than we first conceived. It appears the Regent has asked Montford to act as mediator between the mill owners and the Luddite rioters. Though heaven knows why. He is far too stiff-rumped to be effective in such a role."

Emily had to agree. The thought of Jared—the duke—mediating a dispute with such desperate men made her blood run cold. His idea of mediation would probably be to look down his aristocratic nose at the rioters and demand they follow his dictates.

Lady Sophia took a sip of wine before continuing. "The days of the feudal lords are long past—an unfortunate state of affairs in my opinion, since the system had considerable merit. However, so be it. The fact remains, in these troubled times even a duke must be careful what he says and does. My God if that miscreant Bellingham could assassinate the Prime Minister within the very walls of the House of Commons last month, anything can happen. Is that not correct, Brummell?"

"It is surely something to consider," Brummell agreed when he recovered from a sudden fit of coughing.

Emily shuddered, remembering her horror when she'd read the terrible news in the *Times*, and once again a picture of Jared lying dead in a pool of his own blood flashed through her mind.

"And," Lady Sophia continued in the same grim tone of voice, "if Montford persists in his autocratic ways, I fear *he* may end up with something far more life threatening than a bump on the head."

Emily's thoughts were as tangled as the embroidery skein she had tried to unravel for Lady Cloris before dinner. She suspected she was being led down another daisy path, this time by Lady Sophia. As Lady Cloris had reminded her, Montfords would do anything to get their own way.

Still, as before, there was enough fact woven into the fiction to confuse even the most astute listener. How could she know what to do? And if she chose the wrong course, would she be able to live with herself if some day, safe in her little cottage in the Cotswolds, she picked up the London *Times* and read the duke of Montford had taken a Luddite bullet?

She turned to Lady Cloris and saw the same look of indecision in her troubled eyes. "Very well, Lady Sophia, you win," Emily said with a sigh of resignation. "We will proceed as planned."

A smoky yellow heat haze hung over the streets of London and the stench of sun-ripened horse droppings and human garbage was so overpowering, most pedestrians held cologne-scented handkerchiefs to their noses. It had been years since Jared had been in the city during the summer; he remembered now why he had made such a point of avoiding the dratted place during the dog days—which in some years extended from the first of June until October. This was evidently one of those years.

The handsome grays he had purchased at Tattersall's just the day before were prime goers and required only the softest of hands on the ribbons to control them. He wheeled his snappy new high-perch phaeton along St. James Street, nodding pleasantly to acquaintances he passed. But a knot of anger tightened his stomach when he noted the snide grins with which they returned his greetings.

Apparently the Brynhaven scandal was still the most juicy *on-dit* of the summer and would remain so until some other member of the *ton* provided a new bit of titillation.

A fresh wave of guilt swept through him. If *he* received such a reception in this traditionally liberal all-male section of the city, he could well imagine what Emily had been encountering in Mayfair and Kensington while he languished in the country.

He would make it up to her, he vowed, knowing full well he had purposely put off his return to London to give her time to calm down. A bad mistake. She was probably livid by now, and he dreaded their first meeting under this cloud of scandal almost as much as he looked forward to their first lovemaking as husband and wife.

What could he buy the little firebrand that would pacify her sufficiently to smooth over the first awkward moments? Any other woman he knew would melt in his arms at the sight of an expensive bit of jewelry, but somehow Emily did not strike him as the sort to melt over diamonds and emeralds.

Books. Emily was definitely a book person. He felt inordinately pleased with himself for remembering that helpful little tidbit and decided, if he had to, he would buy every first edition in London to bring a smile to her face.

In fact, he would make a detour to Hatchard's book shop right now and find some particularly fine volume on ancient myths and legends to take as a peace offering when he called on her later that afternoon.

The afternoon sun was at his back when Jared finally turned the grays in the direction of the Earl of Hargrave's town house. He was hot and tired and hungry, and his temper was as short as that of a hunt-bred hound on a short leash—not the best of moods in which to offer for a lady. But he had had an extremely annoying day thus far.

To begin with, his visit to Hatchard's had been most disappointing. With a seemingly inexhaustible supply of books on every other subject imaginable, they had managed to produce nothing but useless pap on ancient myths and legends. He had read Farley Haliburton's erudite pamphlets on the subject, which Emily had apparently edited. Presenting her with one of the volumes from Hatchard's would be like offering a first-year primer to an Oxford professor.

Then he had stopped in at White's for a cool drink and a bite of lunch, only to discover Emily and he had made the pages of the betting book. Men he had known for years were actually laying down wagers on the outcome of the "Brynhaven Scandal." The very idea had so infuriated him he had stalked out leaving a prime cut of mutton untouched.

So, here he was about to rap on the Hargraves' door empty-handed and evil-tempered before he even felt the sting of Emily's well-earned wrath.

The Hargraves' butler, who opened the door, was a seedy-looking old badger who, when Jared offered his card, stared at him with such malevolence Jared felt his skin crawl. The fellow even had the gall to leave him standing, hat in hand, in the vestibule while he inquired if the lady was receiving.

Furthermore, when he was finally ushered into a rather bare-looking salon, he found Lady Hargrave and Lady Lucinda, but no Emily. He gritted his teeth. How many such annoying developments could a man stand in one day?

Lady Hargrave met him at the door, her eyes wide with something that looked suspiciously like hope. Jared groaned. Could the silly old fool actually believe that after all that had happened there was still a chance of an alliance between Lady Lucinda and him?

"Your grace, how delightful to see you again, and looking so well," she gushed. "I was just this very morning telling Lady Lucinda how much I hoped you had no lasting effects from your . . . your accident."

She flushed pink as a schoolgirl. "Just you wait, I told her. Montford will call on you. He is too big a man to hold the disgraceful actions of a shirttail relative against us. Didn't I, my sweet?"

She made a vague gesture toward Lady Lucinda, who sat white-faced and silent on a shabby-looking loveseat, which except for two Hepplewhite chairs was the only piece of furniture in the room.

"Your servant, Lady Lucinda," Jared said, crossing to stand before her with the idea of doing the pretty and kissing her hand since she might one day be his cousin-in-law. She did not offer it, and the eyes she raised to him fairly blazed with hatred.

Jared stepped back, shocked by the girl's reaction, and nearly tripped over one of the chairs.

"You must excuse our lack of furniture, your grace," Lady Hargrave prattled on. "We've sent most of the really good pieces out to be recovered. Renovating the entire house, you see."

Jared nodded stiffly. He'd seen the earl's bay stallion on the auction block at Tattersall's just yesterday, and he suspected the furniture had gone the same way, if the rumors he'd heard of Hargrave's financial straits were true. Lady Lucinda was still glaring at him, and he found himself wondering if she somehow blamed him for her father's problems.

"I would like to speak to Miss Haliburton if she is at home," he said, cutting directly to the purpose of his visit.

"Emily?" Lady Hargrave's face fell and all at once she appeared to be having difficulty swallowing. "I am sorry, your grace, but she is not here at present," she said stiffly.

Jared smiled to himself. The stubborn little minx was apparently still nursing her anger and had decided to punish him by refusing to see him. She was probably hiding out in her bedchamber while her aunt sent him on his way. "When do you expect her back?" he asked innocently. "Perhaps I should wait."

"Oh no! That would not be at all wise. For I have no idea when she will return. She didn't really say, you see." Beads of perspiration broke out on Lady Hargrave's forehead and she cast a frantic glance at Lady Lucinda, as if begging for help. Two spots of color flamed in the girl's pale cheeks, but her lips remained firmly closed.

Jared felt the first twinge of alarm. Something was wrong here. "Miss Haliburton is well, I hope?" he ventured.

"Emily? Oh yes, I am certain she is. Emily is always

well." Lady Hargrave's heartiness sounded as empty as the denuded room in which they stood, and Lady Lucinda rose abruptly, tossed her embroidery onto the loveseat, and marched out of the salon without so much as a by-your-leave or a simple curtsy.

A sudden spate of shivers crawled Jared's spine despite the sweltering heat. Something was decidedly smoky here, and he had had his fill of Lady Hargrave's Banbury tales. "I want some answers," he said. "And I want them now. Where is Miss Haliburton and when may I see her?"

"As to when you may see her, I cannot say, your grace. Because she is . . . she is visiting relatives. Yes, that's it. Emily is visiting relatives."

The woman was obviously lying, but he had to ask. "And the direction of these relatives?"

"I haven't a clue. Emily is annoyingly secretive, you see. Didn't have the common courtesy to tell me how I could reach her." Lady Hargrave was sweating profusely now and she had the look of a fox cornered by a pack of hounds.

Jared could see he was getting nowhere. He was tempted to wring the truth out of the old harridan, but he could not bring himself to lay hands on a woman—not even this disgusting creature.

"Hear this," he said with quiet menace. "I will give you two days to locate Miss Haliburton and inform me of her whereabouts, after which time I will contact Bow Street."

So saying, he bowed slightly and turned to leave the room. He stopped at the door to offer one last admonition. "For your sake, madam, I sincerely hope Miss Haliburton has come to no harm at your hands. For if she has, I will make certain both you and the earl live to curse the day you were born."

He did not bother to pick her up when she collapsed to the floor, but merely informed the evil-eyed butler on his way out.

Chapter Fourteen

Jared paused for a moment outside the Hargraves' town house to gather his troubled thoughts. Where in the name of God was Emily? And why did the very mention of her name make her aunt look as guilty as a murderer about to swing at the end of Tyburn's rope? He would give anything he owned for a minute alone with Lady Lucinda; he knew he could pry the truth out of her.

A tight smile crossed his lips as it occurred to him how such a meeting could be accomplished. Unless lovesick young pups had changed a great deal since the days when he was prone to such foolishness, Percival would be meeting the little pretty on the sly. He would coerce the earl into arranging things for him.

He tossed a coin to the bundle of rags he'd hired to watch his cattle and reached for the ribbons.

"Hold up, guv," the boy cried, his thin young face alive with mischief. "There's an old bird wot wants to chirp at you a bit. Leastwise she give me a first-rate mutton pasty to twig you to where she be hidin', which be right round the corner of this very 'ouse." He grinned broadly. "But you been square wi' me so I'll give you fair warnin'. A nasty-lookin' piece o' goods she be. Never seen none nastier."

Jared glanced toward the spot to which the boy pointed and found himself staring into the sulphurous eyes of the old she-devil who had refused him entrance to Emily's bed-chamber at Brynhaven.

"Pssst," she hissed, crooking a bony finger at him. "If it's news of Miss Emily you want, I can tell you as much as her nibs; maybe more."

Jared moved quickly to the old woman's side. "Where is she, old mother? I'll make it well worth your while if you can tell me."

She drew herself up to her full height, which brought the top of her head not quite to the middle of Jared's chest. "I don't want your blunt. Miss Emily's a friend of mine." She studied him closely. "But before I tell you what I know—which ain't all that much—I need to know why you're lookin' for her. Seems to me you done her enough harm to last her a lifetime already."

Jared swallowed hard. "That I have, old mother, but I swear I mean to make it up to her."

"Words is cheap, but then maybe you do at that. Me and the old butler listened at the door whilst you brangled with her nibs. Done our hearts good, it did." She brushed away a tear which rolled down her gaunt cheeks. "The Good Lord knows it's time someone showed a bit of kindness to the poor scrap."

Jared caught her by her thin shoulders. "For God's sake, woman, spit it out. Where is Miss Haliburton?"

"How can I know, what with fourteen days gone by since she was turned out into the streets, a ruined woman." She stared accusingly at him. "And we both knows the why of that, don't we, your dukeship?"

Jared felt a telltale flush heat his cheeks, but steeling himself, tightened his hold on the old woman, forcing her to look up into his face. "Hell and damnation, what are you saying?"

"I'm saying I heard, with me own ears, the earl tell the coach-for-hire lad to drop Miss Emily off at the Haymarket and no questions asked. 'Let the little tart try selling her wares on the street, 'stead of givin' them away-at my expense' is what he said. Though you just have to look at Miss Emily to know she ain't *that* kind."

She shook her grizzled head. "And the poor little thing without a shilling to her name."

It took Jared a moment to absorb the full impact of the old woman's words, but when he did he felt as if he'd just taken one of Gentleman Jackson's famous punches to the solar plexus.

He braced himself against the wall of the town house, his legs suddenly too shaky to hold his weight. "I'll call him out," he growled, sick with shock and rage. "So help me, I'll put a bullet through the swine's evil heart."

The old woman straightened her mobcap, which had fallen over one eye when Jared grasped her. "You do that, your dukeship, for I'm sure 't'will ease your own black conscience," she said dryly. "But it won't help find Miss Emily, will it?"

"Never fear, I'll find her. To hell with waiting two days to contact Bow Street; I'll have their best runner on her trail within the hour." With a final comforting pat for the tearful old servant, Jared bounded back to his carriage, tossed another coin to the wide-eyed street urchin and headed for Bow Street.

He knew the man he wanted. Sam Haggerty. He'd used him any number of times on sensitive Whitehall business. Sam was the human equivalent of a bloodhound and as much at home on the back streets of London as in his own front parlor. If anyone could find Emily, he could.

But fourteen days! That was a lifetime on the streets. He tried not to let himself think what could have happened to her in that time, but his thoughts chased each other around his brain like rats in a cage—each one wilder and more frightening than the last. Like most other young blades of his day, he'd sowed his oats on those streets some ten years earlier. He knew all too well what evil waited to prey on an innocent young woman fresh from the country.

It was the busiest time of day and the city was crowded with everything from elegant carriages to the meanest of produce carts. Jared paid them no heed. Cracking his whip over the heads of the grays, he sent them flying as if there were not another vehicle in sight, leaving a path of cursing coachmen and overturned carts behind him.

He cared not a whit. For the first time in his life, Jared Neville Tremayne, Eighth Duke of Montford knew what it was to be gripped by a terrible, paralyzing fear . . . and to face the agony of knowing that his careless arrogance had placed the only woman he had ever really cared about in terrible jeopardy.

"La, miss, don't you look grand. And ain't that just the perfect color for you." Martha's eyes glowed with approval as she surveyed Emily in the gown of moss green silk with matching lace overskirt which Madame Fanchon had designed for her "coming-out" at the opera.

There were still three days until the great event, but the finished gown had been delivered just moments before and Emily couldn't resist trying it on. "It is lovely," she agreed, surveying herself in the mirror. "But isn't the neckline a trifle low?"

"Not for the gentry, miss. They're ever so much more forward about such things than common folk. My dad says if he ever caught my mum sporting her 'up-fronts' the way the fine ladies do, he'd take a switch to her backside."

"But *I'm* common folk," Emily wailed. "And I shall feel positively indecent going about in public with so much of my 'up-fronts' showing."

"Ask Lady Sophia or Lady Cloris," Martha suggested. "They'll know what's proper and what isn't."

Emily took the little maid's advice and moments later pushed open the door of the salon where she knew the two ladies were taking tea. To her surprise and embarrassment, both George Brummell and the Earl of Chillingham had joined them.

"I came to show you my dress," she stammered, wishing desperately she had a handkerchief to stuff into the neck of her daring gown.

Lady Sophia nodded her approval. "Madam Fanchon has come through as usual," she said, which for her was high praise. "But straighten your shoulders, girl. Show off your assets. If I'd had such a bosom when I was your age, I could have toppled thrones."

Emily could feel a blush start at her toes and work its way up to her hairline.

"You look beautiful, my dear," Brummell declared. "The rest of the ladies might as well stay home, for you will be the cynosure of all eyes."

"Thank you," Emily said automatically, but somehow his effusive compliment fell short of offering the assurance she was seeking.

"You must change your frock and join us for a cup of tea." Lady Cloris smiled her usual vague smile. "Percival has just brought us some interesting news—and there's no use scowling at me, sister, for I feel Miss Haliburton should know."

"Know what?" Emily asked warily.

"Lady Lucinda told me Montford came looking for you, ma'am," the earl said, his Adam's apple bobbing furiously. "Got his back up something fierce when Lady Hargrave tried to tell him the whisker that you were visiting some make-believe relatives. Gave her two days to come up with you or he's calling in the runners. Near scared her to death.

Last I heard, she'd locked herself in her bedchamber, but it won't do her any good. Knowing Montford, he'll just break the door down."

Emily felt her heartbeat quicken erratically. "The duke was looking for *me*?" Despite herself, she felt a moment of elation just knowing he'd worried what had happened to her, even though she suspected it was nothing more than a brief attack of conscience.

"Humpf! The scallawag's conscience is bothering him no doubt, and well it should," Lady Sophia declared, echoing Emily's very thought.

"But we must let him know Miss Haliburton is safe," Lady Cloris said. "The dear boy is probably worried sick."

"Do him good. Make him think twice before he spins one of his fairy tales for another gullible young innocent."

"I don't know, my lady." Brummell's expressive brows drew together in a frown. "He's liable to be very angry when he learns the truth. I've only seen the duke lose his temper once, but I can't say I wish to see it again."

The earl set his teacup down with a bang. "Please, Aunt Sophia," he begged, "let me tell him where she is. Brummell's right. Montford has a terrible temper once he's riled, and I can't afford to get him down on me, not with him holding my purse strings for another year. He'll cut me off for sure if he thinks I've held out on him, and I'm already in the basket—and my quarterlies are coming up this very month."

"And what do *you* think, Miss Haliburton? We've heard from everyone else." Lady Sophia fixed Emily with one of her ferocious stares.

"I do not know what I think," Emily answered frankly. "Except that I am flabbergasted to learn someone like the Duke of Montford does indeed possess a conscience like the rest of us."

She let her gaze travel from one to the other of her newfound friends. "I certainly do not want the earl, or any of the rest of you, to suffer the duke's wrath because of me." She paused. "But I must admit I shall not be at all sorry if he turns the Bow Street runners loose on my aunt and uncle."

Both Lady Sophia and Brummell burst into laughter and Lady Cloris and the earl soon joined them. "Well, that is that, then," Lady Sophia said, when she could finally speak. "You will simply have to take your chances, Percival, because I say we proceed with 'the plan' as formulated. The duke shall learn of Miss Haliburton's whereabouts on Friday night and not a minute before."

Jared took a firmer hold than usual on the ribbons as he urged the grays along the crowded, stall-lined streets of the London Stews to the location Sam Haggerty had chosen as a meeting place. The stench here was a hundred times more potent than in the more fashionable districts, and both Jared and the groom riding behind him were forced to limit their breathing to short, shallow breaths to keep from gagging.

Everything from battered iron pots to Axminster carpets, all of it used and much of it stolen, was sold on these streets, and vendors, spotting his elegant carriage, left their stalls to hold up their wares and urge "the toff" to take advantage of their prices.

Ragged children with dirt-streaked faces and ancient, knowing eyes trotted beside him, begging for the price of one of the hot penny pies the old women hawked from trundle carts, but tempted as he was, Jared left his coins in his purse, knowing all too well if he tossed so much as a ha'pence to one of the urchins, he'd instantly be mobbed by a hundred others.

He carried a loaded pistol hidden beneath his topcoat and the groom carried another in plain sight for all to see. But night would soon be falling, and no man in his right mind would be caught in this section of London after dark. A cold, numbing horror seized him at the thought of Emily somewhere in this welter of awful humanity, struggling to survive on these fetid streets. Even if luck was with him and he found her, would she ever recover from such a hideous experience?

Minutes later, he pulled to a stop at the appointed place, handed the reins to the groom, and leapt from the carriage. A shadow instantly detached itself from the side of the nearest grimy building, and Sam Haggerty stepped forward.

"This is it, your grace. The place where the girl fitting your lady's description is working. Time's right. According to my source, she just took up the profession a fortnight ago."

"Devil take it. This can't be," Jared choked, as an oily-looking fellow in faded purple knee britches and a stained yellow topcoat ascended the stairs and pushed open the door. "This is a damned brothel, and the lowest kind of brothel at that. Miss Haliburton would never be caught dead in such a place."

Haggerty shrugged. "You said she was a gentlewoman turned into the streets without a penny. In my book that leaves her two choices. One of these"—he jerked his thumb toward the disreputable establishment—"or the Thames. I can check with the lads who drag the river each morning but I doubt they'd be much help. I've seen some of the bodies they've fished out and I doubt their own mothers would recognize them."

Jared swallowed the bile rising in his throat and without another word followed the stoic runner through the shabby doors. They were met by the fattest and most malodorous woman he had ever seen. She was dressed in a shapeless, gray garment bearing the remains of at least a dozen different meals, and at first glance he judged her weight to be a good twenty-five stone.

It was obvious she recognized the runner as an old ac-quaintance, and once she'd accepted the coins he dropped

in her outstretched hand, she led them down a grimy hallway and stopped before one of a long row of doors.

While Jared watched, she pushed open the door, revealing a young woman in a flimsy pink wrapper sitting on an
unmade bed. Her hands were folded in her lap, her eyes
downcast, her rich brown hair cascading about her shoulders like a heavy mantle.

"Emily?" Jared stepped forward, his heart thudding
against his ribs.

The girl raised her head and stared at him through eyes
utterly devoid of expression.

"My name is Mary, sir," she said dully, "but I can be
Emily just as well if it will please you."

Jared drew a deep breath as relief surged through him.
Turning to Haggerty, he shook his head. "She is not the one
we seek."

He returned his gaze to the girl, who still stared at him
with her great, sad eyes. "But hell and damnation, I can't
leave her here. She's no more than a child."

"I'm afraid you have no choice, your grace," Haggerty
said with a chilling lack of compassion. "It's too late; the
chit's been here a fortnight. She's already ruined."

Ruined! The very word the old woman had used to de-
scribe Emily. "The devil she is," Jared said, clenching his
fists to keep from wringing the runner's neck.

He turned to the girl, whose small heart-shaped face had
suddenly come alive. "Are you willing to do an honest
day's work to support yourself?" he asked.

"I'll do anything," she declared fervently. "Anything but
this."

"Very well then. Put on your clothes and come with me.
I'll send you to Brynhaven, my estate some twenty miles
from London. The staff is large enough so one more maid
will never be noticed."

He smiled kindly at the girl, who had leapt to her feet and
was busy scrambling into a nondescript brown frock much

like the one Emily had worn the first time he'd seen her. "I'll give you a note to carry to my housekeeper. She's a good woman. She'll work you hard but she'll treat you fairly."

"Think what you're doing, your grace," Haggerty warned. "You can't just walk out of here with her. She's probably in debt to the house; the girls always are, and don't think that fat old woman listening at the door don't have a team of bully boys ready to see she pays up. You know the way of things down here in the Stews, even if it ain't your bailiwick. How far do you think you'll get with such as them at your heels?"

"I'm taking the girl," Jared said stubbornly, shoving a wad of pound notes into the runner's hands. "Pay the procuress whatever it takes to buy her out of this hellhole."

It was an illogical thing to do; the girl was nothing to him. She was just one of the great multitude of prostitutes who filled London's brothels or walked London's streets. But she did resemble Emily a little, and somehow he couldn't just walk out and leave the sad-eyed child to wait for a parade of unwashed, unfeeling men to defile her.

Odd. He'd never before given a thought to the kind of life a prostitute led. Possibly because he'd never frequented bordellos—not even the high-class ones so many of his acquaintances used. He'd always preferred to keep a mistress under his protection to serve his needs.

He thought about it now—and about all the poor creatures who, like Mary, waited out their dismal lives in such dismal rooms—until they were too old or too ill to wait any longer. He found himself wondering how many of them had been forced into the degrading profession because some titled member of the *ton* had betrayed them as he'd betrayed Emily.

By Friday Jared was at his wit's end. Night after night he'd walked the streets hoping, by some miracle, to find Emily. It was, he knew, a useless exercise in frustration.

Still, it was preferable to lying awake wondering where she was or worse yet, to dropping off to sleep. For on the rare occasions when he closed his eyes, he had the same recurring nightmare of the cold waters of the Thames washing over her pale, lifeless face.

The last thing he felt like doing was attending the opera tonight. But he was obligated. He was, after all, the one who had persuaded Catalani to perform, and the funds raised would benefit the poor devils who lay maimed and dying in the Duke of York Military Hospital. He'd invited his longtime mistress Lady Carolyn Crawley to share his box because she would no longer be sharing his life.

For he couldn't bring himself to touch her and doubted that he would ever be able to do so again. In fact, there were times when he found himself wondering if he would ever again desire any woman if Emily was lost to him.

He would give Caroline her congé tonight along with a very expensive gift. For she had been his friend as well as his lover for the past six years, and he owed her that much.

Then he would return home and drink himself into mindless oblivion.

The note came while his valet was dressing him for the evening. It was on the cheapest kind of paper and he instantly recognized the scrawling, almost illegible handwriting.

I think I have a lead on Miss Haliburton. Highpockets Harry, a cutpurse who works the King's Theatre area, bumped into a lady of her description on the street the night you mentioned. Saw some fancy-dressed toff take her up in his curricle. Don't yet know who he was, but I promise you I will soon. Look at it this way, your grace. At least it is better than the Thames.

Haggerty

Jared was torn between a staggering sense of relief and a monumental wave of anger and jealousy so intense it emptied his lungs of air and left him breathing so hard his frantic valet started burning feathers and plying him with hartshorn as if he were some dowager with a fit of the vapors.

He had half a mind to organize an army of servants to knock on every door in fashionable London until he located her. For he knew his Emily. She would feel so indebted to the lecherous Corinthian who had saved her from the horror of the streets, she would get all weepy and emotional. And a weepy, emotional Emily was a vulnerable Emily.

But by all that was holy, it would be pistols at dawn if the blighter had dared to lay a hand on the future Duchess of Montford.

Chapter Fifteen

"So it is farewell then, your grace?"

Even in the dim interior of his carriage, Jared could see the bitter twist to Lady Carolyn Crawley's lovely mouth as she fastened the exquisite emerald earrings to her earlobes. "You will note I wore my emerald necklace in expectation of your parting gift."

Jared sighed. "You know me well, Carolyn."

"So I thought. But it seems I was mistaken if there is any credence to the gossip running rampant throughout the *ton*. You didn't really ravish that girl, did you? I cannot imagine I was that mistaken in you."

"No, of course not. But I might as well have. I put her in such a compromising position, her reputation is"—he choked on the word—"ruined. I must find her, wherever she is, and offer for her."

"And what of my reputation?" she asked somewhat petulantly. "Everyone in London knows I have been your mistress these past six years."

"And the Earl of Skiffington's mistress before me and Lord Falkener's before him."

"Enough! You have made your point." She laughed softly, ruefully. "What a blackhearted devil you are. I cannot think how I came to fall in love with you."

Jared raised a skeptical eyebrow. "I was not aware love was ever a part of our arrangement, my lady."

"Of course you weren't. How could I tell you how I felt when every time the subject came up, you declared love was simply a term coined by hypocrites to pretty up their natural lust."

Jared searched the face of the woman whose body he knew as intimately as his own and wondered how he could have failed to realize he knew nothing of her heart or mind. "I am sorry," he said gently. "I would never intentionally cause you pain."

"I have survived pain before. I shall survive it again." She tossed her head of gleaming golden curls. "And don't you dare pity me, for that I could not bear. I shall have no problem finding another protector; the wealthiest men of the *ton* will be standing in line to take up where the Duke of Montford left off."

"That will not be necessary, my dear. I have put the Kensington town house in your name and made arrangements for a quarterly allowance to cease only upon your death. With a little clever maneuvering, you should be able to move into a more acceptable level of society. God knows at least half the so-called proper matrons of the *ton* have pasts more colorful then yours."

He turned to stare out the window at the passing scene, avoiding her eyes. "You have given me many good years, and I care too much about you to live with the thought of your having to sell yourself merely to survive."

"You care about me?" Lady Crawley looked genuinely surprised. "I would never have guessed."

Now it was Jared's turn to be surprised. "My God, Carolyn, we have been bed partners for six years. How could you think I had no feeling for you? I have always considered you my friend as well as my mistress."

"Have you really? How very odd. Yet you have never given me permission to address you as anything but 'your grace.'"

Jared felt a humiliating flush spread across his face—something that had happened too often of late. He cringed. "Am I really as stuffy as you paint me?"

"I did not say you were stuffy, your grace. Stuffy implies boring, and that you have never been. You are just exceedingly high in the instep, but then I suppose one must expect that of a duke."

Lady Crawley shrugged her plump shoulders with the same grace she did everything else. "Ah well! It makes no mind now, does it? And I am sincerely grateful for your protection and for all the expensive gifts you have given me—especially this last and most generous one. If I had more strength of character, I would politely refuse it, but a woman with my expensive tastes cannot afford too much pride."

She reached across the space between them and caught Jared's hand in hers. "Find your country miss, your grace, and make her yours. For already I see the changes she has wrought in you. Given time, she might make you as human as the rest of us."

Jared gave a snort of mirthless laughter. "Now you sound like Edgar Rankin. Perhaps there is truth in what you say. But if this past se'nnight is an example of what it is to be 'human,' I am not certain I shall survive the experience."

The Royal Theatre was, as Lady Sophia had predicted, full to overflowing. Emily had scarcely finished settling the two old ladies in their luxurious first-tier box when she realized an odd silence had settled over the crowded auditorium. She looked about her and found every set of opera glasses in the house trained on her—including those of Beau Brummell, who stood in his usual place in the pit with the rest of the *ton*'s leading dandies.

She took a deep, calming breath. It was obvious this was going to be a very long and very difficult evening. Despite the thrill of hearing the great Catalani, she would be immensely relieved when it was over.

Only moments later it was brought home to her just how long and how difficult an evening lay ahead when a cumulative gasp spread through the assemblage like a breeze rippling through a forest.

"Montford must have arrived," Lady Sophia said, leveling her glasses at a box on the opposite side of the great hall. "Just as I thought, and he has 'that woman' with him."

Emily's breath caught in her throat and every bone in her body turned to water. She kept her eyes studiously trained on her lap, for fear she would encounter the duke's gaze if she raised her head.

Lady Cloris lifted her glasses. "Oh, my goodness. Is that Lady Crawley? You must admit, sister, she is really quite beautiful."

"*Lady* Crawley indeed!" Lady Sophia gave an indignant sniff. "A title the chit acquired by marrying a ne'er-do-well baronet who fled to the Americas less than a year later to escape debtors' prison. Furthermore, she is five-and-thirty if she's a day and common as coal dust."

Surreptitiously, Emily stole a brief look at the woman in the duke's box, and her breath caught in her throat at the sight of the stylish golden-haired beauty who was the duke's mistress. Compared to the sophisticated Lady Carolyn Crawley, she felt the veriest country bumpkin, despite her elegant new gown.

"Aha! Montford has seen us." A triumphant smile spread across Lady Sophia's flushed face and she quickly dropped her glasses to her lap.

Lady Cloris's glasses followed suit. She pressed a shaky hand to her bosom. "He looks terribly angry," she managed in a hoarse whisper.

"Angry? He looks ready to commit murder." Lady Sophia chuckled with obvious glee. "And observe that flock of sheep below us. They couldn't be playing their parts more perfectly if we'd rehearsed them."

Against her will, Emily glanced over the railing fronting the box. The entire lower floor looked like a giant pendulum, swinging from left to right—right to left as all heads swiveled back and forth between the Duke of Montford's box and the one in which she sat.

The silence in the vast auditorium was unnerving and when the orchestra suddenly struck its opening chord, she nearly leapt from her seat.

"Do stop fidgeting, Miss Haliburton," Lady Sophia said smugly. "Sit back and enjoy yourself. It bids fair to be a rousing performance."

Emily sincerely hoped she was referring to the one on stage.

Jared still couldn't believe his eyes. At first glance, he had assumed the fashionable young woman sitting in his aunts' box must be the daughter of one of their titled friends. It was only when he took a second look that he realized who she actually was.

Emily!

His first reaction was a relief so profound it made his head swim; his second was total bewilderment.

What was Emily Haliburton doing in his aunts' box at the opera?

He looked again. And what in the name of heaven had the woman done to herself? Her hair was different—not at all as he remembered it—and there was such a disgraceful amount of her generous bosom showing above the neckline of her daring gown she might as well have been sitting there stark naked for all that was left to the imagination.

He lowered his glasses, suddenly aware that every eye in the place was on him.

"Who is the pretty young thing in your aunts' box, and why is she attracting so much attention?" Lady Crawley asked.

"She is attracting attention for the rather obvious reason that she is rigged out like some high-priced Cyprian," Jared declared in a choked voice.

"Nonsense. She is dressed in the latest stare of fashion, and quite uniquely so. Not many women would dare wear that particular shade of green, but it is most attractive on her."

She took another look. "And if it is her neckline you're criticizing, it is no lower than that of any other woman in the room."

"She is not any other woman in the room," Jared growled. "And I have half a mind to haul her out of that box and give her the thrashing she deserves."

A smile of dawning comprehension flitted across Lady Crawley's exquisite face. "Good heavens. Is that your Miss Haliburton? I wonder why the gossips called her plain?" She regarded Jared with puzzled eyes. "I thought you said she was lost."

"She was as far as *I* knew," he replied bitterly.

A sudden movement among the dandies gathered in the pit directly below him caught his attention and he found himself staring directly into the terror-glazed eyes of his heir presumptive.

Some pink of the ton *took her up in his curricle.*

Percival owned a curricle—a garish pink-and-black curricle.

Beside the earl stood a smiling George Brummell, who raised his hand in a brief but telling salute.

With maddening precision, the pieces of the mysterious puzzle fell into place. All the long, agonizing nights he'd haunted the most dangerous streets of the London slums searching for her, Emily had lain safe and snug in one of his aunts' feather beds—and neither she nor his bacon-brained relatives had had the decency to put him out of his misery.

"I am going to strangle the lot of them," he muttered, starting to rise from his chair.

Lady Crawley caught his arm. "No, your grace. Think! You will only embarrass yourself and embarrass me—and unless I am mistaken, that is exactly what the ladies across the way would enjoy most."

Jared sat back down. "Of course. You are absolutely right. I tend to lose my head whenever I am near Emily."

"Lucky Emily," Lady Crawley murmured.

Jared ignored her jibe. "I can understand why *she* would want to take revenge on me—she has good reason. But why are my two aunts aiding her? What have I done to them?"

"You mean aside from publicly humiliating them by failing to choose one of their five candidates after they'd informed the entire *ton* they were arranging your marriage?"

"Oh that!" Jared drummed his fingers on the railing in front of him, pondering the truth of Carolyn's explanation. "I believe you've hit on it. It is not hard to imagine Aunt Sophia's fine hand in this unfortunate business. How a woman can be so clever and so foolish at the same time is almost beyond comprehension."

His mind was made up. "Justified or not, I cannot let them get away with it. I'd be the laughingstock of London."

"Of course you can't, your grace. But what can you do to remedy it? And how may I help?"

Jared caught Lady Crawley's dainty hand in his and raised it to his lips. "Simply by being your usual understanding self, dear lady. For to accomplish the task, I shall have to visit my aunts' box at intermission—which means I must leave you on your own for a few moments. A rudeness I regret most sincerely."

Lady Crawley fluttered the jeweled fan Jared had given her at Christmas with the consummate skill of a practiced courtesan. "Not to worry, your grace. I find I am developing a most annoying headache and cannot endure the thought of sitting through the balance of the opera anyhow."

"I shall instruct one of the attendants to order my carriage."

"That will not be necessary, your grace. If you will be so good as to escort me from the box, I believe we shall find the Earl of Summerlyn hovering about the anteroom, just waiting for the opportunity to escort me home."

Lady Crawley's soft, pink lips tilted in a mischievous smile. "In point of fact, the poor, besotted fellow has been hovering about somewhere or other for well over a fortnight; it is high time I gave him a bit of encouragement. Granted, he may be somewhat of a bore, but he does have the loveliest deep pockets."

Jared chuckled. "Ah, Carolyn. I do believe I shall miss you sorely. Was there ever anyone like you?"

"Never, your grace." Her brilliant smile fell just short of reaching her eyes. "Nor do I expect I shall ever meet anyone quite like you again."

Emily didn't see the duke leave his box at the end of the first act, for she had schooled herself to look everywhere but at the man she most wanted to see. But she knew the exact moment when he did. It was as if all the light in the great auditorium had suddenly been extinguished.

She settled deeper into her chair, part of her waiting with pounding heart for his return—another part hoping she would never see him again. Maybe then she could find some enjoyment in the rest of the opera. She might even eventually find some enjoyment in the rest of her life once the image of the blackhearted devil began to dim in her memory.

"Now where do you suppose the duke and that creature have gone?" Lady Sophia asked. "He has never been one to wander about socializing during the intermissions."

Lady Cloris looked as if she were about to burst into tears. "Jared has probably gone home. I warned you we would ruin the opera for him."

"Did I hear someone speak my name?"

Emily swiveled round in her chair, as did the two ladies flanking her, to find the duke standing at the entrance to their box. Dressed all in black and with a devilish smile lighting his strong, chiseled features, he had never looked more handsome . . . or more dangerous. Emily shivered as a frightening presentiment gripped her.

"Good evening, ladies. Enjoying the opera, I trust. I cannot remember when Catalani has been in such rare form." The duke's gaze lingered momentarily on Lady Sophia. "Something I cannot say for everyone."

Emily heard Lady Sophia's sharp intake of breath and realized she had been holding her own breath since he first stepped through the door of the box. Beside her, Lady Cloris gave a soft, mewling whimper.

His lazy gaze switched to Emily, and she felt her heart plunge to her toes. "May I compliment you on your exquisite gown, Miss Haliburton. I perceive you have engaged a new modiste—Madame Fanchon, unless I mistake the cut. You must allow me to escort you on a stroll around the anteroom. Such excellent taste deserves to be displayed."

Emily's knees were shaking so badly they literally knocked against each other, but she plucked up her courage. "Thank you for your kind offer, your grace, but I am not in the mood for a stroll at the moment."

The duke surveyed her with a look so icy Emily felt the chill penetrate to the very core of her being. "But when shall we find a better time to converse, dear lady?"

Emily gulped. "I have nothing to say to you, your grace."

"Ah, but I have a great deal to say to you, Miss Haliburton. And since we are known throughout the *ton* to be friends—very close friends—I should be courting malicious gossip if I failed to acknowledge that friendship publicly."

A diabolic smile spread across his handsome features. "And as I am certain my lady aunts will attest, malicious gossip is the last thing any person of good breeding would wish to court."

Sparks flared in Lady Sophia's eyes and she opened her mouth, obviously to protest the duke's less than subtle innuendo. But a quelling look from him instantly put paid to her intention. "Oh, for heaven's sake," she grumbled. "Do as he says, child. The game is over and the rogue holds the winning hand."

With quaking heart, Emily preceded the duke through the door to the crowded antechamber and placed her hand on the arm he offered. All eyes followed them as they slowly strolled the perimeter of the vast, ornate room, leaving a trail of fluttering fans and whispered speculations in their wake.

"So, Emily," he said softly, "you have taken your revenge for the hoax I played on you. And what a cruel revenge it was! I do believe you have more than evened the score."

To the eager spectators surrounding them, the duke might appear to be smiling with the easy congeniality of the old friend he purported to be. But Emily could see the pain and anger in his eyes, and her blood ran cold.

"Smile at me, Emily," he demanded. "We do not want the gossips of the *ton* to think we are at odds with each other."

Emily smiled. "Pray tell me, your grace, what have *I* done to you that could compare to what *you* did to me?" she asked, fanning herself vigorously in the hot, overcrowded room. "Surely a few raised eyebrows and a little tittering behind fans will not mark a man such as you for life."

"I do not refer to this tasteless charade you and my lady aunts have carried on tonight," he replied grimly, "though we will most certainly speak later of the disgraceful way you have displayed yourself."

He stared pointedly at her décolletage, and Emily felt her hackles rise. "How I display myself is my own business, your grace, and none of your concern." She looked about her. As far as she could see, her neckline looked positively modest compared to those of many of the jeweled and perfumed women staring so avidly at the duke and her.

She tossed her head. "What does it matter anyway. I am already a ruined woman."

"Hell and damnation, Emily, your own impetuosity was as much the cause of your ruination as anything I did." He scowled fiercely. "But be that as it may, you are now my concern whether you like it or not."

He raised a hand to forestall the objection that rose to her lips. "Do not fight me on this, for I have had all the trouble from you I can tolerate."

"Trouble, your grace?" Emily was forced to move closer to her elegant companion as a couple brushed by them. "I ask you again. Just what is this trouble I am supposed to have caused you?"

The duke placed a protective arm about her shoulder, but his eyes sparked with angry silver fire. "My God, woman, have you no concept of the hell you have put me through? Five days and five nights I searched for you in every back alley of London, thinking it was I who had driven you alone and penniless into the streets. Can you imagine the horrors I pictured? There were even times when I imagined . . . but we will speak of that another day."

Emily stared at him in utter bewilderment, the smile he had commanded still frozen on her face. "I am truly sorry, your grace. I didn't know. It never occurred to me someone like you would care what happened to me."

The duke winced as if she had struck him. "Touché, Emily," he said bleakly. "I doubt the finest swordsman in all of England could have skewered me more effectively."

Without another word, he turned on his heel and headed back toward his aunts' box, literally dragging Emily behind him through the crowd of curious, chattering opera goers.

Executing a stiff bow first to Lady Cloris then to Lady Sophia, he declared, "You may expect my formal call at your residence tomorrow morning at eleven o'clock. I trust that will be convenient."

"Of course, your grace, we shall be pleased to receive you," Lady Sophia replied, looking very much like the kitchen cat when it presented Cook with a captured mouse.

Emily blinked, wondering why she should be so happy her arrogant nephew was making a social call when just moments before he had delivered her a cleverly worded insult. What strange creatures these aristocrats were. She doubted she would ever understand them.

Hours later, as she lay abed reliving her own bizarre conversation with the duke, she pondered another puzzle. Word by word, sentence by sentence, she recounted everything the charming, unprincipled rake had said, but for the life of her she could not determine how he had contrived to whitewash his own evil deeds and make her feel as if she were the one who had sunk herself beneath reproach.

Chapter Sixteen

It was precisely one minute before the hour of eleven when Jared stepped from his carriage and walked up the steps to his aunts' Grosvenor Square town house. The old ladies were waiting for him in the green-and-gold salon on the second floor. Emily was not.

"Where is she?" he demanded, gripped by an uneasy feeling of déjà vu.

Lady Cloris looked up from her embroidery. "Miss Haliburton and her abigail have gone for a walk—in the park, I believe."

"The devil you say! Is the woman trying to drive me out of my mind? Surely she was aware of the purpose of my call."

Lady Sophia chuckled. "Strange as it may seem, your grace, I do not believe she had the slightest notion. We tried to persuade her to await your arrival, but she declined most firmly. As she put it, 'the duke said all he had to say to me last evening—none of it complimentary. I have no wish to be raked over those particular coals again.'"

"Miss Haliburton is from a different class of society than we are, you see," Lady Cloris explained in her usual placid voice. "One I am inclined to think is much more honest and direct. She would not expect to be 'raked over the coals,' as she put it, one day and proposed to the next." She knotted her thread and bit it off. "Do sit down, my dear. She should return shortly."

Squinting, she rethreaded her needle with a different color thread. "But perhaps it would be wise to have one of the footmen instruct your coachman to return in an hour or so. I doubt she'll come in if she sees your carriage."

Jared did as she suggested, although it annoyed him mightily. Still, he found himself intrigued by the idea of taking Emily by surprise with his offer. No telling how she would show her gratitude for the honor he was bestowing on her, but knowing Emily, she would do something quite unexpected.

Thirty long, boring minutes later he was still listening to his aunts' idle chatter when Emily walked into the room. He rose instantly and glowered down at her, as was his fashion. Though, in truth, she looked so delectable in her flowered dimity dress, he was hard-put to keep his hands off her.

"You're still here," she said, obviously flustered.

"His grace has been waiting to speak to you," Lady Sophia said and leaning heavily on her cane, made her way toward the door. Smiling shyly, Lady Cloris followed suit and, to Emily's surprise, closed the door behind her.

"You wished to see me, your grace?"

"I did, Em . . . Miss Haliburton." Jared cleared his throat. Now that the moment had come, he found himself oddly ill at ease. "In my opinion enough has been said on the events which have transpired between us in recent weeks. I prefer not to touch on that subject again."

Emily's eyes narrowed. "I am certain I would feel the same were I you, your grace."

Jared did not particularly like her tone of voice, but he dismissed it without comment. "Suffice it to say, I am aware I triggered events which placed you in a compromising position." Instantly a picture of Edgar stumbling upon them while he lay in her arms with his head on her breast flashed through his mind. The very thought of that softest of pillows caused certain parts of his anatomy to react in ways which were most embarrassing, considering how the new trousers that fool Weston had designed molded his body.

"If this is an apology, your grace, I accept it in the same spirit it was given, though it is long overdue."

"Hell and damnation, Emily. It is not an apology. That is, I suppose it is an apology of sorts, but that is not my primary reason for seeking you out. Honor demands that I offer for you. For while you are a commoner and, therefore not someone I would normally consider qualified to be my duchess, you are a virtuous woman." He breathed a sigh of relief. He had said it and he was heartily glad it was over and done with.

"You are offering to marry me?" Emily stared at him, mouth agape, and Jared had visions of those warm, full lips opening beneath his, that impudent tongue employed in the tantalizing ways he had already begun teaching her in the few passionate kisses they had shared.

She raised her stubborn little chin and stared at him in that same proud way she had that first morning when she'd called him a looby. "You must be mad to think I would consider marrying you," she said. "One day you are a lying, scheming highwayman who takes unspeakable liberties with my person; the next you are an icy aristocrat whose very look freezes me to the bone. I cannot think either of your personalities would qualify you for the role of loving husband any more than my 'commonness' would qualify me for the role of duchess. In short, your grace, we simply would not suit."

Jared chuckled to himself. What a saucy baggage she was; just thinking about her in his bed made his blood race so hotly he had to blink his eyes to clear his vision. "You will learn what is required of you in time," he said confidently. "I do not demand instant perfection; I am not, after all, an unreasonable man. My aunts can instruct you in many of the things you will need to know as my duchess and I will personally instruct you in others." What those others would be he dared not mention until they were safely married.

He stepped forward to take her in his arms and seal their betrothal with a kiss—but to his surprise, she retreated behind a nearby loveseat. "I thank you for the honor you have bestowed on me, your grace," she said through gritted teeth, "but I cannot bring myself to take it seriously. For I have no desire to spend the rest of my life hobnobbing with the aristocracy."

Jared felt a twinge of uneasiness. It was not like Emily to play coy. If he didn't know better, he would almost think she was refusing him. "You have no choice in the matter," he said sternly. "Nor do I. We are involved in a scandal. The only thing which will save you from utter ruin is marriage."

"Utter ruin in whose eyes? The *ton*? I say fie on the *ton*. What do I care for the opinion of people whose only reason for their purposeless existence is their own gratification."

Jared's uneasiness accelerated noticeably. This was not going as he had planned. "Devil take it, Emily, you would not lead such a useless existence as my wife. You could become involved in any number of worthy causes and I have numerous estates which need a mistress." He could see from the expression on her face that the use of the word "mistress," even in the most innocent of connotations, had been a mistake.

"And that's another thing," Emily declared. "When I marry it will be to a man who loves me and me alone. I have no desire to share him with a mistress, as is common in the marriages of the aristocracy."

"If you are referring to Lady Crawley," he said stiffly, "we have gone our separate ways as of last evening. I am not in favor of so-called 'modern marriages.' My own parents' example was enough to sicken me on that score. Besides," he added in an attempt to lighten the mood, "I do not think I shall be in need of a mistress once we are married, little firebrand."

Emily ignored his attempt at levity. She searched his face with wide, inquisitive eyes. "Did you love her?"

"Carolyn? No, I did not love her if you are referring to the kind of emotional rubbish your Mrs. Radcliffe portrays in her novels. Ours was a practical arrangement."

"But you made love to her, probably hundreds of times in the years she was your mistress. You strike me as a man with strong appetites."

"This does not strike *me* as a conversation I should be having with my future duchess," Jared said, attempting to look more shocked than he actually felt. He could see he was going to have the kind of frank and open relationship with Emily that few men of his social status enjoyed with their wives. The idea did not displease him in the least.

He scowled as fiercely as he could manage, considering how close he was to laughing at his impertinent little bluestocking. "What, may I ask, is the purpose of this inquisition, Miss Haliburton?"

Emily's cheeks were flushed, her eyes almost too bright. "The purpose is to determine your attitude toward love. You don't even believe in it, do you?"

He was tempted to lie to her. Somehow he couldn't. There had already been too many lies between them. "No, Emily," he said gently. "I do not. I am afraid such fantasies were bred out of my bloodline shortly after my ancestors crossed the Channel. But if I were capable of believing in fairy tales, I am sure you would be the woman who would inspire me to do so. For I desire you more than I have ever desired any other woman. Is that not sufficient to ease your mind?"

"No, your grace, it is not. For I do believe in love, you see, and I will marry for no other reason—be he a duke or the most impoverished of country vicars."

She swiped viciously at the tears coursing down her cheeks. "Therefore, I must respectfully decline your most generous offer, for I can see we really would not suit at all."

She was sobbing in earnest now and her breasts heaved with the exertion. "You should marry another jaded sophisticate like yourself," she gasped through great, choking breaths. "That way neither of you would have expectations the other could not fulfill."

"What have you done, you foolish girl? How could you refuse the Duke of Montford?" Lady Sophia looked on the verge of apoplexy. "All our hard work for naught! I swear I could shake you until your teeth rattled."

"Calm yourself, sister," Lady Cloris said. "I am certain Miss Haliburton had good reason for what she did—although I confess I cannot imagine what it might be."

Emily sank onto the loveseat to which she had been clinging since the duke had crushed her lips in a brutal kiss, told her to think about *that* while she lay each night in her spinster's bed, and stalked out of the salon just moments before.

Covering her face with her hands, she sobbed openly. She felt certain she had done the right thing. Agreeing to spend the rest of her life with a man who did not love her—indeed, was incapable of loving her—would be tantamount to condemning herself to eternal torment. Especially when she loved that impossible man with all her heart despite his many shortcomings.

Just remembering how strong his arms had felt wrapped

around her and how warm and demanding his lips had felt pressed to hers made her ache in those secret parts of her body she'd only just recently become aware of. She was desperately afraid no other man would ever make her ache in such a delightful way again.

Maybe it would have been better to settle for what he could give her and not demand what he did not have to give. At least then she might have had his children on which to lavish the love he didn't want.

But no! It would have been living a lie and she was the world's worst actress. Sooner or later he would realize how she felt about him—and how embarrassing that would be for both of them.

For he had freely admitted he'd only made his offer because honor demanded it. That folderol he'd prattled later about desiring her above all other women had obviously been nothing more than his clumsy attempt at kindness. She had eyes in her head; she had seen the kind of woman who appealed to him.

She felt Lady Cloris slip a comforting arm around her shoulders and press a handkerchief into her hand. "Was I mistaken, my dear? I was so sure you cared for my nephew."

Emily sobbed even louder. "I do care for him," she wailed. "I . . . I love him. Don't you see, that was why I couldn't accept his offer." She turned her face into Lady Cloris's shoulder and clung to her the way she had used to cling to her dear mama when she'd been hurt as a child.

"Well, I never. If that doesn't make the least sense of anything I've ever heard," Lady Sophia declared, settling herself in a nearby chair.

"It makes perfect sense, sister," Lady Cloris smoothed Emily's hair back from her forehead with gentle fingers. "Miss Haliburton is a romantic and if I know Jared, he probably made his offer sound much like he was placing a bid for a filly at Tattersall's. Her refusal may wake him up to how deeply he cares for her and he will make her the kind of offer every woman in love desires; if he does not, then they are better off apart."

"Humpf! I wouldn't hold my breath if I were you, Miss Haliburton." Lady Sophia's voice was heavy with sarcasm. "For if that was your gamble, it was foolish in the extreme. No man as proud as Montford could ever care enough for any woman to risk such humiliation twice."

Jared had been drinking steadily since he returned home from his aunt's town house yesterday morning—or was it the day before? He wasn't even certain how many bottles of fine French brandy he had consumed. He was, however, certain of one thing: For a man who had always felt nothing but disgust for men who drowned their sorrows in the bottle, he was managing to be unspeakably disgusting himself over his rejection by Miss Emily Haliburton. Even that most obsequious of minions, his butler Pettigrew, had ventured to suggest it was high time he stopped wallowing in self-pity and pulled himself together.

But the problem was, he could think of no good reason to pull himself together. Facing life without Emily was bad enough while one was thoroughly castaway; it would be completely unbearable if one were sober. He reached for the nearly empty brandy bottle at his elbow and poured himself another drink. If any man ever deserved to wallow, he was surely that man.

The library door opened behind him and he heard someone tiptoeing toward the chair in which he was slumped. Who did the idiot think he was fooling? He was drunk, for God's sake; not deaf.

He raised bleary eyes to the intruder and encountered a blaze of color so bright it forced him to close his tortured orbs lest the shock to his senses of daffodil yellow trousers, a scarlet topcoat, and a purple-and-gold waistcoat should bring on an eruption of the nausea already roiling in his stomach. "Go 'way, Percival," he muttered.

"I must speak with you, your grace. It is a matter of terrible urgency. I've already spoken to our lady aunts, but they insisted I must inform you of my plans since you are the head of our family and my guardian as well."

"Go 'way, Percival," Jared said again. "Don't think I can help you right now."

"I don't need your help. I already know what I'm going to do. I wouldn't even bother you if I hadn't promised the lady aunts."

Somehow the urgency in the earl's voice penetrated the fog of alcohol in which Jared had immersed himself. He took another look at the boy and decided the only way to get rid of him was to listen to whatever was bothering him. He pulled himself upright, aware that while he was capable of understanding what was said, he would have a devil of a time if he had to make any intelligent comments.

"Ring. Coffee," he managed, pointing to the pull chord.

The earl did as he asked and moments later Pettigrew arrived with a tray containing a pot of coffee and two cups. He poured one for the earl and spoon fed the other to Jared while the earl paced back and forth in front of the cold fireplace.

Eventually the steaming black liquid took effect and Jared waved Pettigrew and his spoon away. "All right, Percival, I'm ready to listen," he said, rubbing his temples, which were beginning to ache abominably.

The earl stopped his pacing. "It's like this, your grace. Lord Hargrave says he can't wait the year until I come into my inheritance and can offer for Lady Lucinda. He's going to marry her off to Lord Woolsey, who's offered him enough blunt to pay off his debts."

"Woolsey? Good God. The man's a known deviant and old enough to be the girl's grandfather. Already gone through four—no five wives."

"Exactly." The earl looked about to burst into tears. "I have to save her. I love her, you see, and I cannot bear the thought of that filthy old lecher putting his hands on her."

He flopped into the chair facing Jared and held his head in his hands. "And she loves me, too. Oh, I know everybody else thinks I'm a bit of a nodcock and a funny-looking one at that. But Lady Lucinda don't. She thinks I'm smart as a whip and handsome as any exquisite in the *ton*—and the thing is when I'm around her, *I* think I'm smart and handsome, too."

For the first time he could remember, Jared was in complete sympathy with his young cousin. Emily had seen *him* as a dashing highwayman—not the stiff-rumped aristocrat he knew he appeared to most other people. Even in his present alcoholic stupor, he could remember feeling tall as the oak tree under which he'd first kissed her.

"So, you want me to advance you enough money to persuade the earl to let you have her instead," he surmised.

"No, your grace. That ain't it at all. For then it would be you who saved her and what would I have risked?"

The earl raised his head and looked Jared in the eye. "I have a plan, only it will bring more disgrace down on our family and that's why the lady aunts said I was obliged to tell you. But you must know it don't really matter what you say, for nothing will make me change my mind."

Jared could scarcely believe this determined young man could be the same shy, tongue-tied youngster he had judged ill-suited to be his heir. If this was what love did to one, it was more powerful than he had credited it. "What is your plan?" he asked, strangely eager to hear what the boy had come up with.

"I'm going to take her to Gretna Green—tonight. Once the deed is done, the earl can't touch her even if we are under age, can he?"

"He can, but he won't. I'll see to that," Jared replied.
"But Gretna Green! You'll both be in disgrace."

"What do we care long as we have each other?"

Jared found himself humbled by his young cousin's single-minded devotion to a girl he had seen as nothing but a silly little fribble without a brain in her head.

"And how do you propose to support your wife?"

"I've already talked to Tattersall's and arranged to auction off my cattle. They're prime blood and should bring enough to get us by until I come into my inheritance," the earl said offhandedly. But Jared wasn't fooled. "He knew how much the boy prized his stable of fine horses.

"Very well. I won't stand in your way," he said. "What would be the point when you've already informed me it would do me no good."

He thought for a moment. "But I think you must let me help you to this extent. When you return, I'll arrange for you to take over the management of one of my small estates in the Midlands. It's in need of a man who knows horses, and it will provide you and your lady a comfortable living until you come into your own money."

With an impatient gesture, he waved aside the earl's attempts to thank him and watched him rise to leave. "Wait one moment," he said somewhat hesitantly. "Just out of curiosity, I should like to know what makes you so certain you love Lady Lucinda?"

"Why that's easy, your grace," the boy said without hesitation. "I care more what happens to her than what happens to me. Never felt that way about anyone else so it has to be love."

Long after the young earl had departed, Jared pondered his profound words. The boy was right, of course. He remembered those hellish nights when he had searched for Emily in the slums of London, with no thought to the danger to himself. Even now, if she were in harm's way, he would gladly give his life to save her. Hell and damnation, he must have been in love all along and hadn't had the sense to know it.

Absentmindedly, he rubbed his aching temples. And Emily loved him, too. Why, he couldn't imagine, considering all he'd done to hurt her, but she did. She had put his welfare before her own so many times in so many ways, only a blind man—or a pompous ass—could have failed to see the shining glory of her love.

No wonder she had refused to marry him. Somehow he must prove to her his eyes were open at last; somehow he must make her believe he loved her as she deserved to be loved.

It would have to be something spectacular. Something that would leave her no alternative but to agree to become his wife.

It came to him in a sudden flash of light which illumined all the dark and dismal corners of his brandy-soaked mind. Without a moment's hesitation he rang for Pettigrew. "More coffee," he ordered. "Lots of it and black as Satan's heart. And food. Tell Cook to prepare something hearty enough to settle a man's stomach and sober his mind."

He crossed to his desk, found pen and paper, and began writing furiously.

The Earl of Chillingham wasn't the only man in London with a plan to win the heart and hand of his ladylove.

Chapter Seventeen

It had been four days since she had rejected the duke's offer and Emily still could not control the tears that slid down her cheeks every time she thought about him. She found herself wondering how many times a heart could break before it was shattered into so many minute fragments there was no heart left at all.

Even now, as she pushed the lovely breakfast Cook had prepared around on her plate, a tear splashed onto the bite of scone she hadn't been able to convince herself she could swallow.

She was thoroughly disgusted with herself. She had made the only decision that made sense; one would think she could live with it without turning into a hopeless watering pot.

Lady Sophia and Lady Cloris had been kindness itself, but she could tell she was distressing them. It was time she took her leave of the two old dears and let them get back to enjoying the placid life they had led before she had invaded their home.

But what should she do with all the gowns and fans and slippers they had purchased for her? For she could see now they had been secretly supplying her with a trousseau for when she married their nephew, and she felt sick with guilt that she had disappointed them.

All things considered, she wondered if she would have the courage to refuse him if she had it all to do over again. She was beginning to think pride was a poor bedfellow, and that even a few crumbs of affection from the man she loved might be more satisfying than a banquet with any other man.

"You must try to eat something, my dear," Lady Cloris chided. "You haven't consumed enough food to keep a sparrow alive these past few days."

Sparrow. He had called her a plump little country sparrow. Another tear splashed onto Emily's plate.

She looked up to find Finster, the ladies' butler hovering in the doorway. The fellow always looked mightily pleased with himself; today he looked as if he had just been appointed to the post of majordomo of Carlton House.

She looked again. Martha was peeping around one of his shoulders and the housekeeper around the other, and she caught glimpses of two liveried footmen in the background.

"What is going on here?" Lady Sophia scowled. "Why is the entire staff peering at us as if we are animals on display at the Tower?"

"The *Times* has arrived, my lady," Finster intoned in his usual sepulchral voice, but Emily was certain she saw a suspicious glint in his eye. Behind him Martha and the housekeeper dissolved into giggles.

Lady Sophia's scowl deepened. "Is that any reason to suspend all work in the house?" She flipped open the folded paper and perused the front page briefly. "Well, I never! What will that scamp think of next?" Without another word, she passed the paper to her sister.

Lady Cloris's eyes grew wide and she gave a little shriek of delight. "How romantic! I just knew the dear boy would think of something."

"Romantic? Fiddle-faddle! More like attics-to-let if you ask me. Before the fool is finished, he'll have 'Montford' as common a name in London households as 'lemon oil.'"

"Well, I'm sure Miss Haliburton will think it romantic," Lady Cloris declared, handing the paper to Emily.

The entire front page was blank except for a framed paragraph in bold letters in the very center:

Let it be known to all citizens of London, indeed of all of England and unto such far-flung regions as Ireland and Scotland, that I, Jared Neville Tremayne, Eighth Duke of Montford, do publicly declare that I love Miss Emily Haliburton and desire, above all else, to make her my wife.

Emily stared at the incredible paragraph in stunned amazement. She read it again and still couldn't believe what she was seeing.

"Dear God, he loves me!" she exclaimed, laughing and crying at the same time. Clutching the paper in one hand, she pressed the other to the spot where her heart was thumping so madly against her ribs she could scarcely draw breath.

Lady Cloris beamed happily. "Of course he does, my dear. I have known that all along."

"Humpf! The arrogant puppy is monstrously sure of himself to risk the ridicule he'd face if the marriage didn't come off," Lady Sophia muttered.

Emily laughed softly. "There is no denying he is arrogant, my lady, but in this case I rather think I am the one of whom he is so sure. He must have seen through all the dreadful things I said to him and realized I was hopelessly in love with him."

Lady Sophia's smile had an ironic twist. "Perhaps you are right. As I can attest, Montford is devilish clever."

She glanced toward the door and frowned. "What is it this time, Finster?"

The butler held out a small silver tray on which one heavily embossed card rested. "The Duke of Montford presents his compliments, my lady, and requests the pleasure of Miss Haliburton's presence in the music room."

Lady Sophia raised an eyebrow. "What in the world is he doing in the music room?"

"Playing the pianoforte, my lady. A little known composition by Mr. Mozart, unless I am mistaken."

"Well, I never. He is not acting himself at all. Has he lost all sense of decorum?"

The corners of Finster's mouth twitched, which was as close to a smile as Emily had ever seen him come. "It would appear so, my lady. But I understand that is quite common with young men in love."

Blushing furiously, Emily rose to her feet, and still clutching the newspaper to her breast, walked toward the door.

"If you turn him down again, Miss Haliburton, I shall wash my hands of you," Lady Sophia called after her.

Emily smiled. "Never fear, my lady, I have no intention of turning him down this time. For I gave him his chance to escape. Henceforth, whatever comes of this impossible union, the blame is on *his* head."

He was indeed playing Mozart—the very piece she had played that first night at Brynhaven—and playing it very well too. Emily paused in the doorway to listen.

"If you're thinking this is an odd thing for a duke to be doing, you are correct," he said. "But music has always been my secret passion—my only passion, actually, until I met you."

"What I am thinking, your grace, is that you are a man of many talents," Emily said as she stepped into the room and closed the door behind her. "Horseman, actor, blackmailer, and now accomplished pianist."

"Do not forget highwayman," he said as his fingers moved lightly over the keys. "For that is my favorite."

He looked up. "You've been crying. Your eyes are all

red and puffy and you look as if you'd eaten one too many strawberries and developed the hives."

"And you have such black smudges beneath your eyes, you look very much like a barn owl I once had as a pet," she retorted.

"That's because I have been on a three-day drunk, thanks to you, my dear." He ended the piece with a flourish and rested his hands in his lap. "I find myself wondering why I want you so badly. I can't remember when any woman has wreaked such havoc in my life."

"I have to wonder the same thing. For nothing has changed, you know, except that I plan to hold you to this." Emily waved the newspaper before his eyes. "I am still hopelessly unsuited to be a duchess."

He nodded solemnly. "I agree. I could not possibly make a worse choice."

"I have a terrible temper."

He nodded again. "And a tongue as sharp as Wellington's sword. Furthermore, you're hopelessly impulsive—a trait I am certain you will pass on to our daughters, who will most likely be the scandal of the *ton* before they ever make their come-outs." He sighed. "And God only knows what our sons will be like. Avowed revolutionaries, no doubt, who will attempt to abolish the House of Lords."

Emily smiled. "With my help, no doubt, if the members I've met so far are any example of that august body."

The duke stood up and moved to stand directly in front of her. "I suppose I shall be expected to turn my precious library over to you so you may continue your research into ancient myths and legends—even though I consider it a most unsuitable occupation for a duchess."

"I shall insist upon it."

"And, of course, I shall have to give up any idea of keeping a mistress, for not even the most notorious Cyprian will risk the wrath of a woman who thought nothing of turning the Royal Opera House into her own personal battle-ground."

"A wise decision, your grace."

"And considering your lowly background, you will undoubtedly insist we share the same bed like the most common of married couples, rather than maintain your own suite as a proper duchess should," he murmured as one by one he removed the pins from her hair and tossed them to the floor.

Emily felt a laugh start deep in her throat. "I warned you I was hopelessly unsuited for the role, but you wouldn't listen and now it is too late."

He buried his fingers in her heavy locks and drew her to him—closer and closer until she could feel every muscle and sinew of the lean, hard body pressed against hers.

His long, sensitive fingers cupped her chin and he searched her face with his molten silver eyes. "I can see it now. I shall never have another moment's peace. My quiet, orderly life will be turned completely upside down."

He brushed his lips across hers ever so lightly. It was not a kiss—merely a tantalizing promise of things to come, and Emily felt a terrible hunger start in those secret feminine places deep inside her.

"Why, if I am such a trial, did you trap yourself by telling all the world you loved me?" she asked innocently.

"Why, little sparrow?" His warm, seductive mouth hovered just a breath above hers; his soft laughter whispered across her lips. "Because with all the trouble you cause me, life with you is so much better than life without you, I shall probably never realize how miserable I am."

It was not precisely the romantic declaration Emily had hoped for, but as it turned out, it was of little consequence. For it soon became apparent that while the Eighth Duke of Montford was no Lake District poet when wooing a lady with words, he was truly a man without equal when it came to action.